Dear Reader,

I hope you'll enjoy your third visit to Cape Cod in *Reading the Clues*, and further getting to know Mary Fisher and her sister Betty Emerson. Since I don't have a sister, it was fun to write about sisters who are so close and loving. And, of course, the beauty of the Cape Cod area is a great locale for any story with historical elements.

The Emerson gristmill plays a large role in this story. Somewhat to my surprise, a good number of my California friends were only familiar with the lumber mills that are scattered across the Sierra Nevada Mountains. One friend thought a gristmill might be something like a "gossip mill." Of course, gristmills were actually used to grind grain, and virtually every small town had one in the early years of our country.

I have to commend the other authors of Secrets of Mary's Bookshop for the fine work they've done to set up the series. I know you'll enjoy returning to Ivy Bay again and again.

Happy reading!
Charlotte Carter

SECRETS *of* MARY'S
BOOKSHOP

Reading the Clues

Charlotte Carter

Guideposts
New York, New York

Acknowledgments

Every attempt has been made to credit the sources of copyrighted material used in this
book. If any such acknowledgment has been inadvertently omitted or miscredited,
receipt of such information would be appreciated.

"From the Guideposts Archives" originally appeared in *Daily Guideposts 2008*.
Copyright © 2007 by Guideposts. All rights reserved.

Cover and interior design by Müllerhaus
Typeset by Aptara, Inc.

Printed and bound in the United States of America
10 9 8 7 6 5 4 3 2

ONE

From Mary Fisher's perspective, there was nothing more exciting than opening a carton of new books—like the one the UPS man had just delivered to her bookshop. She loved the scent and texture of the paper as she rifled through the pages. She supposed that was why she'd spent much of her working life as a librarian and now owned Mary's Mystery Bookshop in Ivy Bay on Cape Cod.

It was August, and the height of tourist season in Ivy Bay. During the summer, she'd become inspired by how history and mystery often collided, so she'd established a theme for the month of August at her store. Across her front window, she and her sister Betty had displayed a banner: Ivy Bay—History, Romance, Intrigue . . . Mystery. Ever since the sign had gone up, alongside Betty's seaside-themed window display, sales had been so brisk that she'd just this morning had to order more books.

The sweet scent of freshly baked cupcakes hung in the air. Mary tried not to sample treats from Sweet Susan's Bakery next door too often, but after smelling them all day, it was sometimes all she could do to resist. She distracted herself by shelving the books she'd received in their respective sections, leaving some for the display table in the front, and stepped back to admire her work.

"What do you think, Gus?" she asked her gray cat, who was snoozing near the front counter. He briefly opened one eye, then closed it again.

She decided that was a sign of approval.

The chime over the front door tinkled, and Betty rushed into the shop as though she was being chased by a rabid dog. Her cheeks were bright with exertion, she was breathing hard, and her lightweight cardigan flapped open. Even her blonde hair, the same shade it had been when she was a young woman, looked disheveled.

"What is it? What's wrong, Bets?" A trickle of fear slid down Mary's spine. Had someone been hurt? Was the house on fire?

Even Gus stood, arched his back, and stretched, his nap disrupted by Betty's arrival.

Betty scanned the shop as if making sure the coast was clear. There were no customers in the shop, so Betty began. "It's terrible. I don't know what to do!" Betty's words spilled out in a staccato voice, which was very uncharacteristic of her typically calm, even dignified demeanor. "I called Evan at his office, but he was out in the field with a client looking over a building site."

"*Sh*, now, take it easy. I'm sure Evan will call you back as soon as he can." Mary's sister, who was two years older, wasn't usually so excitable and rarely called her son in a panic. And given her rheumatoid arthritis, she seldom ran anywhere. She clutched a large brown mailing envelope in her hand.

"Come sit down and catch your breath. Then tell me what has happened." Mary led her sister to the pair of overstuffed chairs in the back of the shop where customers could browse through books at their leisure. Once Betty was seated, Mary dashed to the nearby refreshment table to get her a glass of water and put on some water for tea.

"Now then ..." Mary sat in the chair next to her sister. "Take a drink and tell me what happened."

Betty's hand shook as she took a sip. She swallowed and exhaled. "I'm being sued," she said, her voice calmer but no less anxious.

Mary sat back and blinked. "Sued? By whom? And why?"

"A process server came to the door no more than an hour ago. He served me these papers." She handed Mary the envelope. "Daniel Hopkins is the one suing me. He claims the Hopkins family owns—" She put her hand over her heart. "He says the gristmill belongs to the Hopkins family."

"The *Emerson* gristmill?" Mary tried to imagine why anyone would say such a thing about the mill that had stood on the edge of town since sometime in the 1600s. She and Betty had played there as children during summer visits to their grandparents, even before Betty had married Edward Emerson, a member of one of the founding families of Ivy Bay. Now the only Emersons left in town were Betty; Edward's sister Eleanor Blakely, the self-proclaimed family matriarch; and Betty's son Evan and his young family. All the other Emersons had moved away.

"I couldn't make sense of those papers the court sent me." She shook an arthritic finger at the envelope. "Edward told me the Emersons had owned the gristmill since the day it was built. Since Edward passed away, I've faithfully paid the property tax every year. And Evan has even been talking to a contractor about restoring the old place. A considerable expense, but we both think it's the right thing to do. Why would Daniel say it isn't ours?"

Mary recalled a passage in Leviticus 6 where the Lord warned Moses about people stealing or extorting others for their property and how they must make restitution in full plus a fifth more. Betty had certainly not stolen the gristmill from the Hopkins family, and she didn't believe Betty's late husband Edward had either.

Hearing the teakettle whistle, Mary went to fill the teapot in the back room. She put milk in a pitcher and carried that and cups out front to Betty.

While the tea was steeping, Mary pulled the thick sheaf of paper from the envelope, adjusted her glasses, and skimmed the contents. The suit claimed that, in 1792, Isaac Emerson sold the gristmill to James Hopkins for the price of five British pounds.

She lifted her head. Gracious, 1792! That was going a long way back in history. Why was the sale and ownership of the mill just now being disputed?

"Do you have any idea what five British pounds in 1792 would be worth today?"

Betty shook her head. Her breathing had slowed to normal, and she had regained control of herself. "Probably a lot more than it was then. Evan thinks the property itself is worth quite a lot even though the mill is in disrepair." Still agitated, Betty ran a fingertip along the fabric seam on the arm of the chair.

"Sounds like there may be greed at the bottom of this suit." Mary leaned back in her chair to read the legal papers more thoroughly. "Do you have the original deed for the property?"

"I suppose it's possible, but I don't know that there ever was a deed, per se. Edward's ancestors built the mill so long ago; the area was part of the royal charter given to the Massachusetts Bay Company."

Mary appreciated her sister's depth of knowledge about the history of Ivy Bay, but for the moment, she was more worried about Betty's very contemporary problem. "I'm trying to think how to counter this suit. Surely there must be some sort of a record *if* the mill was sold as Hopkins apparently claims." She poured tea into their cups.

"All I know is that I have records of paying property taxes for years and years. The county certainly believes we own the mill. As far as I know, there's nothing in the file Edward kept that gives any suggestion the mill was ever sold." She sounded offended by even the mere suggestion that the mill didn't belong to the Emersons. That was understandable. So what evidence was the suit based on?

From the paperwork, it looked like Marc Dougher, an attorney on the Cape, had filed the suit for Hopkins. Mary wondered what sort of a man he was.

The chime over the door announced the arrival of a customer, a youngish woman dressed in shorts, halter top, and flip-flops.

"Hello," Mary said. "Is there anything I can help you find?"

"No, I'll just browse, if that's okay."

"Of course. Let me know if I can help in any way."

Mary turned back to Betty and lowered her voice. "Tell you what, after dinner tonight, let's go through what records you do have. I'm sure there's a way to put this suit to rest in a hurry."

Betty squeezed Mary's hand. "I'm sure too. Being served with papers caught me totally by surprise."

"I can sure understand that. Speaking of which, what do you know about Daniel Hopkins?" Although Jill Sanderson was in her prayer group, Mary hadn't ever met the man who was Jill's grandfather-in-law. Jill had expressed concern about Daniel's temperament since he'd moved in with her and her husband.

"Not much. I see him occasionally around town, but the Emersons have never been friends with the Hopkinses. I do know that they're a family of commercial fishermen and they live on the other side of town." She pursed her lips together and her brows lowered. "I don't want to speak unkindly of anyone, but from what I've seen, Daniel Hopkins is an angry man. I've always avoided him."

Mary nodded, encouraging Betty to go on.

"Edward didn't have anything to do with the Hopkinses either. I do remember he mentioned a couple of times something about a feud between the two families."

"What was the feud about?"

"He didn't know or wouldn't say. And you know how these stories start up and get distorted over time. Edward believed in 'live and let live.' He had no interest in pursuing whatever it was that had come between the two families generations ago."

As Mary slipped the papers back into the envelope, she wondered if Betty's sister-in-law Eleanor knew more about the feud than Edward had. "Apparently, Daniel Hopkins isn't into 'live and let live.'"

"I really can't let him take the mill away from us, Mar. It's such a big part of the Emerson family history. Edward was so proud—"

"Bets, try not to worry. I'm sure we'll find a way to stop this ridiculous suit."

Forcing a brave smile, Betty nodded.

Taking a sip of tea, Mary considered the situation. She realized in order to defend against the suit, someone would have to prove Isaac Emerson did not sell the gristmill to James Hopkins or anyone else. No easy task considering the sale was supposed to have taken place more than 220 years ago.

And proving something didn't happen was far harder than proving it did.

The young woman who had been browsing waved goodbye and went out the door.

"Maybe we should go talk with Mr. Hopkins," Mary said. "At least to find out what he bases his claim of ownership on," she suggested, her voice filled with caring. Betty's face still looked troubled, but Mary could tell her sister was comforted to have Mary by her side.

Betty shook her head. "I'm so upset that I'm not sure I could even be civil to the man. Edward and his family were honorable people. How dare Hopkins accuse them of being anything but? As much as I want to know what's going on, I don't think I'd have anything productive to say to him. I'm sure Evan will hire an attorney to represent us. Let's wait to see what the attorney advises."

That might be wise, Mary mused. But she had learned that it was often possible to solve a problem by having an honest, open conversation in order to get to the crux of the matter.

"You know what?" She stood and put the tea things back on the tray. "It's a lovely day, and I could use some exercise. Let's take a walk. Maybe it will clear our heads."

"Take a walk?" Betty's forehead wrinkled. "I suppose I could use a breather."

Mary carried the tray into the back room and retrieved a light jacket. Despite the heat of the day, there was always a breeze blowing off the ocean.

"I haven't been out to see that old mill since I moved back to town," Mary said. "Maybe we'll see something that triggers an idea about how to prove you own the mill."

Betty stood. "That's a good idea. But I should warn you, it's really run-down. Evan thinks it's unsafe."

Even though Rebecca Mason, Mary's one employee, was off for the day, Mary wasn't worried about closing the shop for a bit. That was the beauty of owning your own business, anyway. She flipped the antique Open/Shut sign on the door to SHUT. Letting Betty out first, she locked up behind them.

As they walked, a light breeze coming off the ocean fluttered Mary's gray curls. She reflected not for the first time on how much she loved the little town of Ivy Bay. On the north side of the Cape, it was separated from the mainland by a channel. Two bridges provided access to Ivy Bay, with its charming shops and Victorian homes, some of which were on the historical registry.

"Evan was looking at the mill recently. He wants to either restore the mill or tear it down because of its poor condition. In fact, the city may insist on us doing something soon. But you see"—Betty's voice caught—"this is all my fault. In one of my last conversations with Edward before he passed away, he told me he was sorry he hadn't done something with the mill. Made it something more that all his descendants could be proud of. You remember that we were at the mill when he proposed to me."

"Yes, I remember. I thought it was very romantic of him."

"And then when he was dying, I promised—"

Mary rubbed her sister's back to soothe her. "It's all right, Bets. We'll make it all right."

They walked past Meeting House Grocers, which had recently become one of Mary's favorite places in town, and up Meeting House Road. Cars passed by on the street, and pedestrians were strolling along peeking in shop windows.

"Evan was going to get something started, and then he got so busy. I couldn't ask him to drop everything to take care of the gristmill. But I should have done something before now. Evan has asked a contractor to take a look at the mill and give him some cost estimates."

Evan, an architect, lived nearby and had a busy life with a wife and two daughters. Even so, he had taken over some of Edward's business interests after his father's death.

"Evan is doing the right thing, and so are you." Betty's emotional response to the lawsuit had surprised Mary until she'd learned of Edward's final comments about the mill, Betty's nostalgic memories, and the promise Betty had made. No wonder her sister didn't want to lose the mill and fail her late husband.

Betty exhaled and pulled herself together.

Once out of the business district, houses appeared, many of them separated by white picket fences. When the road came near the shallow end of a pond, Mary stopped and held up a finger to get Betty's attention. "Do you hear that? Sounds like we have some saltmarsh sparrows." One of the stocky gray birds flitted so fast from one low-growing plant to another that it was hard to see the yellow markings on its face.

"They are the busiest little birds. They wear me out just watching them flit around."

As they turned the corner, the mill came into sight. Water for the gristmill ran from a pretty pond down a raceway past the mill to turn the waterwheel. Unfortunately, the aging wheel was now tilted at an odd angle, which prevented it from turning on its axis.

Sturdy gray rocks quarried from the mainland formed the mill's foundation. Someone had chiseled "1667" into the cornerstone block.

Wood siding on the building, weathered gray by hundreds of years of sun and rain, showed signs of decay, and the shutters for the windows were missing.

The mill had been used for hundreds of years, but it had stopped operating in the 1930s. Edward's father moved the grain production to the new commercial baking facility he opened in Provincetown after the worst of the Depression was over. From there, he began delivering bread daily to grocery stores on the Cape. The company eventually expanded to a broader market, distributing specialty breads and rolls throughout much of New England.

Edward had followed in his father's footsteps, becoming the CEO of the company when his father retired, but the family had always made their home in Ivy Bay, and the mill had always been a part of their family history.

They approached the mill slowly. Years ago, someone had placed two water-worn logs across the raceway for a bridge. Mary scurried across, and Betty followed more slowly.

"Seems to me, there was an easier way to get here when we were children," Betty commented.

"Or maybe we were both more agile back then."

"Speak for yourself, little sister."

"I fear age is going to creep up on us whether we want it to or not." Mary laughed and slipped her arm around Betty's waist, hugging her.

"You remember when we were kids and came back to stay with Grandma during the summer?" Betty asked. "The older boys would try to scare us about a ghost that haunted the old place. One time a boy made such a scary noise, you went running out of there screaming."

Mary twisted her lips into a wry smile. She had all but forgotten that embarrassing incident. She couldn't have been more than seven or eight. "A few months went by before I built up enough courage to go back to the mill."

"The boys swore there were snakes inside the mill and a buried treasure left there by pirates. And there was something about colonial soldiers hiding there while a whole regiment of redcoats marched by."

"What grand imaginations we all had as children," Mary said with a laugh. "I remember one time some of us used the mill as a fort. We piled up grass-and-dirt clods. When anyone approached, we'd bombard him or her through the windows."

Although the mill door was still in place, it hung crookedly from old metal hinges. They eased their way into the dim interior, the small windows admitting little light even on a sunny day. The huge four-thousand-pound buhrstone— Mary recalled hearing it was originally from France—looked just as it always had, ready for a load of corn to be brought in.

Mary remembered learning as a child that to make cornmeal, the miller would haul the corn up to the second level and pour it down a shoot. The two matching grinding stones, driven by the waterwheel in the race, would grind it into a gritty product, probably accompanied by a great deal of noise.

During the early years of America, almost every town had a gristmill. Local villagers would bring their corn to the mill to be ground for a fee. If the person didn't grow his own corn, he'd buy cornmeal from the miller. Everyone needed cornmeal, so the miller did business with just about everyone in town. The Emerson who had built this mill had been wise. It had provided the foundation for the family's later wealth.

"I should have brought a flashlight." Mary walked gingerly across the dusty wooden floor. "Be careful. Some of the floorboards look rotten to me."

Betty stepped slowly back toward the door. "I don't think it's safe to walk around in here, Mary. We've seen the place, now let's—"

Mary let out a cry as her foot broke through an aged floorboard.

"Mary!"

"I'm all right." The end of the rotten wood next to the foundation had given way and scratched her leg, but she hadn't fallen more than six inches. Thank the good Lord.

Feeling foolish, since she was the one who had warned Betty to be careful, she shook her head. Hoping to release her foot from the grasp of the rotting wood, she grabbed hold of the end of the plank that had snared her and lifted. The board squeaked and groaned. Then the rotten wood snapped about three feet from where she was standing.

"This place really is rotting," she said. "No wonder Evan wants to either restore the mill or tear it down. It's a lawsuit waiting to happen." Which made Mary wonder why anyone would want to sue for the right to own a piece a property that would be a money pit.

"I hate the thought that some children might be playing in here and get hurt," Betty said.

"If that happened, you and Evan might want to agree that it's owned by Hopkins and let it be his problem."

Betty giggled. "Sometimes you can be very devious, Mary."

Maybe so, but right now Mary's shoe was caught by something under the floorboards. A rock, or perhaps some leftover construction material.

With one leg in the hole, she knelt on the other knee and reached down to feel for whatever was pressing on her ankle and foot. Her fingers brushed something slick.

She tensed. On second thought, she might not actually want to know what was under the floorboards. But her innate curiosity—

"Really, Mary, I think we ought to get out of here before one of us is seriously injured. Those overhead beams don't look all that sturdy to me."

Mary chose to ignore her sister as her hand closed around the slick object. It was not all that big. She felt what she believed was the spine of a slender book. Interesting . . .

Carefully, she pulled the package out of the hole.

"What's that?" Betty asked.

"Some kind of book, wrapped in oilskin." She set it down next to her and reached her hand back into the hole. "Give me a minute to see if there's anything else down here."

"You'd better hope it's not a bed of snakes."

Mary shuddered. Her sister would have to mention snakes. Worst case, she might find a hognose snake under the mill. It was an ugly creature, but it was harmless, as were all the snakes on Cape Cod. Or so Mary had been told as a child.

Her hand closed around something hard and cold. Smooth like a bone. Oh dear . . .

Grimacing, she pulled her find out of the hole.

Not a snake, she thought gratefully. But whatever it was, it was covered in dirt and grime. She rubbed her finger over one end of the object. A white spot appeared.

Not a bone either, she realized, rubbing more dirt away.

"What have you got?"

"I'm not sure." Holding the white object, she struggled out of the hole and found more secure footing. Then she picked up the book. Interesting. As far as Mary knew, oilskin hadn't been used as a wrapping in many years. Her heart rate picked up. "These items are old."

"Old? Antique? Show me." Betty, an avid antiquer, took a few more tentative steps farther into the mill house.

"Let's go outside where we can see better."

"Good idea," Betty said with a relieved laugh.

Glad to be out of the gloom of the mill, Mary studied the unfamiliar object. Maybe six inches long, it weighed no more than six or eight ounces.

Betty peered at Mary's find, and Mary could see her anticipation rising at the possibility of having found an antique. "Let's wash all that dirt off in the pond. It's probably a piece of some old pottery."

It didn't feel like pottery to Mary, not quite heavy enough, but she agreed they needed to get rid of the dirt.

At the pond, she knelt and swished the thing in the water. Layers of dirt melted away, revealing a porcelain doll standing on a chipped porcelain base. Around the base were the words *Only the Very Best* painted in a bright blue script.

"What a pretty little girl," Betty said. "A sweet face and a charming bonnet. It could be a child's doll."

"Maybe." Looking for a maker's mark, Mary turned the doll upside down. The base and doll were hollow. But she couldn't see an indication of who had made the doll.

After handing the doll to Betty, Mary carefully unwrapped the oilskin package. It wasn't a book, exactly, but rather some sort of bookkeeping ledger with page after page filled with odd markings.

Standing, Mary said, "What do you make of this?"

"*Hmm*, it looks a lot like the record book Edward used to keep track of our expenses. Of course, he changed to using his computer years ago."

The oilskin had kept the binding and pages in good condition, but the notations were indecipherable as far as Mary could tell. Just from the flourishing handwriting on the title page, she thought the ledger must be old. On each page, there were rows and columns, symbols of some sort. On the left, there were tally marks and what looked to be box-shaped markings across the rows.

She wasn't sure what it meant. She would have to spend some time studying it to try and learn more about it.

But why had the ledger and the doll been left under the floorboards? Had they been hidden for some reason? Or simply tossed away?

Could they possibly lead to answers about the ownership of the mill?

TWO

—◆◇◆—

Betty went home to see if Evan had returned her phone call, while Mary returned to her shop. She turned the sign on the door to Open and carried her finds from the mill inside. Gus was still curled up in his favorite patch of sunlight and barely opened his eyes to greet her.

"I do so like a warm welcome home, Gus," she teased. "No need to overdo it, though. I know you need your rest."

She smiled as he appeared undisturbed. For a cat that had once been a stray, he'd certainly found a good home and a softhearted owner. In payment, he'd provided love and solace, particularly when she'd lost her husband John.

After putting the wrapped ledger on the counter, she took the doll into the back room to wash it more thoroughly. She used soap and a soft scrub brush to get rid of the remaining grime stuck in the creases. She wiped it dry with a paper towel and then held it up for examination.

"Well, you are a pretty little thing." The doll wore a bonnet and old-fashioned skirt and had puckered red lips. It didn't look like a child's toy. Maybe a knickknack a woman would display on a shelf, discarded because of the chip in its base. "I guess whoever made you thought you were 'Only the

Very Best,'" Mary said, reading the inscription on the doll. Or perhaps that was a reference to whoever had received the doll as a gift.

Smiling to herself, Mary took the doll back into the shop and placed it near the cash register. Later, she might try to identify the maker by checking online. The slogan on the base, if that was what it was, could be a good lead. It still wasn't evident how the items she found had anything to do with the ownership of the mill, but she was curious about them nonetheless.

When she started to unwrap the ledger, Gus roused himself. He jumped up onto the counter and sniffed the oilskin, then the ledger that she'd placed next to the wrapper.

"What do you think, Gus?"

His answer was to lie down with his paws on the wrapping. It must have carried a scent that interested him. Plain old dirt was the best Mary could imagine, but maybe the oilskin itself had an odor only a cat could appreciate.

Carefully, she opened the ledger. The handwriting on the first page was so arcane and filled with swirls it was hard to make out. But she was pretty certain it was in English. She saw what could have been a date on the first page, but she couldn't even be sure about that.

As she turned the pages, she frowned. The handwriting went from swirly English to what looked like Chinese-style characters, followed by rows of symbols and tally marks. What could those odd characters mean? There weren't many Asians in Ivy Bay now, and she couldn't imagine an early Emerson able to write in Chinese, but who knew?

After closing the ledger, she slipped the oilskin out from under Gus's paw, wrapped the ledger again, and put it on a shelf behind the counter. It probably wasn't valuable in any way except its connection to the mill, but maybe it would help her figure out more about the mill's history.

Mary thought again about Betty's promise to her husband. This mill was important to Betty, even more so now that she might lose it. Mary knew she needed to help her sister.

She mentally put three chores on her list. First, she'd look through Betty's files and make sure there was no record of sale. Even though she was confident she wouldn't find such a record, she needed to at least double-check. Second, despite Betty's determination to avoid him, Mary would drop by Daniel Hopkins' home tomorrow, after she found out where he lived. With any luck, she might be able to get him to drop the suit, or at least discover the reason he claimed to be the owner.

If those efforts failed, she'd head for the county clerk's office. The clerk's archives contained records back to almost the founding of Ivy Bay. Surely she could find who were the original owners of the mill—the first Emersons in town, according to Betty. It shouldn't be that hard.

And then she could check to see if the property had ever changed hands. If it had, a bill of sale would have been recorded and the title to the land changed.

She suspected whatever Daniel Hopkins claimed, he was going to lose his suit. The mill had been owned by the Emerson family forever. Everyone in town seemed to acknowledge

READING THE CLUES ～ 19

that. Unless Daniel Hopkins had incontrovertible proof otherwise, surely that wouldn't change.

The chime over the door announced the arrival of Henry Woodrow, longtime resident of Ivy Bay. Henry was a good friend of Mary's from back when they were youngsters, and when she moved back to Ivy Bay, they had reconnected. They'd become close friends again, and Henry often came into the shop to visit. His silver hair was windblown, and from his casual attire, nonslip shoes, and captain's cap, Mary assumed he'd been out on his boat *Misty Horizon*.

"Hi there, Henry. How was your boating adventure today?"

"How'd you—?" He looked down at his outfit and chuckled. "It was very pleasant, thank you. I took a tour group over to Wellfleet. The bay was so smooth."

"Sounds perfect." Mary suspected his days on the boat helped him to maintain an optimistic outlook. He'd recently lost his wife Misty and, just as Mary filled her life with the bookshop, his boating business kept him very busy.

"Yep, it was a good outing. Caught a couple of nice striped bass after lunch." Henry wandered over to the shelves of mystery titles. "I finished the last book you sold me—kept me up way too late at night—and I'm ready for another of your killer recommendations."

"No pun intended," Mary said with a smile.

"Nice one," Henry said, then began perusing the shelves. While he browsed, Bob Hiller, longtime mailman for Ivy Bay, walked into the shop. He placed the day's mail on the counter and gave Mary a wave.

"Thanks, Bob," she called out, then returned her attention to Henry. "Just this week, I got copies of Archer James's new book." She joined him at the historical mysteries section. "I haven't had a chance to read this one yet, but he writes wonderful mysteries based in the Scottish isles." She plucked the hardcover from the shelf and handed it to him.

He briefly considered the cover, then flipped to the back where there was a photo of the gray-haired author holding a pipe.

"Distinguished-looking gentleman," Henry said.

"I understand he's a bit of a recluse, but a lot of authors are. There always seems to be a ruined castle and lots of fog in his books."

Henry laughed and his smile crinkled the corners of his eyes. "Sounds sufficiently spooky. I'll take it."

He handed her the book, which she carried to the cash register. While she rang up the sale, Henry petted Gus.

"You have a pretty soft life, Gus. I hope you appreciate how well Mary takes care of you."

With his eyes squeezed shut in pleasure, Gus pushed up against Henry's hand to encourage more petting. Mary smiled at the sight of Henry cooing over Gus. A man who could love a cat was definitely a good man.

"I'm lucky to have Gus." She gave Henry the total, and he passed her his credit card. "I can talk to him and people don't think I've gone 'round the bend talking to myself."

"Sounds perfectly reasonable to me. I've been known to do a little muttering myself." He chuckled. "Well, I should get going."

"Big plans?"

"Dorothy Johnson stopped me at the Meeting House Grocers the other day. She asked me to drop by sometime and take a look at her house."

"Oh?" Dorothy, who was a member of Mary's prayer group, frequently expressed an interest in Henry, which tickled Mary. She thought for sure Dorothy had her eye on the town widower for something more than casual conversation.

"Yep. She says some of her windows don't open and close right, and a couple of doors get stuck now and then. Hopes maybe I can fix 'em without a whole lot of trouble."

"Nice of you to help her out."

"I'll do what I can. I'm a little worried the house needs more than a few minor repairs."

"Oh, I hope not. It's such a lovely place, and on the historical register."

"It being old might be at the root of the problem."

"Good point." Mary finished ringing up the sale, slipped the book into a bag, and handed it to Henry along with his credit card. "Receipt's inside. Let me know what you think of the book."

"I will." He tipped his hat to her. The chime tinkled again as he left the store.

"Well, what do you think, Gus? Should we call it a day?" Tomorrow was Friday. Weekenders would start arriving by noon, and business would pick up again. Rebecca would be in tomorrow, so Mary decided she'd spend the morning trying to track down Hopkins.

She got her jacket from the back room and put Gus in his cat carrier. "Let's go see if we can help Betty with dinner."

Betty and Mary's home was located on Shore Drive and had a lovely view of Little Neck Beach and Cape Cod Bay. A two-story Federal-style house, it was painted a light green with darker green shutters on the front windows. Betty had planted rhododendrons along the property line with her neighbors, low shrubs across the front of the house, and had beds of annuals that provided bright colors all summer long. Given her arthritis, Mary couldn't imagine how Betty managed so much planting and weeding, but she was definitely glad for it. Betty had a wonderful aesthetic style.

Inside, Mary discovered Betty on the phone. From the conversation, she knew her sister was talking to her son. She released Gus from his carrier, and he scampered upstairs to one of his favorite napping places.

A couple of chicken breasts were on the kitchen counter. Mary washed her hands and started to prepare the chicken for baking.

Betty was a wonderful cook, but sometimes her arthritis made it hard for her to stand at the counter for any length of time.

When she finished her phone conversation, Betty joined Mary in the kitchen. She wore a rose-colored cardigan over her pretty housedress and had changed into her comfortable slippers.

"Evan is going to send a messenger over tomorrow to get a copy of the lawsuit. As I suspected, he's going to hire an attorney. He has a college friend Robert Dunlap, who he thinks could handle the case. Apparently, Rob is very experienced in property disputes."

"That sounds perfect. Unless Daniel Hopkins has a change of heart and drops the whole thing." Mary thought of her plans to visit the man tomorrow but decided it would be better not to mention them.

"Wouldn't it be nice if Hopkins forgot the whole thing." Sighing, she rubbed the knuckles of her left hand as though holding the phone had caused them to ache.

"Would you like me to get your hand cream from your room?" Mary asked. Her sister had a special prescription cream to soothe the pain in her hands when it flared up.

"Oh no, I'm fine. Just worried, I guess." She sat down at the kitchen table. "Evan asked me if I had any idea of why Daniel would claim the mill was his. I told him about the feud, but that's about all I know."

After sprinkling on some spices, Mary put the chicken in the oven, set the timer, and sat down with Betty. An arrangement of iris and daisy mums Betty had picked from the yard served as a centerpiece and lent a light floral fragrance to the room.

"You know," Betty said, "after our visit to the mill, so many memories of the mill and the fun we had there came back to me. Of course, as I recall, neither Mother nor Gram were pleased with that grass-clod stunt you reminded me of. You and the neighbor boys got into a lot of trouble."

"True." But Billy Joe Nesbitt had been the leader of the gang, and Mary had had a childish crush on him at the time. "The Emersons probably weren't all that pleased with us playing in the mill either. I'm surprised they didn't run us off."

"My in-laws were dear people and loved children. I suppose they thought God would watch over us."

Mary wondered if they could have possibly anticipated, years later, that Daniel Hopkins would try to claim the gristmill as his own.

After dinner, Mary and Betty went into Betty's bedroom, where her files and financial records were kept in a tall filing cabinet.

Betty opened a drawer. "Edward always told me we only had to keep financial records, like receipts for tax purposes, for seven years. I confess I haven't cleaned out the files recently, so they probably go back a little further." She indicated a group of manila file folders all carefully dated by year.

"Does that include a receipt for your property taxes?" Mary asked.

"Oh my, yes. That's a big tax deduction." She pulled out the folder with the oldest date and placed it on her nearby desk. Opening the folder, she flicked through the stack of receipts. "Here it is."

Mary picked up the sheet of paper. Clearly it was the bill for the mill's property tax. "From the date, it looks like the county knew you owned the mill back ten years ago."

"They certainly did. And they still do. There's a property tax bill in every one of these files."

Mary continued to flip through the papers. "And you're sure you don't have a copy of the deed?"

Shaking her head, Betty said, "I really don't think so. I've never seen anything like that." Betty and Mary continued scanning through files, but they came up short.

"I guess since the Emersons were granted the land from the Massachusetts Bay Company, you'd have to check back to the 1600s."

"Now *that* would be some research project." Mary closed the file folder. "Let's hope we only have to check as far back as 1792."

"When Daniel claims his ancestors bought the mill." Betty made a dismissive sound. "This whole suit business is so annoying. And stressful. After all this time, why would Daniel start fussing about the mill now?"

That's what Mary hoped to find out when she spoke with him tomorrow.

———

First thing Friday morning, Mary dropped into the shop to leave Gus and make sure Rebecca was okay being alone for a while.

"Hi, Rebecca. Ashley, you're looking very summery with that blue bow in your hair." Rebecca's daughter was the quickest and nicest seven-year-old imaginable, which made her a big help to both Mary and Rebecca. Today, she'd pulled her ash-blonde hair back in a ponytail.

"Mom pinned the short hairs back for me." She tossed her head, making her hair swish back and forth.

"You look lovely," Mary said as she gave Ashley a light kiss on the head. She set Gus's cat carrier on the floor and released him. He went directly to Ashley and rubbed up against her legs. Ashley dutifully knelt to pet him.

"I have a couple of errands to run this morning," Mary told Rebecca. "If you need me, call me on my cell."

"No problem. I'll do a little dusting and sorting to keep me busy until some customers show up."

"Wonderful. I so appreciate you being here." She smiled at Ashley. "Both of you."

Mary had checked the church directory at home last night and found Jill Sanderson's address. Jill had been widowed for several years before marrying Harry Hopkins. When she remarried, she had kept her married name from her first marriage for the sake of her children. She had mentioned at prayer group that Daniel was her grandfather-in-law and now lived with them. It was a situation that apparently troubled her. Since Mary didn't want to alert Daniel by calling first, she decided it would be better to arrive unannounced.

She drove her car to Water Street, then turned left. She slowed as she drove past older, one-story houses with attics. Scattered among them were what amounted to mansions in comparison, new houses recently built by wealthy owners.

She pulled over to the curb across from what she believed was Jill Sanderson's house. It was one of the larger homes on the street.

Resolving to be honey sweet with Daniel Hopkins, she climbed out of the car and walked across the street. She stepped around a skateboard, no doubt belonging to one of Jill's two adorable sons, and knocked on the door.

A moment later, Jill opened the door. Dressed in jeans and a tank top, the young blonde woman gave Mary a puzzled look.

"Mary? I, ah . . ."

"Hi, Jill, nice to see you. I'm sorry to drop by without calling first, but you mentioned that Daniel Hopkins is living with you now. Does he happen to be home? I'd like very much to talk to him."

"Daniel's here, which is unusual. He gets too restless to stay around the house all day and would rather be outside."

"Would you mind letting him know I'm here?"

Looking unsure of herself, Jill glanced over her shoulder. "I know what this is about, Mary. I'm sorry, but I'm not sure he'll want to talk to you."

"It'll just take a few minutes," she pressed, keeping her voice as light as possible.

"Really, it might be better if—"

"Who's at the door?" a male voice bellowed from a back room. "If it's one of those fool salesmen, send him away."

Jill flinched. "I'm sorry."

Leaning into the door, Mary called out. "Mr. Hopkins, my name is Mary Fisher. I just need a few minutes of your time. I won't keep you long."

The man marched down the hallway toward her. Tall and wiry and wearing a sailor's cap, he had to be in his eighties. As he drew closer, Mary noted that his wrinkled face resembled a topographical map and spoke of a life spent outdoors. The tiny veins in his cheeks and the reddened tip of his nose suggested an equal number of years of heavy drinking.

His expression seemed permanently frozen in a frown. "What is it? I'm busy."

Mary straightened her spine. "Mr. Hopkins, I'm Mary Fisher. My sister is Betty Emerson." She kept her tone level and calm. "I'd like to ask you about the suit you've filed against her."

He snorted. "You got questions, you talk to my lawyer." He started to turn away.

"Mr. Hopkins, please. I'd just like to know why you believe you own the mill. It's been in the Emerson family since 1667, when it was built."

"Lady, your sister's got a real surprise coming." Leaning into Mary's personal space, he lifted one corner of his lips in a sneer. She got a whiff of alcohol on his breath. "I got the bill of sale that says otherwise."

Wrinkling her nose, Mary took a step back. "If you have such a piece of paper, I'd very much like to see it. If you don't mind."

"I do mind."

"Well, then, would you tell me why you've brought the suit now instead of years ago?"

"Because I hadn't found the evidence yet, that's why. Didn't find that piece of paper 'til I was packing up my stuff to move in here with my grandson." He stepped out of the door and spit off the side of the porch. "We'll be showing the bill of sale when my attorney says it's time, and not before. I wouldn't trust it to an Emerson for so much as two seconds." His face flushed, a muscle flexed in his jaw, and his hands balled into fists at his side.

Instinctively, Mary retreated another step. "Mr. Hopkins, I know very little of the history of your family. I understand the Hopkinses and Emersons have been feuding for years."

His salt-and-pepper eyebrows angled downward. "Yeah. With good reason too." His beady eyes arrowed into her with laser precision.

Mary swallowed hard and pressed on. "Would you mind telling me what caused the feud?" She heard a tremor in her voice, though she hoped Mr. Hopkins wouldn't notice.

Or become aware of the beads of the perspiration that had formed on her upper lip.

"Because all them Emersons are thieves and murderers."

He spoke the accusation so loudly, with spittle coming out of his mouth, Jill grabbed his arm. "Come back in the house, Grandpa. Doctor says you shouldn't get all in a fuss. High blood pressure is bad for you."

He shook her off. "What I'm saying is the truth. William Emerson murdered my great-great-grandpa Caleb Hopkins because he wouldn't give over the mill that was rightfully ours."

Stunned, Mary's mouth dropped open. *A man was murdered over the ownership of the gristmill?* She shuddered. Surely that wasn't possible.

"When … when did this …" Mary was so taken aback by such a wild statement that she seemed unable to get the words out.

"I'll tell you when. Was October 1841, that's when."

"That's over 170 years ago," Mary blurted out. "All these years—"

"It's like yesterday for us Hopkinses. We know what's right and what's not."

Mary lifted her chin, appalled that an angry feud could go on so long without resolution. As far as Betty knew, Edward was vaguely aware of a feud but had no idea how or why it had started, and he had no interest in finding out.

Whether someone had been murdered or not, people had clearly been hurt. "Mr. Hopkins," she said politely, "I will be searching county property records. If there is a deed of transfer or a title change, I believe that I will find it. And if there isn't—"

"The mill is ours; has been since 1792 when it was sold to our family. No county records or nothin' will change that."

We'll see about that, Mary thought. But rather than upsetting Hopkins any further, she smiled. "I'm sure your attorney will be hearing from my sister's attorney soon."

Jill, poor dear, gave Mary a weak smile, obviously not happy with the situation or Daniel's behavior.

Shaken by the encounter, Mary eased backward down the steps, then hurried across the street to her car. It appeared Daniel Hopkins wasn't in the mood for honey.

He wanted to fight. For him, the feud had never ended.

Back in her car, Mary wondered if Daniel's attorney would be any more forthcoming about the lawsuit, particularly the bill of sale, than Daniel had been.

She checked with Information to get Marc Dougher's phone number. When the receptionist at his office answered the phone, Mary introduced herself and asked to speak with the attorney about the Emerson case.

While the young woman placed Mary on hold, she watched Jill's house. The last thing she needed was for Daniel to come outside and catch her talking with his attorney.

Finally, the receptionist came back on the line. "I'm sorry, Mrs. Fisher. Mr. Dougher says he would be happy to talk to Mrs. Emerson's attorney, but any conversation with you regarding the case would be inappropriate."

Inappropriate? So much for her bright idea to talk to the attorney. But that wouldn't stop Mary from investigating Daniel's assertion that he had a valid bill of sale.

THREE

━━━◆◆◆━━━

From Jill's house, Mary headed to the county clerk's office, still unsettled by her encounter with Daniel.

When she arrived, the uncomfortable feeling she had from her conversation with Daniel Hopkins was replaced by the strange comfort she felt in the office's musty corridor.

Beatrice Winslow, the county clerk, was a tiny woman with short, closely trimmed silver hair and reading glasses she wore perched on the end of her nose. A counter covered with copies of the *Ivy Bay Bugle*, flyers about Cape Cod activities, and the county selectmen's next meeting agenda separated her from visitors.

Since the old records had been shifted from what was now Mary's bookshop, Bea's work area was crowded with filing cabinets and cupboards and smelled distinctly of aging paper.

"Hi, Bea. How are you?"

She glanced away from her computer screen, looked over the top of her glasses at Mary, and smiled.

"Mary, hi! I'm great, thanks. Except for a knee I twisted training for the 5K race in Provincetown next month, I'm feeling quite fit. How about you?"

For a woman who had to be close to seventy, Bea was in admirable shape. Which reminded Mary she ought to make a

point of taking long walks more often now to take advantage
of the summer weather. If only she could find the time. A
convenient excuse, she admitted.

"I'm good, thank you. I'm doing some research on the
old gristmill for my sister." Mary didn't have any trouble
revealing the situation to Bea. Not only did she need Bea's
help, but she knew the clerk was the soul of discretion.
She'd never reveal a word she heard or secret she learned
as county clerk. Probably not even under the threat of tor-
ture. It was why she'd been reelected more times than Mary
could count.

Bea raised her gray eyebrows. "Is there a problem?"

"We're hoping it's much ado about nothing. Daniel
Hopkins is challenging the ownership of the mill. Claims it
belongs to his family."

"Oh, stuff and nonsense." Chuckling, she waved her hand
in front of her face as though shooing a fly away. "Daniel
Hopkins is so crazy that he couldn't even find his own house,
let alone the mill. Everyone knows that."

Mary would have laughed except for the seriousness of
the situation. "Well, he actually filed suit against Betty, so he
must have found his way to an attorney." Although some attorneys weren't entirely ethical—taking on a case they knew
they couldn't win just to claim the fee from their hapless
client. "I thought I'd check the county property records to
see if there was ever a title change or a new deed recorded. I
need to know if there's any merit to his claim. I'm sure Betty's
attorney will be searching too."

"How far back do you want to check?"

"As far as possible. How far back do the records go?"

"Ivy Bay was founded in 1639, but the county wasn't established until 1685. The records were a bit sketchy back then."

"I'd like to take a look at whatever you have."

Glancing at her computer screen, Bea typed a few keystrokes. "There wasn't enough room for all our records up here, so we stored the oldest ones down in the basement."

She got up and plucked a light-blue duster from the coatrack to cover her dress. "I hope you don't mind getting your clothes a little dusty. There's enough dust and dirt on the oldest boxes of records to build a new sandbar. I was joking the other day with the selectmen that we ought to put in some big lights and start a hydroponic garden down there to raise tomatoes all year long."

"Sounds like a good fund-raising project for the county," Mary joked. She was wearing a pair of washable khaki slacks and a light sweater over a blouse, and she wasn't worried about a little dirt.

Bea led her down a flight of steep stairs that would be dangerous if they hadn't had a solid handrail. The dim overhead lighting barely provided enough illumination to read the labels on row after row of boxes stacked on shelves six feet high. Certainly not enough light to grow tomatoes.

"I really appreciate you letting me look at the old files," Mary said.

"All part of the job," she said cheerfully. "Walking up and down the stairs makes for good thigh muscles."

They'd reached the end of an aisle, and she pointed to a sturdy cardboard box with a green label on the highest shelf above the others. "Looks like 1689 is the oldest we've got for property records."

"Then I'll start there."

Bea dragged a rolling ladder over, climbed up, and handed down the top box.

Taking the weight of the box, Mary grunted and sneezed. It was heavier than she'd expected, and just as dusty as Bea had promised. No wonder Bea was in such great shape if she moved these boxes around with any regularity. She carried the box to the table in the center of the room.

"You're all set now," Bea said. "This box contains lists of property records. Each list is dated and indicates the name of the property owner. You shouldn't have any trouble figuring it out. Let me know if you need anything else."

"I will. Thanks, Bea."

Bea left her to go back to work upstairs, and Mary sat down at the steel table. Though the room was dungeon-like, it admittedly was more spacious than the dungeons described in historical novels. Perhaps she could use a musty-smelling basement in the mystery novel she had been writing for a half dozen years. She intended to finish the story someday, but not with publication in mind. Really, her writing was a hobby for cold, wintry days.

When she lifted the lid off the box, she sneezed again. Gracious, she should have brought a dust mask to cover her mouth and nose, and a dust cloth.

She started with the first file, dated 1689; the record listed all the properties in the county, along with the respective owners.

Unfortunately, the paper was so fragile that Mary probably should have worn white gloves to avoid damaging the records with body oil. The once-flourishing handwriting had faded, making some of the entries hard to decipher.

She laboriously worked her way through page after page that listed specific properties, describing each plot of land, the size and use at that time, and the owner's name. Many of the plots included a large amount of acreage, probably claimed by early settlers and sold off over the years for a profit.

The county was larger and had more residents than she had realized, certainly more than she'd expected for the late 1600s. She searched several pages before she found the name of Emerson mentioned.

She squinted and fussed with her glasses to read the faded ink. The corners of the property were given in degrees, minutes, and seconds of latitude and longitude. "Usage: residence and gristmill. Owner: Ezra Emerson."

"Well, there you are," she said to herself. "That proves the Emersons owned the property and the mill as early as 1689." Given the timeline, Ezra, or perhaps his father, had built the mill, though that would have no bearing on Hopkins' suit and the current ownership of the mill.

She leaned back in the hard metal chair. That didn't, however, prove the owner hadn't sold it in 1792, almost a hundred years and generations of Emersons later.

She skimmed down the page and turned to the next. An Arnold Hopkins was listed as owning a residence in Ivy Bay, presumably Daniel Hopkins' ancestor and another original settler.

She made copies of the records she'd found and returned the originals to the file box. After hefting the heavy container into her arms, she carried it down the aisle and struggled to lift it back into its proper place. She sneezed again and waved the dust she stirred up away from her face.

Glancing at her watch, she realized she didn't have time to look for the 1792 records. She needed to get back to the bookshop to give Rebecca a break. In fact, since this was

Friday, with a busy weekend coming for the bookshop, she wouldn't be able to check more records until Monday.

———

A little after lunchtime, Mary had just finished with a customer when Betty entered the bookshop carrying a potted rose. She wore jeans, a man's old shirt that used to be Edward's, and her gardening gloves.

"Hey, Bets. What are you up to?"

"I got tired of fretting about the lawsuit, so I decided to go to Tanaka Florist and Garden Center and buy some plants to spruce up the bookshop's backyard." Mary knew Betty had planned to work on the backyard, but it was a surprise to see her there this afternoon.

"That's wonderful," Rebecca said from behind the counter. "It certainly could use some landscaping and some bright color."

Ashley looked up from the book she'd been reading. She was in the small area Mary called the children's nook. The centerpiece was a porcelain pedestal bathtub lined with a light-blue rug that children loved to sit in while they read. It was a gift from Betty for the shop's grand opening.

"Can I help you garden?" Ashley asked. "Sometimes I help my mom."

Betty eyed the girl. "I'd love for you to join me, but you have to get permission from your mom. You'll probably get dirt all over your pretty outfit."

"Eh, it's all washable," Rebecca said with a resigned smile. "It's fine with me."

With a big grin, Ashley popped up and joined Betty.

Mary was grateful for her sister's green thumb and that she'd found a diversion to take her mind off the lawsuit. Before Mary had bought the property, the county had used the building for archives. Although she'd always loved the structure and its history, the county had done little to the small plot of ground in the back, and it had grown up in weeds. Except for a wild raspberry bush, she'd had the yard cleaned out shortly after she bought the building. To have flowers growing there would be a delight. Something both she and her customers could enjoy.

"I don't want you to overdo it," Mary said.

"Don't worry. Digging a few holes won't hurt me if I'm careful, and it will get my mind off my troubles. I bought a chokeberry bush, one like I have in my yard, and two of these antique roses. The berries attract migratory songbirds."

"Sounds great, Betty. Thanks. Yell if you need any help with the planting, okay?" Mary offered.

"Ashley will do just fine." She smiled down at the child. "Right now, I came in to get a glass of water. Gardening is thirsty business in the summer. Which reminds me, the plants will have to be watered every day for a few days. As soon as they're established, once a week should do it."

"I'd be happy to do that," Rebecca volunteered.

"Me too," Ashley echoed.

"Perfect. That will be wonderful." Betty moved to the refreshment table to get her drink of water, Ashley right with her.

"I bet you two had lots of fun and were close when you were young," Rebecca commented to Mary.

"I'd say so. Of course, we did our share of sisterly bickering. And as my *older* sister," Mary said with Betty still in earshot, "she used to boss me around whenever she thought she could get away with it."

"I did not!" Betty said. "Besides, sometimes you were a pest."

Stifling a laugh, Mary shook her head for Rebecca's benefit. "I was always a complete angel," she whispered for her employee's ears only.

The arrival of a middle-aged woman halted their teasing banter. Not one of Mary's regulars, the woman was probably from the mainland for the weekend. The local hotels and bed-and-breakfasts often referred customers to her since she'd opened.

"May I help you find something?"

"Absolutely. Silly me—we're here for the weekend, and I forgot to pack anything to read."

"Well, it's the perfect excuse to visit a bookstore." Mary smiled. "Tell me what sort of books you like to read, and I'm sure we can find something you'd enjoy."

When she had found a book for the customer, Mary stepped out the back door to see what progress Betty was making. It looked like she and Ashley already had the chokeberry in the ground and were now working on the rosebushes.

"Everything all right?" Mary asked.

Betty wiped her forehead with her gloved hand, which left a streak of dirt. "We're fine. Ashley's a good little helper."

Mary smiled and slipped back into the shop.

As Mary had predicted, the shop had a small but steady stream of customers drop in to browse and buy books throughout the rest of the afternoon, enough to keep Mary busy answering questions and Rebecca ringing up sales.

After her gardening, Betty washed up and browsed in the shop until closing time. Rebecca and Ashley had already gone home when Mary closed the shop with her sister.

Once back home, Mary helped Betty put away her gardening tools. Betty warmed up some chicken-and-barley soup she'd made earlier in the week. They sat at the kitchen table.

Mary spooned some soup into her mouth and considered how to tactfully bring up the murder comment Daniel Hopkins had made. "So, I know you said Edward never mentioned why there was a feud with the Hopkinses. But do you remember *any* rumors that may have been brought up?"

"No, I haven't been able to think of anything. I'm not sure Edward knew."

"So there was nothing ever said about a murder?"

Betty visibly shuddered. "Dear me, no."

Mary sighed. "I figured as much. Seems like something Edward or someone in the family would have mentioned." Mary set her spoon down and looked squarely at Betty, who looked sufficiently confused. "I went to see Daniel Hopkins this morning, in the hope I could convince him to give up the suit, or at least hear his explanation for why he filed it."

Betty's eyes widened, but Mary continued. She told her sister about his accusation that William Emerson had murdered Caleb Hopkins in 1841, over the question of mill ownership.

"That's ridiculous! Certainly if Edward knew about it, he would have said something."

"If there was a murder back in the 1800s, it sounds as though the Emersons had forgotten all about it." Mary buttered a whole-grain cracker.

"Because no such thing ever happened. I'm sure of it."

Mary looked at her sister tenderly. "Of course, I agree with you. But Daniel Hopkins certainly thinks there was."

Betty bristled and put her spoon down. "Really, Mary, I would know, wouldn't I, if the family had some deep, dark secret like that?"

Not necessarily, but Mary didn't want to press the point. Her sister was already upset enough. But her defense of the Emersons, her pride in having married into the family, left her less than objective about their role in Ivy Bay history. In the case of her husband's family, she'd always been fiercely loyal. Mary would have to tiptoe gently not to offend her.

Pensive, Mary and Betty finished their soup in silence. Finally, Mary spoke. "I think it will be important to learn as much about the history of the mill as possible. According to Daniel, William Emerson must have at least thought he owned the mill in 1841. It should be easy to check the census records for 1840, which will show where the Emersons and Hopkinses lived at the time. I'll do that after I've searched the property records up through the 1790s, when the suit claims Isaac Emerson sold the mill to James Hopkins."

"You won't find any record of the mill being sold, Mary, I guarantee it. And there was never a murder either. Daniel Hopkins has simply made it up. He's probably jealous of how prosperous the Emersons have always been." In a huff, she stood and carried her bowl and spoon to the counter.

Mary had another thought. "I wonder if Eleanor knows more about the feud than Edward did. Women tend to keep their ears more in tune with what's going on."

"I have no idea. She's never talked to me about any feud, and I've never asked."

"Maybe we can catch her after church on Sunday. See if she has any thoughts on the subject."

Turning, Betty eyed her sister. "If you insist. But I know no Emerson was involved in any murder."

As Betty left the kitchen, Mary whispered one of her favorite Bible verses: "The end of a matter is better than its beginning, and patience is better than pride. Do not be quickly provoked in your spirit, for anger resides in the lap of fools" (Ecclesiastes 7:8–9).

Both she and her sister would have to be patient until they could prove Daniel Hopkins' assertion was false.

Before she could get her dirty dishes in the dishwasher, Mary's cell phone rang. Her daughter's name flashed across the screen.

"Hi, Lizzie!" she said. She was always pleased to hear from her. "How are you, darling?"

"We're good, Mom. Luke wanted to tell you about his soccer game this afternoon. I'll put him on."

After a pause, Luke said in an excited voice, "Grandma, I made a goal today!"

Mary grinned. Hearing Luke's voice was just the pick-me-up she needed. "Congratulations, young man. I'm so proud of you."

"Yeah, I'm proud of me too. Love you."

With that, Luke handed the phone back to his mother, which made Mary laugh. Boys were so much less articulate than their sisters.

Since Emma, her granddaughter, was at a sleepover for the night, Mary and Lizzie talked awhile, catching up, but

Mary didn't mention the gristmill and the latest mystery that had embroiled her. She didn't want her daughter fussing over her or worrying about Betty. Not yet, anyway.

Not unless the court case went very badly against the Emersons.

———

Saturday afternoon, Betty dropped into the bookshop.

"I'm going over to the park to check out the summer festival," she told Mary, who was straightening books on a shelf. "I want to take a look at the craft guild's booth. Do you have time to come along?"

Mary slid a book into place and glanced around. They'd had a steady but small stream of customers that afternoon.

"You okay on your own for a bit?" she asked Rebecca.

"Oh, sure. I'll be fine."

"Okay. Call me if you need me."

The Albert Paddington Park, named after an early settler who'd given a nice chunk of land to the town, wasn't far away. As Mary and Betty stepped out onto the sidewalk, they could hear the high school jazz band playing in the park gazebo.

A committee chaired by Dorothy Johnson arranged entertainment in the park for each Saturday afternoon during the peak summer weeks. There was always music of some sort, ranging from string to barbershop quartets. Food booths sponsored by local businesses or organizations were set up around the perimeter of the park. The youth group of Grace Church of Ivy Bay had a hot dog booth, Sweet Susan's Bakery was always represented, and so was the Bailey's shop, which sold ice-cream cones.

The festival drew not only local residents but also tourists and visitors from other towns on the Cape.

"Are you looking for anything in particular?" Mary asked her sister. The temperature was warm, but the air smelled clean and fresh as it blew in off the bay. And it felt good to be out walking.

"Oh, you know me. I like to browse, and if I see anything I like, I like to buy." Betty shot Mary a quick grin. "Edward never wanted to go shopping with me but was terrified to let me go out alone."

Mary laughed, knowing that Edward had been a generous husband who never would have denied his wife anything. For her part, Betty was always on the lookout for decorative pieces that would sparkle up her house. Her taste had made her home a showcase for local artisans.

The music grew louder as they approached the park. Teenagers had put up a volleyball net on the grass and had a pickup game going. Several fathers and sons were playing catch, and toddlers were running around in bare feet, having a wonderful time. Families sat in the shade of maple and poplar trees that put on a spectacular leaf display in the fall.

Several booths were set up in the craft guild's area. Betty headed in that direction.

Mary reached out to stop her sister. "Isn't that Dorothy Johnson over in the corner?" She squinted to see what Dorothy was selling on her table.

"Yes. It looks like she's got a table full of antiques. Now why would she be selling those?"

"I don't know." But Mary did know Henry thought Dorothy's home was in need of some serious repairs. "Should we go say hello?"

"Maybe later. There's something else I want to see first." Betty stopped to visit with a local artist. While they chatted, Mary examined the watercolors displayed on easels. Lovely scenes of children playing on the sand dunes at sunset, and sailboats, spinnakers blooming, racing across the bay. Idyllic scenes around the Cape.

Mary wondered if she ought to buy one or two to display in her bookshop. She was sure Betty, who had a much better artistic eye than she did, would help her select something appropriate. When she'd first bought the shop, she'd found a couple of framed old photographs, one featuring her uncle George in front of the shop, and one of the back of the building. But after one of the photographs was stolen, and Mary learned of some unsavory history behind them, she decided they'd be better suited for storage than display.

They wandered past the various booths until Betty stopped again at a table filled with handblown-glass pieces.

"Oh my," Betty murmured. Carefully, she picked up a pulpit vase, the colors progressing from a dark green at the base to a pale shade of green around the fluted edge.

"Are you the artist?" she asked a bearded young man wearing shorts and T-shirt, who was slouching in a chair behind the table.

"I am," he said without standing.

Betty turned the vase over to check the markings. "JK?"

"Jack Kerns. I work out of what used to be a boat repair shop in Falmouth."

"This is an extraordinary piece." She set it back on the table and picked up another vase, examining it with equal care. She returned that to the table and pointed at the first vase. "I assume it's for sale?"

A cute grin brightened his expression and he stood. "Yes, ma'am."

Within a few minutes, Betty had become the proud owner of a Jack Kerns original vase.

As she and Mary walked away, Mary said, "That was a pretty expensive impulse buy."

"Sister, dear, mark my words. That young man is going to have pieces of his glass in museums within a few years. This one piece will double or triple in value. Besides"—she smiled—"it's going to look perfect in our living room."

Betty's uncanny sense of taste and artistic value always stunned Mary. Lucky for her, she'd married into a wealthy family, Mary thought without envy. The life Mary had led with John and their children had been all she could have asked for.

"Now then," Betty said. "I saw you eyeing some watercolors earlier."

A flush warmed Mary's cheeks. "I was just thinking about buying a couple for the shop. You know, to give the walls some color. But I don't need to—"

"Of course you do." Betty hooked her arm through Mary's and marched her back toward the art display. "Buying art is not only good for starving artists, but it's therapy for those who buy and enjoy the artist's talents. Now then, let's take a closer look."

The two of them wandered around the displays of half a dozen different artists who worked in oil, watercolor, and even charcoal. Many of the paintings were of Cape Cod scenes, but Mary kept being drawn back to those first paintings she'd noticed.

The fully rigged sailboat was a traditional subject, but this painter had caught the wind in the sails with such accuracy, Mary could almost feel the wind in her face and hear the zip of the boat racing over the water.

The scene of the two young girls making castles in the sand took her back to her youth. She and her sister could have been models for the artist.

Betty engaged in a little bargaining, and in no time, Mary was the proud owner of two lovely watercolors perfect to display in her bookshop.

By the time they were ready to drop by Dorothy's table, she appeared to have closed up shop for the day.

Mary wondered again what she was selling. And why?

After church on Sunday, Betty and Mary made their way through the departing crowd.

"Do you see Eleanor?" Mary asked, peering around. She hadn't seen Edward's sister during the service but knew Eleanor faithfully attended virtually every Sunday.

"There she is." Betty struck off across the patio area. Mary followed.

A striking woman of seventy-five years, Eleanor had a regal carriage and wore a stylish silk lavender suit with low pumps. Her hair was impeccably arranged in an upsweep.

"Eleanor," Betty called. "Do you have a minute?"

Holding a cup of coffee in her hand, Eleanor turned. She raised her finely shaped brows. "Of course, Betty. Did you need something?"

"Actually, we wanted to ask you a few questions," Mary said.

"You appear very serious, Betty. Is something wrong?"

"Yes." Glancing around, Betty gestured to an area of the patio where no one was standing. "Let's step over there so we won't be overheard."

Straightening her spine, Eleanor stood even more erect than she had been. "If you insist."

When they were away from other members of the congregation, Eleanor, in a firm, tight voice said, "Now tell me what this is all about."

Betty took a deep breath. "Eleanor, I'm being sued. Daniel Hopkins claims he owns the gristmill."

For a long moment, Eleanor simply stared at Betty as though she'd spoken in some alien tongue. "That's impossible."

"We know that," Betty said.

"But we were wondering if you'd ever heard any claims of that sort," Mary said.

"Absolutely not!"

"Daniel claims he has a bill of sale," Mary added.

"Utter nonsense." She set her coffee on a low wall and folded her arms across her chest.

"He also says there's been a feud between the Emerson and Hopkins families since 1841. And that the feud was over the death of Caleb Hopkins."

Eleanor gave an unladylike snort. "Those Hopkins people have created more difficulties for our family than I can even count. They made up some story about unrequited love between a Hopkins and an Emerson girl in the early 1800s. When she turned the boy down, he went to sea and drowned. Fishermen drown all the time, but they blamed the girl."

"That doesn't sound reasonable," Betty commented.

"It wasn't." Eleanor held up two fingers as though counting transgressions committed by the Hopkins families. "Then there was another story around World War I. A Hopkins girl claimed one of our ancestors got her pregnant. He denied it was true. We Emersons don't trifle with the Hopkinses."

Mary wondered if that applied to Jill Sanderson, who was now married to Harry Hopkins, Daniel's grandson. But Eleanor might not know that information.

"There were earlier stories too," Eleanor continued. "Thievery. Fighting. All sorts of skullduggery."

Betty had paled. "Edward never said a word to me."

Eleanor waved off the comment. "Men are not usually involved in the social life of the community in the same way we women are."

"What about a murder?" Mary ventured.

"The Hopkinses started a rumor blaming our family for the death of one of their clan years and years ago, but nothing ever came of the story. Purely fiction, I assure you." Eleanor sniffed. "I really must get home now, but please keep me informed about the ridiculous suit over the mill ownership."

"Just one more thing," Mary said. "Would you happen to have any old records related to the mill? Anything at all would help."

Eleanor hesitated, her nicely arched brows pulling together. "There are boxes and boxes of old family records in the attic, most of which I've never examined at all."

"There might be something in them that would be helpful to Betty's case," Mary said. "If you have time, could you please take a look?"

"Of course," Eleanor said. "I'm as anxious to defend against this frivolous suit as you are." She nodded an abrupt good-bye.

Eleanor walked with purpose and made her way through the crowd without acknowledging anyone.

Mary turned to her sister. "Do you think Daniel Hopkins has made up this whole story to somehow get even for past injustices?"

"I think Eleanor knows the history of the Emerson family better than anyone else."

Mary certainly agreed with that. "I do hope she can find something useful in those boxes in her attic."

Evan had arranged for Robert Dunlap, his college friend and the attorney he had hired, to meet him at Betty's house Monday morning.

A tall man in his forties, Rob had a receding hairline, a slight thickening around his waist, and an easy smile. After introductions, he sat on the chair opposite the sofa where Betty and Evan sat. Mary took the matching chair.

"I've read the suit," Rob said, his leather briefcase across his lap. "As near as I can tell, it rests entirely on the claim of a bill of sale from 1792."

"It's absurd. I just can't imagine where he would have gotten such a document," Betty said. "The mill has always been owned by the Emersons. The bill of sale Hopkins claims he has must be a forgery."

"That would be our hope," Rob agreed. "We'll just have to prove it."

"How?" Evan asked.

Rob raised his brows, acknowledging the problem. "*If* Daniel really does have that document—which his lawyer claims he does—then the first thing we'll need to do is authenticate the signature. If we had a sample of Isaac Emerson's signature, that would be helpful."

Mary leaned forward. "Perhaps there is something in the county clerk's office that has Isaac's signature on it."

"I'll have my assistant look into that," Rob said.

Mary thought she'd do some searching herself too. She owed Betty her best effort to clear up the mess as soon as she could.

"I should mention," Rob said, "that the opposing attorney is Marc Dougher. He doesn't have a sterling reputation, but he does win a good percentage of his cases."

Mary didn't think that was good news. "Is there anything we can do to help you? And Betty's case?"

Rob chuckled a bit. "If any of you can convince Mr. Hopkins to withdraw the lawsuit altogether, that would save everyone a lot of time and trouble."

Mary agreed. But based on her one brief meeting with Daniel, she didn't think that would be possible.

———

After the meeting with the attorney, Mary went directly to the county clerk's office.

"Good morning, Bea. How was your weekend?"

Looking up over the top of her glasses, Bea said, "Wonderful, thank you. I took in a play in Barnstable with some friends, and it was hysterically funny. Back for more research?"

"Yep!"

"Go on down," Bea said with a wave of her hand.

Mary headed downstairs, daunted by the task ahead of her. In all these files, where would she find a signature? But she squared her shoulders and got to work.

She started by looking through the 1792 property records she hadn't had time to look through last time, but she didn't find anything to indicate that property had changed hands. Then, she spent the next several hours flipping through files during the mid- to late 1700s and early 1800s—the time of Emerson's adulthood—only to come up short. There were no examples of Isaac's signature, let alone any indications that the mill had been sold.

When she left the clerk's office, she was surprised to see Daniel Hopkins leaning against the wall of Cape Cod Togs across the street. The store sold clothing Mary liked to think of as country club casual and had high-end prices to match the designer duds.

She frowned. Why would Daniel, wearing overalls and his captain's cap, be loitering around Cape Cod Togs? Navy blazers, white slacks, and loafers definitely did not seem his style.

She glanced up and down the sidewalk. No one was in sight, and Daniel was looking right at her.

A cool breeze raised the hair on the nape of her neck as she considered approaching him. But considering the menacing look on his face, and knowing how he'd reacted the last time they'd interacted, Mary thought it best to avoid him. She turned and hurried back to the bookshop.

FOUR

Mary reached the shop somewhat breathless, not from exertion but from a sudden case of nerves. Daniel Hopkins had rattled her simply by standing across the street. Her skin was still crawling from the way he'd stared at her. The fact that he seemed so confident about his right of ownership to the gristmill made her all the more uneasy about him. Maybe she was just being silly. Jill had told her Daniel liked to wander around town.

"Are you all right?" Rebecca asked. "Your cheeks are flushed."

Ashley came in from the backyard and hopped up on the stool next to her mother. A few splashes of water on her shoes suggested she'd been watering the new plants. "You look like I do when I hold my breath too long and my face turns all red."

"I'm fine, sweetie." Despite her anxiety, she smiled at young Ashley and drew a settling breath. "I guess I walked back from the clerk's office too fast."

Gus roused himself enough to greet Mary by rubbing up against her legs.

Feeling foolish that she'd reacted to Daniel's presence so strongly, Mary looked for a distraction. Her gaze fell on the old ledger from the mill, which she'd left on a shelf behind the counter.

"How are you at reading old-fashioned handwriting?" she asked Rebecca.

"How do you mean?"

Mary retrieved the ledger and placed it on the counter, then opened it to the first page. "I'm having a hard time reading this. Can you make anything of it?"

Rebecca took a look. "Artistic doodling?"

Peering around her mother, Ashley said, "A map of a river that's gone silly?"

Chuckling, Mary shook her head. "Artistic, I agree. But I don't think it's a river map or doodling."

"Oh, I see it now. At least I think this bit ..." Rebecca pointed at a grouping of swirling lines. "Does this say 'Lord'?"

"Lord?" Mary took another look and a tingle of excitement skittered through her stomach. "I think you're right. But what about the rest of it?"

Slowly, Rebecca shook her head. "The best I can guess is that it's the artist's idea of what God looks like. Sort of all swirly around the whole universe."

An interesting guess, but Mary didn't think it was the answer she was looking for. "Maybe it's a phrase that ends in the word *Lord*?"

She opened the ledger to one of the pages with peculiar marks. "Does this look like anything to you?"

Rebecca studied the page. "It almost looks like the marks I used to use in high school to keep score of a baseball game. You know, hits and runs and outs marked in little diamond shapes in the columns." Rebecca frowned. "But it looks like there were a lot of players on the team."

Eyeing the rows and columns, Mary supposed it could be a record of scores in some sort of game, although the shapes looked more like boxes than the diamonds John used to make when he was keeping score of a Red Sox game. She had never understood why he did that, since the score was posted right where everyone could see it, but he enjoyed it.

And why would a record of scores be hidden or thrown away under the gristmill's floorboards? That made little sense to Mary. Then again, maybe the ledger had fallen off of something and been forgotten. Over time, perhaps it had simply tumbled into a crack between the rock foundation and the floor of the gristmill. All she knew was that it was likely some kind of ledger, and she couldn't ignore the distant possibility that it might shed some light on the ownership of the mill.

"Well, whatever this is, we know that it's old," Rebecca said. "Maybe Rich or Jayne Tucker at the antique store could figure it out."

Mary lifted her head. "What a good idea! I should have thought of that myself." She wrapped the ledger in its oilskin and picked up the porcelain doll. Might as well take that along as well. "I'll pop over there now to see if they can help me out."

She headed out across the street and waved to Jeremy Court, who was walking his dog down Main Street. Jeremy owned Meeting House Grocers with his wife Kaley and though they were young and could come across as aloof, they were actually quite warm and kind. Mary headed to Gems and Antiques, the store Jayne Tucker and her husband Rich had opened more than twenty years ago. Every winter the Tuckers closed up shop for up to a month and toured Europe in search of gems and antiques they could bring back to sell. During the rest of the year, one or the other of them would slip away to estate sales all over the Northeast.

Mary suspected they'd chosen the business in order to have an excuse to travel.

Mary had come to love the antique shop. It was a maze of New England heritage—antique quilts, desks and dressers handcrafted in the 1800s, Paul Revere silver, wooden rocking horses, and old cradles. The European side of the maze featured silver, exquisite china, brooches, and jewelry chock-full of gemstones.

Just as some of the original buildings in town had their own stories, so did each of the antiques Jayne had on display.

Jayne, a vibrant woman with auburn hair to match her personality, was sitting on a stool behind the counter.

"Hey there, Mary. Haven't seen you in a while."

"Hi, Jayne. Good to see you. How's everything going?"

"All's well. Rich is just back from a Maryland estate sale, in fact. Amazing jewelry and stones, plus some original paintings from the 1700s. If you're in the market . . ."

"You're talking to the wrong sister," Mary said with a smile. "But I'll be sure to tell Betty about your new stock. I just dropped in to see if you or Rich can tell me anything about a couple of items I've come across."

"Sure. What have you got?"

Mary placed the doll on the counter.

After picking it up, Jayne examined the doll, turning it around and checking the bottom much as Mary had when she found it. "There aren't any markings, which means there's no way to date it. I don't think it's worth much, but let me ask Rich."

Jayne vanished behind a curtain into the back room, and a moment later Rich appeared. In contrast to Jayne's incredibly beautiful hair, Rich's head was shaved bald. Fortunately, he had a well-shaped head and was somehow equally attractive in a masculine way, particularly with his intelligent blue eyes.

"Hello there, Mary. What brings you to our modest shop today?"

She smiled since there was nothing modest about the value of the antiques they sold. "Just doing a little research."

Jayne handed her husband the doll. "Does this speak to you?"

"*Hmm.*" As he examined it, he shook his head. "Only the very best. But best what?"

"I have no idea," Mary said. "That's what I'm trying to find out."

"Sorry. Can't help you."

"That's all right. Here's something else I'd like you two to take a look at and tell me what you think."

After unwrapping the ledger, she placed it on the counter beside the doll. Rich flipped open the pages. "Now this looks old; at least the handwriting on the front page does."

"I thought that too." Mary turned a page. "But what could all of this mean?"

Shoulder to shoulder, Jayne and her husband studied the ledger pages.

"Some kind of game? Like dominoes?" Jayne guessed.

"I suppose something like that." Rich rubbed his palm over the top of his head. "I know who could probably help you. A guy named Lincoln King. He's an expert on antiquities, though he's mostly retired now. But if you could entice him to take a look . . ." Rich rummaged around in a drawer and came up with Mr. King's card. His address was on the outskirts of town.

Excited to have the name of an expert, Mary expressed her appreciation and hurried back to the bookshop. She'd try to reach the gentleman right away.

To her delight, she reached the soft-spoken Mr. King in one call. He was currently working on a project with a tight deadline, but she arranged for the expert to visit her shop a week from Wednesday. Apparently, he had heard of her store and had been curious about it. That plus the situation she described—and the fact she volunteered to give him a selection of mystery books in exchange for his services—helped her to close the deal.

Glad to have arranged the appointment with Mr. King, she rolled her shoulders in an effort to relax the tension she'd been feeling.

Her gaze fell on the porcelain doll from beside the cash register. Picking it up, she weighed it in her hand. *Only the Very Best.* What could the doll, or the phrase, mean as they related to the mill? And where did the doll come from? She figured it was probably unrelated to the ownership of the mill, but she wasn't willing to entirely ignore the artifact either.

With a sigh, she put the doll down and went into the back room to get a stepladder. She hadn't had a chance yet to hang the paintings she'd bought at the festival. No one, including herself, could enjoy them if they weren't on display.

She found a hammer and some nails. She positioned the stepladder where she wanted it and climbed up.

The chime over the door sounded.

"What are you up to?" Henry strolled into the shop. "I saw you through the window. Need some help?"

Keeping herself steady on the ladder, she looked over her shoulder. "I'm hanging a couple of paintings. I think I've got it okay."

"She doesn't look too steady to me," Rebecca commented.

"I agree. It doesn't look like she's measured right either."

Mary scowled. "This isn't rocket science." She banged a nail into the wall, climbed down and picked up the painting.

"A painting that size needs two nails or it will hang lopsided. And you need to measure the distance between them and between the bottom of the crown molding and the top of the pictures to get it right."

She eyed Henry with a mock glare, yet felt nothing but warmth for his friendship. "I don't suppose you know any handyman who's really good at hanging paintings?"

He grinned broadly. "I thought you'd never ask."

Laughing, she stepped off the ladder and out of the way, so he could climb it. "Thank you, Sir Galahad."

During the lunch hour, Mary was alone in the shop. Henry had finished hanging the paintings, which looked perfect on the wall. *Very Cape Coddish*, she thought with a smile.

Rebecca and Ashley had left to pick up some items they needed for dinner and had then gone home for a quick bite.

As Mary was reshelving some books, the chime sounded above the door. She turned to see Jill Sanderson glance up and down the sidewalk, then slip inside.

"Hello, Jill." The young woman's furtive manner and the way she stepped away from the front window troubled Mary. "What can I do to help you?"

"I just came by to apologize." She spoke in a low voice and glanced over her shoulder out the window. "My grandfather-in-law can be a little rude sometimes, but at heart, he's a good man."

A little rude was an understatement. "Thanks, Jill. But you have nothing to be sorry for. You certainly aren't responsible for your grandfather-in-law's behavior."

"I just . . . I can't get involved in the whole lawsuit thing. But I wanted you to know that I felt bad about the other day when you came by the house. You've always been so kind and friendly to me, and I love our prayer group."

"It was not your fault, Jill. And I feel the same way about you."

Jill smiled weakly and started to leave.

"Jill, can I ask you something?" Mary said tentatively. She didn't want to push Jill, but she couldn't help asking this one question. "Have you seen the bill of sale Daniel claims he has?"

She quickly shook her head. "Like I said, Mary, I really can't get involved. I'm sorry." She ducked out the door and was gone without another word.

Mary puzzled over Jill's visit. She supposed Jill sympathized with Mary's quest for information but was afraid to say anything. Assuming she had any firsthand knowledge of the lawsuit.

Mary mentally tucked away her questions. There might come a time when she would need to test Jill's sympathies for more information. But she'd have to tread very lightly if the need occurred.

⸻

The following morning was the ladies' prayer group. This time, they were meeting for breakfast in the Grace Church chapel.

Mary had formed the women's prayer group shortly after she'd moved to Ivy Bay and found it a good respite from her everyday worries. Somehow an hour or so contemplating the Lord's message in the company of fellow believers and praying for others lifted her spirits.

Facing Water Street, the church was only a block from her shop. In typical New England style, the church was painted white and boasted a tall spire that could be seen for miles. The church and setting were so striking that during the tourist season, the sidewalk across the street was virtually lined with people taking photos of the church—especially true when the maple trees changed color.

Mary arrived for the meeting in the church's prayer chapel at the same time as Dorothy Johnson, one of the group members. Mary felt dowdy next to Dorothy, who wore a stylish navy dress that emphasized her slim figure, matching pumps, and her ever-present string of pearls.

Mary greeted her. "How are you this morning?"

"Quite well, thank you." Dorothy angled directly toward the coffeepot next to the serving plates filled with a selection of sweet rolls and a variety of fresh fruit.

Mary decided one roll and a slice of melon wouldn't hurt her. She took a plate and served herself.

"Henry came by yesterday," Dorothy said, her tone casual. "Such a sweet man. I'm just useless at house repairs. So he volunteered to fix a couple of my windows that have gotten stuck." She stirred some creamer into her coffee.

"Oh, that's so nice of him. I remember he mentioned something about you asking him to do that."

Dorothy's head snapped around so fast, her coffee nearly sloshed out of her cup, and she narrowed her eyes. "He mentioned it to you?"

Immediately, Mary regretted saying anything. She had no desire to compete with Dorothy. "Oh, it was no big deal. He dropped by the bookshop looking for a new mystery to read."

"So he was just shopping. I see. Does he come in often?"

Mary hesitated. She was good friends with Henry, and she didn't mind if Dorothy knew that. She just didn't want to hurt Dorothy's feelings. Still, there was no reason to pretend she and Henry weren't close. "He comes in fairly often. We were childhood friends, so it's been nice to reconnect."

"Oh." Dorothy's voice went to ice. "How nice." Lifting her chin, she walked away as though Mary had suddenly developed an unpleasant odor.

Mary couldn't help but feel sympathy for Dorothy. She didn't sense any attraction to Dorothy from Henry, but it was clear how Dorothy felt.

Mary sighed and checked the clock on the wall. It was time for the prayer meeting, which was a refreshing distraction from both the mill case and Dorothy's unwarranted jealousy. "Ladies, I think it's time to get started." They'd gathered around a grouping of chairs and a soft glow from a nearby stained-glass window illuminated the small room.

Carrying her plate, Mary found a seat next to Tricia Miles, the pastor's wife, who had recently joined the group. A lovely woman in her late forties, she was almost as soft-spoken as her husband.

"Good morning, dear." Tricia squeezed Mary's free hand. "I'm so glad to see you this morning."

"You too." Mary squeezed back, then found her notes for the meeting. "We have quite a number of folks needing our prayers this morning." She read off a list of church members or their relatives who were ill or struggling with problems—a gentleman recovering from a heart attack, a child with chicken pox, a woman who was trying to repair a breach in her family.

When she concluded the list, Mary invited those present to request prayers for themselves or for others in need of the Lord's help.

Tricia spoke up. "There's a teenage boy in town who has recently lost his father. He's having a hard time adjusting to his loss. I'd like you all to pray for him."

The ladies all nodded sympathetically, promising to pray for the unnamed boy.

Amy Stebble, who was the principal at the elementary school, asked for prayers to help her husband, who was an artist, through an advanced online course in Web site building. "It's really hard, but when he finishes, he might be able to do some freelance work."

Lynn Teagarden wanted to give praise that her husband had found a good-paying, steady job.

When everyone had expressed their prayer needs, Mary said, "We'll now have a few moments of silent prayer asking the Lord's help for our friends and families who are in need. By all means, pray for yourself and your loved ones as well."

Mary bowed her head and beseeched God's help for those in pain and those who were suffering in their personal lives. And then, during a lull in the prayer circle, she silently asked the Lord to protect her family and guide her as she tried to find the truth about the Emerson gristmill.

When everyone had finished praying, Mary concluded by quoting 2 Thessalonians 1:12: "We pray this so that the name of our Lord Jesus may be glorified in you, and you in him, according to the grace of our God and the Lord Jesus Christ."

She glanced around the room and at the group of women she was coming to know and love. "This morning, Millie Russell has agreed to present our Bible lesson." She nodded to the dear little lady who was fast approaching her ninetieth birthday.

Millie's lesson was about having grace in the Lord. Mary couldn't help but recognize how little grace she'd had in her heart dealing with Dorothy, and she vowed to do better. Sometimes doing the *right* thing, loving your neighbors, didn't come easily.

"That was a wonderful lesson, Millie," Mary said. "I know it reminded me to live with more of the Lord's grace in my everyday life. Now then"—she glanced around the room— "next week, do you want to meet here again or somewhere else?"

Lynn Teagarden, a tall, friendly woman with dark brown hair, raised her hand. "I'd like to have the group come to my house. I could prepare a buffet lunch for us all."

"That's a very generous offer, Lynn. Thank you. Do you all like that idea, or would you rather meet at another time or place?"

After a bit of discussion, the ladies agreed to meet at Lynn's house but insisted it be a potluck affair rather than imposing on Lynn's generosity.

After Mary closed the meeting, several members left to go about their days. Mary stayed to visit and help the cleanup committee. When she finally said her good-byes to the last of the helpers, she left the meeting, her heart lighter for companionship of the church ladies.

———

Once again, Mary stopped by the county clerk's office before going to the bookshop. After she made an appointment with Mr. King, she realized there was another angle, aside from signature comparisons, that she could pursue toward potentially proving that Daniel's so-called bill of sale was a forgery.

Bea smiled broadly when she saw Mary. "Hello again, Mary. Still on your search for information about the mill?"

Mary returned her smile. "I am getting to be a pest, aren't I?"

"Not at all. I love helping people search through our records. It means they're important to someone besides me."

"Well, this time I have a bit of a challenge. The attorney suspects whatever paperwork Hopkins has is a forgery, but since I wasn't able to find a sample signature, I'm wondering if an expert could tell something about the age of the paper and maybe even the ink that was used?"

"I've seen that on the *History Detectives* television show, so I guess it's possible."

She and Betty occasionally watched that program. "Do you think it would be possible for me to borrow a bill of sale from the same time period that Hopkins claims the mill was sold—1790s? I have an expert coming next week and—"

"Oh, I'm so sorry, Mary. Your expert is welcome to come here to examine public records. But I cannot release any of the county's official documents."

Rules are rules and not to be broken. "I understand. I'll ask my expert if he has time to take a look while he's in town. And if you do think of somewhere else Isaac Emerson's signature might appear—"

"I'll be sure to let you know."

Mary reached the bookshop in time to open for the day. Ashley had a dentist's appointment that morning so Rebecca was taking a few hours off.

Gus, whom she'd brought to the shop before going to the prayer meeting, jumped up on the counter. Automatically, Mary stroked him and scratched under his chin. She was rewarded by such loud purring, Gus sounded like a motorboat warming up at the marina. Because he traveled back and forth with her, Gus had a food dish and litter box in the back room of the shop as well as at home.

"I seem to be stuck." She continued to stroke and pet her big gray cat, musing out loud. "What records I've found indicated Isaac Emerson never sold the mill. But that makes me wonder why Daniel is in such a snit over this whole thing. I can't believe he actually has a bill of sale, but that's what he claims." He also refused to show it to anyone before a hearing, which made her even more suspicious.

The bell chimed over the door, admitting the first customer of the day.

"Good morning," Mary said. "Anything special you're looking for?"

The woman was probably in her thirties. She had lovely long blonde hair and perfect makeup, and wore expensive jewelry. She'd stopped in front of the special Ivy Bay display.

"I think I've found it already." Her accent was pure Southern sweet tea. "This is my first visit to Cape Cod, and I always try to learn something about the history of the areas I visit."

"Then you've come to the right place, although each of these books focuses on some of the mysteries and mysterious features of our town." Mary joined her at the display, pointing out and describing what each book offered, and telling her a little about each author. "In addition to these nonfiction books, we also have some mysteries written by local authors who include a lot of the flavor of the Cape in their stories."

The young woman nodded her head with interest. "These books all sound fascinating."

The woman browsed through several books, selecting three. She put those books on the counter, then wandered around the shop, a book lover enjoying herself.

Meanwhile, Mary returned to the front of the store to ring up the sale.

"I could stay here all day," the young woman said, "but my husband will be back from his run on the beach by now. We're going to do some sightseeing."

Mary bagged the books the young woman had purchased and handed them to her. "Well, then, have a good day and come back when you can. We love to have browsers drop by."

As she left, Mary contemplated what her next step should be to learn more about the gristmill's history.

With a spark of inspiration, she decided to do some research, in between serving customers, right here on her own computer.

FIVE

◆◆◆

Two more customers dropped in before she could get to the computer. But then, selling books was her business. She wasn't going to complain when business was booming.

When she was finally able to sit on the tall stool behind the counter, she booted up the computer and Googled the US census from 1790. She was amazed to discover that these early records had been digitized, and she was actually able to pull up information from over two hundred years ago with the click of a few buttons. The first census the government had conducted was in 1790, which meant there would be no census record of the original settlers in Ivy Bay, like Ezra Emerson and Arnold Hopkins. But she wanted a better picture of who the Emersons were, as well as the Hopkins family.

When she pulled up the census for the county, she scanned down the names. A few of the first names caught her eye, including many biblical names, some of them quite unusual like Bezalel and Zepheniah. But the really special ones made her chuckle: Remember, Comfort, and Thankful. She imagined a mother standing on her front steps calling her children to dinner, and wondered what sort of nicknames they might have acquired. "Dinnertime, Memsy!"

Shaking her head, she got back to the question at hand. She found Isaac Emerson easily enough. Apparently, Isaac had been a prolific man. The record showed there were three males over the age of sixteen in the household, four younger males, and a total of six females. He'd been blessed with twelve children!

That was a lot of mouths to feed, but did that mean he'd had to sell the mill and his livelihood for five British pounds so the family could survive? After the five pounds had been spent, how did the family live if they no longer owned the mill?

"That doesn't seem reasonable, does it, Gus?" The cat had leaped onto her lap in search of attention. She dutifully scratched him under the chin. "Certainly Edward believed he and his family owned the mill. That makes me believe his father and grandfather held that belief as well. And, until now, apparently no one had claimed otherwise."

Balancing Gus on her lap, she searched further in the 1790 census report and found the listing for James Hopkins and his family. He'd had two boys and two girls.

Multiple generations would have been born, lived, and died by 1841 when William Emerson supposedly killed Caleb Hopkins.

Leaning back in her chair, she decided she hadn't learned much about the situation in 1790 except that both men had families. Hardly an earthshaking revelation.

Gus climbed up her chest and purred in her ear.

"You'd be a lot more helpful, Gus, if you'd been around in one of your nine lives way back in the 1790s. We'd have this mystery solved in no time."

Rebecca walked in the door. Gus jumped down to the floor and headed toward the back room to his feeding dish.

"Good morning, Mary. How has the day been so far?"

Mary turned away from the computer. "All's good. How did Ashley do at the dentist?"

"One little cavity in a baby tooth, but she behaved like a lady." A proud smile graced Rebecca's face. "I dropped her off at a friend's house for a playdate. The dentist gave her a stern lecture about brushing regularly. It was pretty cute."

"So much more effective coming from a doctor instead of a mom, I imagine."

Rebecca laughed, her brown eyes sparkling with amusement. "You're absolutely right, which is why I quietly asked him to do just that."

Slipping off her sweater, she said, "Anything I can help you with on the computer?"

"No, I don't think so." Mary told her about the census and that she was investigating the gristmill ownership. She didn't go into *why*. She wasn't hiding anything from Rebecca; she just didn't sense there was any reason to share Betty's troubles with her for the time being. "The census only gives the name of the head of household and the number of people living at that address. There's no other information."

Rebecca frowned. "Boy, for the last census, we had to fill out a huge form about ages, occupations, and I don't know what. It took forever."

"That's right, I remember. If I'd had a large family, it would have been a real bother." She turned back to the computer. Maybe a later census would include more information.

Rebecca went to work tidying up the display table, and Mary continued to work on her computer. With a few quick keystrokes, she brought up the 1840 census. If Daniel's story was right, Caleb Hopkins ought to appear among the names of those counted that year.

Sure enough, she found him right off. Caleb Hopkins, head of household, four children. Occupation: fisherman. Not miller, she noted. Apparently, the fishing occupation had been passed down from father to son through many generations of Hopkinses including to Daniel. Now his grandsons were in the same business.

That, at least, was new information. But she couldn't imagine what motive an owner of a gristmill would have to murder a fisherman. Certainly an argument over ownership of a mill wasn't reason enough to commit murder. Nothing was, Mary knew. Still, Mary couldn't help but wonder where Daniel's accusation had come from.

If it had any validity, Mary didn't think her sister would accept it at all well. It might be pride and loyalty to the Emersons that drove Betty's insistence that the mill had never been sold. But behind that insistence was a deep pool of emotion and the promise she'd made to Edward. She knew Betty wouldn't give up the gristmill easily.

She'd fight with all she had to save her family's legacy.

⁓

Late that afternoon, Betty called Mary at the shop.

"I don't feel much like cooking," she said. "How about after you get home, we'll drive down to Sam's Seafood? It's going to be a beautiful evening, and I'm in the mood for shrimp and chips."

"Sounds delicious." Mary's stomach rumbled in agreement, and she realized she hadn't taken time for lunch. "Maybe we can get outdoor seating on the deck." Sam's Seafood, right by the marina, was a bit of a dive but remained popular with both locals and tourists. Plus it was a great place to watch the boats come and go.

An hour later, Rebecca had tallied the sales for the day and gone to pick up Ashley on the way home. Mary straightened the counter and looked for Gus. He was not in his usual place, in a sunny spot in the front window, which meant he was hiding out to avoid the ride.

"Come on, Gus. I've got a dinner date." She looked under the display tables and then found him snoozing in one of the comfortable chairs at the back of the shop.

She squeezed the reluctant cat into his carrier and headed for home.

Only taking enough time upstairs in her room to freshen up, Mary was quickly ready to leave for Sam's.

"Was the shop busy today?" Betty asked as she backed out of the driveway.

"About the same as usual. And I've done some more research into the case."

"Any luck?"

"Not much, but I'm at least gathering some puzzle pieces. There is no record I can find of the property being sold, and there doesn't seem to be anywhere to find Isaac's signature."

Betty stopped momentarily at an intersection and waited for oncoming traffic to pass before turning right.

"Then there's no way Daniel can win the suit, right?"

Mary gnawed on her lower lip. "I certainly can't find any justification for the suit. But Daniel was able to find a lawyer willing to take on his case, and as Rob said, he's a lawyer who wins a lot."

Betty just shook her head in disgust.

Mary looked out the window. Could Daniel Hopkins be so mean-spirited and angry about ancient history and an old feud that he'd filed a suit without any merit as a way to get back at the Emersons? Make them run up attorney bills? That seemed crazy, considering none of the Emersons even remembered the original cause of the quarrel. Eleanor had related other incidents that wouldn't make for good neighbors, if they were true, but surely they weren't worth suing over.

The parking lot at Sam's was three-quarters full even at this early dinner hour. Betty found a place to park, and they walked to the restaurant, which was housed in an old, low cottage down by the marina. The building was one of the oldest in town and started its life as a fisherman's shack but had had many incarnations since then. The ceiling was low, and the walls of the vestibule where guests wait for a table were dark wood decorated with old black-and-white pictures of Ivy Bay. They were all scenes of the town—a swimsuit competition in the 1930s with the women covered from neck to toe, the commercial fishermen lounging on the dock near their boats, even a picture of the Emerson gristmill when it was in far better condition than it was now.

Mary inhaled deeply. It smelled like fried seafood. Her mouth watered. There were a few small mismatched tables scattered around the small dining room, but they were all occupied, and Mary waved to a couple of women she recognized from church as they made their way to the counter to order.

The menu was printed on chalkboards hung above the low counter. Mary studied the menu, but Betty knew what she wanted.

"Mary, Betty," Sam greeted them when it was their turn to order. Sam, the owner of the restaurant, was a fixture around Ivy Bay. Over eighty, he was still spry and sassy to his customers, and he still came to work at his restaurant every day. Sam started out doing all the cooking at the restaurant, but he preferred to chat with everyone who came in, so now he took orders and left the cooking to the help. The line moved slowly, as he chatted with each person who came to the counter, but Sam earned loyal customers.

"What'll you have?"

"Shrimp and chips for me," Betty said.

"Make that two," Mary said, glancing up at the menu one last time. The lobster roll was tempting, but she'd have that next time.

"Coming right up."

A few minutes later, they carried plastic trays out to the outdoor deck, which was lined with weather-worn wooden picnic tables. Mary spotted a couple of free seats available at one end of a table and threaded her way through the crowd toward it. Sam's wasn't fancy, but the food couldn't be beat, and the view out over the marina was stunning. Mary took in the panoramic view of the narrow rows of fishing shanties along the waterfront, as well as the small boat marina and the commercial fishing fleet.

While there were several people in the small boat marina washing the salt off their boats or loading up their gear, the commercial docks appeared deserted. Fishing trawlers rode easily on the shifting tide, leashed by heavy lines to the dock. Big piles of fishing nets sat at intervals on the dock like giant mounds of forgotten debris. Out in the bay, motorboats arced through the water, leaving a wake of V-shaped waves moving toward both shores of the bay.

As they ate, Mary looked out over the dock where the commercial fishing fleet was tied up. As usual, most of the boats had probably left the harbor as early as two in the morning, returning by noon with their day's catch.

Betty liberally sprinkled pepper over her meal and squirted ketchup from a plastic container onto her fries.

"I can't get the suit out of my mind," Betty admitted. "And I've been going over and over what Daniel said to you. He seems to think his great-great-grandfather was murdered because he was trying to claim the mill from William Emerson."

"Right ..." Mary wasn't sure what her sister was suggesting. She wiped her hands on a paper napkin that was somehow already coated in grease. No one ever claimed Sam's served health food.

"It seems to me that since there's no record of the sale, William Emerson wouldn't have had any reason to kill Caleb Hopkins." She sat back, content with her line of reasoning, and took another bite of bread.

She had a point. "Well, playing devil's advocate ... Maybe the mill wasn't a motive. They could have just gotten into an argument." She thought of Daniel Hopkins and the chip he had on his shoulder. If Caleb had had the same volatile personality, perhaps that caused the rift between the two families. "If things got overheated, William Emerson could have accidentally—"

"Really, Mary." Betty set the ketchup bottle back down with a thud. "I don't know why you persist in thinking the worst about Edward's ancestors."

"Oh, Bets. I'm not thinking the worst of anyone, and I dearly loved Edward. But I am trying to get to the bottom of this suit. Naturally, I have to consider all possibilities." And perhaps, since she was stumped in determining ownership of the mill, she should investigate Daniel's story about the murder of his ancestor.

Betty sniffed and turned away to look at the marina.

Mary's hand trembled slightly as she reached for a fried shrimp.

"I promise, Bets, I'll do what I can." She reached across the table and held her sister's hand. "I'll look into Daniel's story about the murder of Caleb Hopkins."

Betty gave a nod of acceptance. "Thanks, Mar. And when you're done, I'd love to be there when you tell Daniel Hopkins he'll have to stop maligning the Emersons' name or we'll . . . we'll . . ."

"I hate to be the voice of reason, but I do remember there's something in the book of Romans about not taking revenge but leaving room for God's wrath. Instead, we're supposed to feed our enemies."

"There are days, sister," Betty said good-naturedly, "that I'm sorry you've memorized so much of the Bible. There is no possible way I'm going to feed Daniel Hopkins a bite of food out of my cupboard."

With the tension between them eased, Mary and Betty ate for a time in companionable silence, accompanied by the murmur of voices around them and the shrill call of seagulls soaring overhead.

Betty asked how the plants at the shop were doing, and Mary told her how eager Ashley was to care for them. Their conversation then touched on their respective grandchildren's accomplishments, news of mutual friends, and the county's proposal to widen the beach by dredging sand from the bay.

While they chatted, the sun dropped lower in the sky, the boat masts in the marina casting longer and longer shadows. Seagulls vied for a spot on top of the tallest masts with the best perch for spotting luckless fish for their evening meal.

When they'd finished eating, Mary stood and took one last look at the view. She scanned the commercial fishing fleet with its wide-beamed boats tied up to the dock. That made her wonder . . . .

"Sam!" The restaurant owner must have been taking advantage of a lull in business to come out and say hi to his patrons. Sam finished chatting with a woman holding a new baby and then leaned in to caress its cheeks before making his way over toward Mary and Betty. The light breeze ruffled his little gray tufts of hair at the back of his head.

"Did you enjoy your meal?" Sam noted the empty plastic baskets in front of them.

"It was delicious." Mary brushed the crumbs off her hands. "Clearly."

"Glad to hear it. It's a beautiful night." Sam smiled out over the marina. The sun was just starting to slip down below the horizon, casting a warm orange glow over the boats.

"It sure is." Mary paused, trying to figure out how to phrase her question. "We've loved looking out over the marina. There are some beautiful boats. But do you know if one of those fishing boats is owned by Daniel Hopkins?"

Sam glanced toward the boats. "Not by old man Hopkins. The family beached him some years ago after he fell off the boat and almost drowned. His son captains the *Queen Ann* now, with his sons as crew."

"Oh. I just wondered." For a moment, she imagined the hard life of the early fishermen on the Cape. Their struggles. The lives that were so often lost.

Suddenly, her throat tight with sympathy for generations of Hopkinses who had gone to sea, she took Betty's arm. "Let's go home."

SIX

———◆◆◆———

Friday morning, Mary headed to the library. Although she was on a serious errand, she couldn't help but reflect on how much she loved libraries and had ever since she was a child. She'd devoured books by the dozens, including the original *Doctor Dolittle* series and *Black Beauty* during her animal-lover stage. However, a visit to a working farm with horses and pigs and all manner of earthy smells quickly dissuaded her from a career as a large-animal veterinarian.

Although the Ivy Bay library was of modest size, it was perfect, in Mary's mind; she always found it comforting and familiar.

She walked in and immediately looked up and smiled at the library's skylights in the vaulted ceiling, which made the space feel light and airy. She also noted the small statue of her stepgrandfather Adam Franklin, who had once been the mayor of Ivy Bay. As she had several times before, she felt a stab of pride at the representation of the long history her family had in Ivy Bay.

She moved to the front desk, where Victoria Pickerton stood in front of four bronze sculptures lined up on the wall. The sculptures commemorated important men in Ivy Bay's

history, including Franklin, who had been influential in pre-
serving the library's historic building.

"Hi, Victoria. Good morning," Mary said with a smile.
Mary had spent so much time at the library since she'd moved
to Ivy Bay that Victoria was quickly becoming a good friend.
The woman had an amazing memory for details—she could
put her finger on the most obscure facts within minutes.
Mary hoped to put that skill to good use today.

"Love the new glasses." An energetic woman in her forties, Victoria seemed to have an endless selection of cat's-eye
glasses. Today's pair was a sparkling blue.

"Hi, Mary. Thanks! Haven't seen you in a little while.
How are you?" She removed her glasses momentarily, looking
at them as though she were surprised to see which pair she
was wearing.

"Busy with the bookshop as always, and then these little
mysteries keep popping up. I can't seem to stop trying to solve
them."

Victoria clapped her hands. "Wonderful! I do love a mystery. How can I help you?"

She made sure no one was around, then told Victoria
about the lawsuit and how that might be linked to a murder
in 1841.

"A murder?" She gasped, her eyes widening.

"That's the accusation."

"Oh dear. Was there an arrest or trial?"

"I don't know, but it seems unlikely. According to Betty,
Emerson family lore hasn't included any mention of someone
sent to prison for murder. In fact, I don't know if there even
was a murder. It could be nothing more than an old rumor

passed down through the generations with no merit at all. Purely gossip or envy-based."

"*Hmm*, I suppose you could check court records." Victoria closed up the material on her desk that she'd been studying.

"Actually, I thought I might check for a newspaper account of the incident first, assuming there was one. What do you think?"

"Excellent idea. Archives, it is." She waved toward the room with a bow. "My lady."

Mary laughed. "Why, thank you."

Victoria led Mary into the humidity-controlled room where the most fragile archives were safely stored under lock and key. Several microfilm readers were set up at desks. The rolls of microfilm were stored in a bank of shallow drawers in a large cabinet.

"The *Ivy Bay Bugle* wasn't around then, but the *Ivy Bay Observer* was published weekly starting in 1839," Victoria said, "and all through the 1840s. I suppose by then, larger papers were being published and put the *Observer* out of business. But that's probably a good place to start."

Victoria ran her fingertip down the drawers marked with the relevant date. When she came to the appropriate drawer, she stopped and pulled it out.

Mary took the roll and sat down at one of the familiar machines and threaded the film through rollers. A front page headline appeared: Fleet Reports Record Catch. The subhead indicated record numbers of cod and haddock had filled the holds of returning fishing boats.

"Looks like exciting times," Mary commented.

"I'm sure it was to the fishermen who hauled in the catch." Victoria stood behind her, watching the screen change. "We have a very complete collection of the *Observer*. I believe the publisher's family passed them on to us."

"How generous." Mary loved the commitment citizens old and new had to Ivy Bay.

"I'll leave you to it," Victoria said. "But if you have any questions or problems, I'm right outside."

"Thanks, Vic."

The librarian hesitated before she walked out. Her eyes, magnified by her glasses, flashed with amusement. "I've always wanted to help catch a murderer."

Mary laughed. "If there is a murderer, I'm sure he's long dead. So at least we won't be in any danger." Not in danger from the deceased, anyway. Daniel Hopkins might be a different matter.

Daniel had claimed his ancestor had been killed in October 1841. Just to be safe, she started with issues dated in late September. She carried the drawer marked with those dates to the table and sat down to study the papers.

Each edition of the newspaper consisted of only four pages. The headline-making news appeared on the front page, often including some affront a politician or the state legislature had committed. Inside were more local stories of weddings and births, county affairs, fishing and harvesting reports. A few official government notices appeared on page three, as well as merchandise offered for sale—horses, pigs, hay, wagons, and the like.

She even found a small ad placed by the Emerson gristmill: Cornmeal half-barrel—$2.25.

In addition to identifying the effect of inflation between the 1790s and 1841, this showed the mill was still owned by the Emersons. At least the name hadn't changed.

Mary made a note on the yellow notepad she'd brought along.

She continued to browse. The issue of Wednesday, October 6, reported that a huge storm with the power of a hurricane had swept through the area, damaging the fishing fleet and destroying the saltworks. But there was no mention of the murder of Caleb Hopkins.

She moved on to the following week's edition, October 13. There, in the bottom right-hand corner of the front page, below the fold, the headline read: Ivy Bay Man Reported Missing.

Mary's heart jumped as she read the article: "Late on the afternoon of October 6, Mrs. Martha Hopkins reported that her husband, Caleb Hopkins, had been missing since the prior Saturday night, October 2, when he went to the Horse Head Tavern."

Apparently, Mrs. Hopkins' report to the constable had just missed the paper's deadline for the prior week.

"Constable Greenstock has been investigating the case. He determined that Mr. Hopkins was last seen outside the Horse Head Tavern arguing with William Emerson at approximately midnight Saturday."

Mary drew in a quick breath. "Oh goodness. Daniel could be telling the truth." But no, she immediately corrected herself, just because Emerson argued with the missing man didn't mean he had killed Caleb Hopkins.

And why, she wondered, if Caleb hadn't come home on October 3, had it taken until the sixth for Martha Hopkins to report her husband was missing? Was she used to him going off on his own for days at a time? Did she think he was out fishing on his boat? Or had she delayed the report for a more sinister reason?

Shaking her head, Mary studied that paragraph one more time. She'd never heard of the Horse Head Tavern.

As she mulled that over, she continued reading the article.

"Prior to this incident, the tavern barkeep Mountie Baker admitted throwing Hopkins out of the tavern for rowdy behavior and starting a fight with one of his patrons."

Mary wondered once again if Daniel's cranky temperament had been passed down through the generations, going at least all the way back to Caleb.

The article went on to indicate the constable had questioned Mrs. Hopkins and her eldest son at length, and had discovered a bloodstained butcher knife in the Hopkinses' kitchen. Both Mrs. Hopkins and her son Peter claimed not to have seen or spoken to Caleb Hopkins since early on the day he went missing.

Mary stopped reading. Would a bloody knife in a kitchen be that unusual? They would have kept animals for food back then. There wasn't any way at the time to determine whether the blood was human or not. Yet the constable had taken special note of the knife. Interesting.

She resumed reading.

"Interviews by this reporter with the Hopkinses' neighbors suggest the constable was well acquainted with the Hopkinses' household, as he was frequently called to break up loud arguments between the husband and wife, sometimes involving injuries to Mrs. Hopkins.

"Other reports indicate Mr. Hopkins had a loud argument with Irving Smith, a fellow fisherman, earlier in the day. Mr. Hopkins had accused Mr. Smith of running through and destroying his nets on purpose.

"No arrests have been made, and the case is still being investigated. The Hopkinses' boat, though slightly damaged in the recent storm, remains moored at the Ivy Bay dock."

Mary pondered that last sentence. A big storm had damaged the fishing fleet, but apparently Caleb's boat had survived intact. She would presume, then, that Caleb hadn't been lost at sea in the storm.

Leaning back, Mary let out a long sigh. Based on the argument they'd had at the Horse Head Tavern, William Emerson was an obvious suspect for Caleb's murder. But Mrs. Hopkins, who might have tired of being abused, was a viable suspect as well. So was Irving Smith, who had possibly damaged Caleb's fishing gear on purpose, perhaps because of prior disagreements between the two men.

Mary tried to visualize a possible scenario—William Emerson left Caleb standing in front of the tavern and went home alone. Still angry, Caleb could have stormed back inside the tavern, started another fight and been somehow killed, perhaps accidentally, in the ensuing melee with the barkeep and his patrons.

A gruesome thought came to her then. If Caleb wasn't popular among the locals who patronized the tavern, they might have disposed of the body and kept the secret of his death in order to avoid arrest. Yet surely, if there had been more than a few patrons in the tavern, one of them would have let slip something about Caleb's death. The truth would have leaked out.

In any event, how on earth could she prove that or any other possibility after so many years had passed?

She scanned through several more editions of the newspaper but found no update to the story and no further information regarding the whereabouts of Caleb Hopkins.

Still mulling the problem, she returned the microfilm to the file cabinet. She'd have to see what information she could discover about the Horse Head Tavern, and she still wanted to ask Victoria for suggestions where she could find a sample of Isaac Emerson's signature.

She also needed to get hold of a copy of the original police report for the case of Caleb Hopkins' death, if that still existed. Did they even do police reports back then? Mary wasn't sure, but she knew how to find out.

"Did you find what you were looking for?" Victoria asked as Mary stepped out of the archive room.

"I guess the answer is yes and no. I found an article that said Caleb Hopkins was reported missing and that he had last been seen with William Emerson."

"Is that the yes or no part?"

Mary laughed. "I'm not sure. The fact is, based on that one story, there seem to be four possible suspects."

"Well, I suppose the first thing you need to figure out is if you're trying to prove guilt or innocence?"

"Exactly." Mary straightened her spine and tried to determine how she should approach the problem. "I'm not looking for a guilty man. I just need to know once and for all that William Emerson is *not* a murderer."

"So you can begin by attempting to *eliminate* the suspects."

"My plan exactly."

"Anything else I can do to help?"

"I hope so. I'd like to find a sample of Isaac Emerson's signature or handwriting. He owned the gristmill in 1792."

"In 1792?" Laughing, Victoria placed her hand over her chest. "You're really trying to give me a challenge, aren't you?"

"Well, I can't think where I'd find his signature. I did check in the county records, but there was nothing. There might have been a signature on a bill of sale if a copy had been kept in the files. But there is no copy in the county records. And no transfer of title, that I can find. Thus no signature." Mary gave her an innocent smile. "Any thoughts?"

"*Hmm*, let me see if there's any mention of Isaac Emerson in my archives." She sat down in front of her computer. "We have some very old church records, including records of births, deaths, and marriages. The clerk's office only keeps public records, activities that involve the government in some way." As Victoria's fingers clicked away on the keyboard, her frown deepened. She shook her head. "I'm not finding any mention of Isaac except in the census reports." She looked up. "Sorry, Mary. There's not a thing in our archives that would contain his signature."

"Well, I do appreciate you checking. I think I'll use your computers to see what I can find out about William Emerson or his family while I'm here."

"Good luck!"

In the back of the library, there was a separate computer room, which had access to the Internet as well as an interlibrary loan system. Mary sat at one of the computers. Maybe she could find a reference to an old journal. Anything that would hint that William did—or rather did not—kill a man.

As she browsed various sites, she found lots of mentions of the gristmill, including a reference to a birthday party held there in 1907. Hardly the information she needed. She worked on the computer for quite a while but found nothing of use.

The lack of results, however, meant there were no direct avenues to pursue William's guilt, or hopefully, his innocence. With no records, and no one in the Emerson family with any specific knowledge of the murder, she had quickly reached a dead end.

Once outside, Mary took out her cell phone, hoping to catch Benjamin McArthur, the police chief, in his office.

After talking with the clerk first, Mary waited on hold until the chief answered his phone. Mary briefly explained the situation about the mill and the Daniel Hopkins lawsuit.

"It sounds crazy to me that Daniel would be trying to claim the mill is his after all this time."

"I completely agree," Mary said. "That's why I called you. Do you store old police reports in your office?"

He paused a minute. "Yeah. What did you need?"

"The original constable's report about Caleb Hopkins going missing in October of 1841."

He snorted. "You've got to be kidding."

"They did police reports back then, right?"

"I'm not even sure."

"Would you mind looking? I know it's a lot to ask. But I've already checked with Victoria at the library and went through old newspaper accounts. The problem is Daniel Hopkins claims William Emerson murdered his great-great-whatever in 1841. Apparently, that was the start of a feud between the two families and, I suspect, somehow related to Daniel suing Betty and her family over the ownership of the gristmill. I'm having trouble getting to the truth instead of hand-me-down rumors. If you can come up with the police report, it could really help."

In the background, Mary heard the police chief's chair creak, and she pictured him adjusting his position. "It's possible the report is still around, but it's not going to be easy to find."

"Could someone in your office look? If that's too difficult, I could search for the record myself, if that would be easier," Mary volunteered.

"Let me talk to my clerk. Maybe it'll be easier to find than I expect. I'll get back to you."

"Thank you, Chief. I really appreciate your help." And just maybe the original report would help her get to the bottom of the mystery.

That evening, while Mary and Betty relaxed in the living room and watched the shadows lengthen across sand dunes, Mary brought Betty up to date about what she had learned.

"So Caleb Hopkins really was murdered?" The dejection in Betty's voice touched Mary's heart.

"I don't think we can jump directly to that conclusion, but according to the newspaper article, his absence was being investigated as suspicious."

"That's terrible. I can't even imagine any Emerson—"

"Remember there are other possible suspects as well. William Emerson is simply the last person who admitted being seen with Caleb before he went missing."

Betty brightened. "A murderer wouldn't have admitted that, would he?"

"That's what I'm thinking." *Unless he was trying to lead the constable off track or knew there had been witnesses*, Mary considered.

"So which suspect do you think killed him?"

"I don't know. They all seem likely suspects with perfectly good motives. I'm thinking about trying to eliminate them one at a time."

"How are you going to do that?"

"I don't know that either," she said with a discouraged sigh.

Betty frowned, which was happening more frequently since she'd received the copy of Daniel's lawsuit. "You know, I have a vague memory of seeing some old photos of the gristmill around here somewhere. I wonder if they would hold any clues."

"Really? Where?" Mary asked.

"I think they were in a box in the attic."

Hope sparked in Mary's chest. "Let's go take a look. Maybe there's more in the box than photos."

They climbed the stairs to the second floor, then lowered the pull-down stairs to reach the attic.

Betty was breathing hard when they reached their destination. "I'd forgotten how hard it is on my arthritic knees to come up here."

"I had forgotten how much heat an attic holds in. It must be a hundred degrees in here." Sweat beaded on Mary's forehead.

The attic was filled with cardboard boxes, children's toys, an old rocking chair. A metal sewing mannequin stood guard in one corner.

Betty made her way through a narrow path between boxes. "I think what I'm looking for is over here." She lifted one box out of the way. Groaning, she knelt in front of another and opened it.

"What have you got?" Mary asked.

"A few of Edward's books. An old tie. I have no idea why I saved that." Finding a manila envelope, she opened it. "And pictures."

Mary knelt beside her sister as she pulled a handful of black-and-white photos out of the envelope. An old town map came out with them.

"These pictures look like they were taken in the 1930s, before the mill was so run-down."

"Those will be useful if Evan decides to restore the mill." Mary opened the map, which was dated 1939. She recognized the layout of Ivy Bay, but there were also notations on the map regarding historical features. After turning the map over, she skimmed through the interesting details until her eyes fell on the words *Horse Head Tavern*. The caption read: "Originally, the tavern served as a popular spot for local fishermen and for overnight travelers passing through the Cape Cod area. The interior has been remodeled and is now a private home owned by the Stebble family."

"Look at this," Mary said. "The old Horse Head Tavern, where Caleb Hopkins and William Emerson were seen fighting, was converted to a house and was owned by the Stebble family in 1939. I think that's where Amy Stebble, who is in my prayer group, must live now."

"Really? Where is it?"

Mary flipped over the map. "Looks like it's just off Meeting House Road, quite close to the mill."

That was definitely a place Mary wanted to see.

SEVEN

◆◆◆

After a restless night, Mary awoke especially groggy. She definitely needed a cup of coffee to get the day going.

She noticed she was moving a little slower than usual as she got ready to go to the bookshop. She chose comfort over speed, opting for a pair of dark-colored jeans instead of slacks and a slightly overlarge white cardigan over a sea-green boatneck tee. Carrying her laptop, she made her way to the kitchen and noticed that Betty was still sleeping. She moved quietly to not wake her sister; she knew that especially with her arthritis, Betty needed a healthy amount of sleep.

Mary made a small pot of coffee and sat at the kitchen table to enjoy her coffee and let the caffeine take effect. She was looking at another long day of running a bookshop and investigating a mystery.

She smiled. *Investigating a mystery*. She knew she wasn't anything close to a real detective, but she still couldn't help but enjoy the feeling of being helpful in times like these. As she often had before, she thanked her grandmother for getting her hooked on mystery books, which seemed to have permeated her brain and given her the instincts of a sleuth.

After booting up her computer, she searched again for the 1840 census. It didn't take her long to discover the listing for Caleb Hopkins and his address, which looked to be in an older and poorer part of town. She jotted the address on a slip of paper.

She took a final sip of her coffee and glanced toward Gus, who had meandered his way into the kitchen. She'd leave Gus home so he could keep Betty company. Her sister pretended to be a curmudgeon when it came to cats, but the number of times Mary had caught Betty snuggling with Gus belied her claim.

"Sorry, Gus. Today, you'll be staying home," she said to the gray cat, who seemed to almost visibly shrug in indifference and then padded toward Betty's room.

Mary smiled, put the coffee mug in the sink, then made her way to her silver Impala and drove to the bookshop. Rebecca was already inside getting the store ready to open for the day.

"How is everything this morning?" she asked Rebecca.

"Quiet, for now. But I noticed we've sold several of the books you featured about Ivy Bay and Cape Cod, and we're entirely sold out of two of them. Again, if you can believe it."

"That's great news."

"Would you like me to make a list of those we need to reorder?" Rebecca asked.

"That would be perfect." Since Mary had been gallivanting around town so much lately trying to solve the mystery of the gristmill, she felt doubly blessed to have Rebecca working for her.

Ashley called from the children's area. "Mrs. Fisher, I really like this book about the mysteries of the *Mayflower*. I think you ought to include it in your history display."

"Why, thank you, Ashley. That's a good idea. I'll order a couple of extra copies too. Grandparents love to buy books for their grandchildren."

She winked at Rebecca, who rightfully looked proud of her daughter's suggestion.

Mary went back to the original town plot map and spread it out to examine. She checked the street address she'd found in the census record. She had decided to start with understanding Caleb's wife's role in his disappearance, if there had been one.

The address was within easy walking distance of where the commercial fishing fleet docked, and not too far from the location of the Horse Head Tavern. Caleb could have easily walked home in the dark of night. He could have still been angry about whatever had transpired between him and William Emerson when he arrived at his house. And he could have been drunk.

It was possible Caleb's wife knew more about what happened that night than she'd let on.

———

That evening, they ate a dinner of a delicate cold potato-and-leek soup and tuna sandwiches on toast. Betty took a bite of her sandwich and washed it down with a sip of iced tea. "Henry came by this afternoon. He caught me trying to replace the stake for the young poplar tree I planted last spring. Somehow the old one got broken."

"Oh? I hadn't even noticed." The garden was under Betty's purview, not Mary's.

"At any rate, Henry stopped to help me set the new stake properly and stayed for a cup of tea."

"He is the nicest man. Always volunteering to help others. Sometimes I worry that we all take advantage of his good nature."

"He seems to thrive on being helpful," Betty said, and Mary tended to agree.

When dinner was finished and the kitchen cleaned up, Mary invited her sister to walk into town to get an ice-cream cone and stroll around a bit.

Betty raised her brows. "Where are we going?"

"I want to see how far the mill is from the Horse Head Tavern."

"Horse Head Tavern? You mean where Amy Stebble lives now?"

Mary ran her hand over her hair, hoping to smooth the flyaway ends. "Unfortunately, it's also where Caleb was last seen arguing with William Emerson."

They both grabbed light jackets and went out the door and up the block. They strolled along the sidewalk, cracked in places, and passed by well-tended yards bordered by white picket fences.

"After we check how far the mill is to the tavern, I want to do the same thing between the tavern and Caleb's house."

"Where did he live?"

"Quite near the docks. Probably one of those small shanties."

As they turned on Main Street, Mary explained the information about Caleb's wife, and how Mary was trying to figure out if she could have been responsible for his disappearance.

Tourists, most of them sunburned, filled Bailey's Ice Cream Shop, sitting at small tables or waiting to order a cone from Jamie, a daughter of the owners. Jamie's auburn hair was short, and she wore a white bib apron with the name of the shop embroidered in pink floss across the front.

When it was their turn, Mary ordered a vanilla chocolate chip, and Betty ordered Mary's special ice cream of the month, peach and pralines. It tickled Mary that Bailey's had latched on to her talent for making different flavored ice creams soon after she moved back to Ivy Bay and now featured a different flavor of hers every month.

They made their way out of the shop and headed for what was now the Stebble home. Enjoying the warm air and the cold ice cream, they took their time, checking out late-blooming roses in various gardens and watching the flight of birds in search of their evening meal.

"There it is." Mary stopped across the street from the Stebble house. Two stories, with wood siding, it had a straight, flat-sided look.

"Not exactly inspiring architecture," Betty commented.

"No, but look how close it is to the mill. And it's close enough to the docks that Caleb could easily have walked home." The three points of interest were virtually on a straight line with the old tavern in the center.

Mentally, Mary tried to picture what could have happened. "If Caleb walked home that night, mistreated his wife, who then, for the sake of argument, killed him, what would she have done with his body?"

"*Hmm.* Well, first of all, I don't imagine there were this many houses around in the 1840s."

"Good point. And since it was several days before she reported him missing, she would have had plenty of time to dispose of a body."

"Like digging a grave?"

Mary rubbed her chin and considered the possibility. "If the grave was only a few days old, you'd think the constable investigating Caleb's death would have noticed."

"Couldn't she have taken him down to the water?"

"I suppose it's possible. But could Mrs. Hopkins have carried or dragged Caleb that far? How would she have gotten him all the way to the bay?"

"I don't know. You're the professional."

"Hardly!" Mary laughed. "And anyway, a murder mystery is a whole new ball game." Just then, Mary noticed a curtain move in the upstairs window of the Stebble house.

Not wanting Amy or her family to think they were gawking at their home, Mary took Betty's arm and they walked toward the marsh that was between the mill and the center of town.

They turned left at the corner, and Mary continued to think out loud about Martha Hopkins' possible actions. "So if Martha had access to a carriage or wagon, she could have used the knife the constable found, probably in self-defense, then dragged him outside, lifted him into the wagon—"

"All by herself? I wouldn't have been able to drag Edward two feet, much less lift him into a wagon."

Her sister was right. The scenario she'd imagined simply didn't make sense.

She would love, for Betty's sake and her family's, to make the morbid conclusion that Martha Hopkins was guilty of murder just so she could exonerate William. But there simply weren't enough facts. Yet.

By Sunday morning, Mary was ready for a quiet day and a chance to worship the Lord. After getting ready for church, she went downstairs, a Bible verse of grateful praise in her heart: *Shout for joy to the Lord, all the earth. Worship the Lord with gladness; come before him with joyful songs* (Psalm 100:1–2).

Betty, purse in hand, was waiting for her by the door. She wore a summery skirt with a border print and a lightweight sweater over a silk blouse with cap sleeves.

"Sorry to keep you waiting," Mary said.

"No problem. We have plenty of time."

They had no trouble finding a parking space in the lot outside Grace Church, and they leisurely strolled inside. As they stepped into the vestibule, organ music greeted them.

So did Dorothy Johnson. She looked striking in a turquoise dress topped with a cropped white jacket and pearls.

"Hello, you two. Lovely day, isn't it?"

"It is," Betty agreed. "And you're looking lovely yourself."

"Thank you." Dorothy flushed modestly. "Mary, you remember me telling you that Henry was going to do some repairs around the house for me?"

Mary admitted she did with a slight nod. Why Dorothy felt compelled to bring this up again made Mary feel a mix of irritation and amusement.

"Well, that dear man spent almost all Friday at my house." She beamed with feminine pleasure at relating her day with Henry. "He worked very hard to get my windows working again. He was so sweet I invited him to stay for dinner. I'm sure he doesn't get many homemade meals since his wife passed on."

"I'm sure Henry enjoyed your home cooking." Mary spoke softly, her lips tight. Dorothy acted as though she wanted to either make Mary jealous . . . or warn her to keep her hands off.

Mary forced herself to remember her vow to deal with Dorothy with God's grace and smiled. "And I'm glad he could fix your windows."

"Oh yes, he's a wonderful handyman."

Mary took Betty's arm. "We'd better get seated. I'll see you at the next prayer group." She hoped it wasn't obvious that she had practically dragged her sister into the sanctuary.

When they were halfway down the aisle, Betty whispered, "Poor Dorothy certainly has her eye on Henry. I hope he doesn't mind."

"I don't imagine so."

"He might not be so willing to help if she gets too pushy."

They slid into a pew and sat down. The high ceiling soared above the congregation. Tall windows down each side of the sanctuary admitted sunlight. Behind the pulpit, a stained-glass window depicted a scene of Jesus praying.

The choir took their places. A moment later the congregation stood to sing the first hymn, "When Morning Gilds the Skies."

While Mary wasn't blessed with vocal talent, she loved to blend her voice with those around her and with the choir and organ. The music lifted her spirits to the Lord and opened her heart to His salvation.

When the hymn concluded, Pastor Frank Miles led them in prayer.

Pastor Miles had been the pastor of Grace Church of Ivy Bay for quite some time, and Mary loved worshipping under his leadership. He had an uncanny way of making his sermons relevant to the lives of ordinary people and offering up solutions to problems.

This morning's sermon was typically profound and very timely. He spoke of asking the Lord to heal past hurts rather than letting them fester and grow.

The dispute over the ownership of the mill certainly represented an injury that had occurred years ago, which had now festered in Daniel Hopkins' mind. Mary prayed for the Lord's help in resolving the issue so that the wound could be healed.

After the service, as they passed through the crowd of churchgoers enjoying cups of coffee or tea, Mary spotted Jill Sanderson and her husband, Harry. She started to speak to Jill, but the young woman turned away.

Mary got the disheartening feeling that Jill was avoiding her in order not to cause conflict within her family. Mary hated the thought that Daniel's suit had put a barrier between herself and Jill. She prayed she'd find a way to restore their budding friendship.

Her musings were interrupted by the voice of her nephew Evan. "Hello, Mother. Aunt Mary."

Betty turned and embraced her son. "How are you, dear?"

"We're good, Mom." He reached out to his wife Mindy, whom Betty hugged as well. "Beautiful day, isn't it?"

"Not quite as hot as it has been lately." In turn, Mary gave Evan and Mindy hugs.

"Where are the children?" Betty asked.

"They're around somewhere visiting with their friends," Evan replied. Mary spotted ten-year-old Betsy in the middle of a group of girls standing by the doughnut table.

Betty glanced around, then spoke in a lowered voice. "How's the attorney coming along with our case?"

"Rob went out to the mill last week to look around. And his assistant has also been poring over old records at the county clerk's office."

"I hope she wore old clothes," Mary commented. "It's really dusty down in the basement."

"I don't know about that, but she doesn't seem to have had much luck finding Isaac's signature or any records that indicate the mill has ever changed hands."

Mary chuckled. "I could have told Rob that, and I wouldn't have charged him a penny."

Evan laughed. "I can believe that, but I'm sure Rob wants to make sure to cover every possibility and earn his fee."

"I'm confident Rob is doing a good job for us," Betty said.

Mary was sure that was the case. Still, she wished either she or Rob's assistant would come up with something concrete that would prove the Emerson mill rightfully belonged to Betty and her family.

For the rest of the day, Mary mulled over Martha Hopkins' potential guilt in the murder of Caleb Hopkins. How could she have disposed of his body without anyone being the wiser? It simply didn't seem possible. But, then again, some of those early pioneering women were pretty hefty. They certainly hadn't had a soft life, carrying buckets of water to wash and bathe with, chopping wood for the stove and fireplace. Perhaps Martha Hopkins was a lot bigger and stronger than Mary had imagined.

But how could she possibly find out?

Mary and Rebecca were in the process of opening the shop Monday morning when she happened to glance out the window. As though her thoughts about Martha Hopkins had conjured up the perfect answer, Jill Sanderson walked past on the sidewalk carrying a shopping bag.

Impulsively, Mary grabbed the latest book in the cupcake mystery series Jill enjoyed.

"I'm going to dash out for a minute," she told Rebecca. "I shouldn't be gone long."

Rebecca grinned. "I'm used to your coming and going by now, and it doesn't bother me one bit. That's what I'm here for. Take your time."

Mary thanked Rebecca, then hurried after Jill and spotted her going into the Black & White Diner. Perhaps she was stopping for a cup of coffee or breakfast.

As Mary opened the door, the smell of bacon sizzling and fresh-roasted coffee brewing drew her inside. Jill had settled on a vinyl-covered stool at the counter. Mary walked up next to her.

"Hi, Jill. I saw you walk by. May I join you?"

Startled, Jill looked up. "I, um, hi. Of course."

Mary slid onto the seat next to her and put the book on the counter. "I wanted to catch you. I just got copies of the latest cupcake mystery and thought you would like to know."

A smile brightened her face and she picked up the book, examining the cartoonish cover. "Oh, isn't that cute? I love her stories."

"I knew you'd like it." The waitress arrived to take their orders. "Let me buy you a cup of coffee and some breakfast, if you'd like."

"Oh no. You don't have to do that. I only want coffee and a sweet roll."

"Make mine the same," Mary told the waitress. "My treat."

Jill flipped over the book to read the back cover.

"I just wanted to reassure you," Mary said. "Despite the dispute about the mill, I don't blame you in the slightest. I know the suit is none of your doing."

"No, it's not. In fact—" Jill hesitated. "Never mind."

Mary could tell that Jill was close to confiding in her, so she pressed forward, treading lightly. "It's really okay, Jill. I know that it's complicated. You can trust me."

Jill's shoulders sank, and she began to talk. "I believe you, Mary. It's just that . . . my husband and his brother have tried to talk Grandpa out of this whole thing. Harry keeps asking Grandpa what on earth we would do with the mill if we owned it. It's pretty run-down. All the Hopkinses have been fishermen for as long as anyone can remember. We don't know anything about restoring an old mill."

"So what does Daniel say when your husband asks that question?"

"He blusters. A lot." She half laughed at that. "Then proceeds to tell Harry that the mill is going to make us wealthy."

"How?"

The waitress brought their coffee and sweet rolls. Jill stirred a teaspoon of sugar into her cup and added milk.

"He won't say." She swiveled to face Mary more directly. "The truth is, Grandpa Daniel has been getting more and more cantankerous since Grandma Judith passed on. And now his sons won't take him out any longer to fish because he's unsteady on his feet and not safe on the boat. Staying at home makes him restless and at loose ends, which makes him extra grumpy, so he goes out wandering a lot. I think that coming up with this mill business has made him feel important again. My boys are thrilled they're going to be rich if Grandpa is right."

Mary could understand the need to feel useful. But Daniel's claim on the mill would leave him feeling even worse when he lost the case. *If* he lost, she corrected herself.

Mary took a sip of her coffee, hot, rich, and creamy.

"I'm concerned about this feud for a lot of reasons, Jill, and one of them is Daniel's insistence that there was a murder involved. Do you know anything about that?"

"I know he doesn't have anything good to say about the Emersons. And I've heard him make the claim before, but he doesn't seem to say anything of substance about the matter. And Mary, really, I shouldn't be talking with you too much. I don't want to betray my grandfather-in-law, even if I disagree with him."

"I understand." She patted Jill's arm to reassure her. "I do need your help with one more thing, though, and this doesn't really have anything to do with the mill. By chance, do you know anything about Caleb Hopkins' wife, Martha?"

Jill thought for a moment, then shook her head. "I haven't been real interested in genealogy or anything like that. My mother-in-law did give me a box full of old family pictures and stuff, even a couple of tintypes and miniatures, but I've barely looked at them."

Possibility fluttered in Mary's chest. "Do you think there might be a picture of Martha Hopkins in that box?" Probably not a photograph. The 1840s were before the technology was in common use. But there could be a different kind of image.

"I don't know. I guess I could look."

"Only if it won't cause problems with your family. But I would definitely appreciate it."

"I can try." She used her fork to break off a bite of sweet roll. As she chewed, her eyes lit up. "These sweet rolls are so good; I'm tempted to have one every day. But that wouldn't do my weight much good, would it?"

"Oh, I think we should enjoy a special treat now and again without guilt."

Jill agreed by taking a hearty bite of the roll, and Mary laughed. They took the time to enjoy their sweet rolls and moved on to a conversation about the cupcake mysteries. Mary paid for their check and was glad she'd given the book as a gift to Jill. It seemed like the least Mary could do.

During the lunch hour, the flow of customers at the bookshop slowed. Since they weren't busy, Rebecca and Ashley decided to eat their lunch in the back room; they'd brought packed lunches and had stored them in the small refrigerator. They could sit and visit while they ate.

Mary, enjoying the brief quiet moment, picked up the porcelain doll beside the cash register and again weighed it in her hand, wondering where it had come from and how it had ended up at the gristmill. It still looked familiar, yet she hadn't the slightest idea why.

With a sigh, she put it aside and glanced at the ledger. *Loose ends.* She'd be so glad when Mr. King came to look at it. Hopefully she'd learn something worthwhile from him.

While she had a minute, she sat down at the computer and opened her Internet browser. Her home page was her store's Web site, and even though she saw it every time she logged on, she still got a thrill. She opened a search window and typed in "Only the Very Best slogan." A whole page of references to Hallmark cards popped up.

She doubted Hallmark had been around in the 1840s. Could the doll be a contemporary knickknack sold with greeting cards as a promotion or sales gimmick? Might it not be old, after all?

Continuing her pursuit, she did find a Hallmark porcelain doll Christmas ornament. It was lovely in a pink dress and bonnet, but it wasn't the doll she was searching for.

She tried including the words "family crest" when she Googled, and she got even less useful information.

Next, she searched "porcelain dolls" and found dozens of examples, but none that looked like the doll she'd found at the mill.

She still couldn't imagine what the doll would have to do with the ownership of the mill, let alone Caleb's presumed murder.

Discouraged, she sighed and looked for a Web site to convert British pounds to US dollars in 1792. She found a site that came close. With a bit of math, she concluded five British pounds at that time would be worth about three hundred dollars. That's what Caleb Hopkins claimed his ancestor paid for the gristmill.

Add in the inflation rate after so many years, and the amount became quite substantial. Five pounds would have been a great investment. If Daniel's story was true.

She clicked off the Internet. Rather than waiting for Jill to produce a picture of Martha Hopkins, Mary decided she should try to investigate either one of the other suspects: Mountie Baker, the barkeep at the tavern, or Irving Smith, the fisherman accused of tearing up Caleb's nets.

Mary pondered where she might find information about a sea captain who lived in the 1840s.

Standing, she stretched, and then she strolled around the bookshop, touching a book here or there, picking up an odd scrap of paper. Just being near books often jogged her memory.

As she stood staring at a bookshelf of mysteries, her gaze landed on *The Seafarer's Wife*, a novel that had created a stir a few years ago when it was first released.

She started to reach for the book, and then it hit her. Down near the docks was a Seafarers' Hall. Originally, the hall had provided hot meals, showers, and cots for fishermen who were temporarily without ships. Now the hall could be rented for parties or special events, and the funds were used to help seamen who were down on their luck.

The octogenarian who ran the hall, Strom Engle, had a wealth of knowledge about the fishermen who had sailed from Ivy Bay.

When Rebecca finished her lunch, Mary told her she was going out again.

Seafarers' Hall was a block off Route 6A. Built of red brick, it had stood in welcome to fishermen for more than a hundred years. Mary walked to the side office entrance and knocked on the door.

"It's open!" came a reply from inside.

While Strom's office was shabby by most standards, the lean former fisherman stood straight and tall, his blue shirt spotless, his summer-weight slacks carefully pressed. He came around to her side of the desk.

"Why, Mrs. Fisher, haven't seen you in an age. How's your bookshop doing?" His voice was laced with the sea and the accent of a longtime New Englander.

"I do believe I've found my calling, and business is thriving."

"Would you be thinking of celebrating your success, then?"

"Not today." Her gaze skimmed around the room, where boxes were stacked haphazardly. "Today, I'm looking for information about an old sea captain. I couldn't think of anyone who would be better able to help me out than you."

"And who might this sea captain be?"

"His name is Irving Smith. He fished these waters around 1840."

Strom's white brows lowered. "That's a bit before my time." He clasped his hands behind his back and stared at the plank floor. "His name does ring a bell. Let me think. A cod fisherman, I think. Of course, most were at that time."

"I'm specifically looking for something that would tell me where he was on October 3 in 1841." She laughed. Of course, she didn't really expect him to know but was surprised when he lifted his head.

"During the October gale?"

Mary marveled at Strom's knowledge of the area's history. "I guess so. I read something about that in an edition of the old *Ivy Bay Observer*. It must have been quite a storm."

"Aye, it was a fierce one. Hurricane-force winds. Took out the old saltworks and wiped out half the fishing fleet, taking the men onboard to their watery graves."

"Do you know if Irving Smith died in that storm?" she asked. Depending on what time the storm came through, that might give Captain Smith a solid alibi for Caleb's murder.

"I actually know that he did not." He walked over to a wall and pointed to an old photograph, probably circa 1920. "There's a memorial monument out on the spit. It lists all the souls that were lost that day. Irving Smith is not listed."

She joined him to get a look at the memorial. Although the photo was a bit fuzzy, she could make out a large, probably brass anchor set on top of a concrete base. On a brass plate was a long list of names, which she couldn't make out.

"We lost eighty-one fishermen that day," Strom said in a low, respectful voice. He couldn't have been more grave if he'd known the men personally.

"What a tragedy." A wave of sadness welled in Mary. So many gone. Hardworking men who tried to harvest a life for themselves and their families from an unforgiving sea. She thought of the debris of broken ships that had washed ashore: planks that had once been the deck of a boat; masts snapped by nearly two-hundred-mile-an-hour winds; seat cushions, bedding, and waterproof boots that had floated above men who had drowned and slid beneath the waves. Those bits and pieces, the detritus of lives taken too soon, that came to rest on the shores of Cape Cod.

Perhaps even the remains of those who had died at sea had washed up on beaches along the Cape.

She pressed her lips together. "But Irving Smith wasn't among those lost?"

"Nope. His name would be up there with the others."

Sighing, she wondered what to do next. "Would there be a record anywhere of his life?"

"Well, now"—he jingled some change in his pants pocket—"used to be the old-timers who stayed here liked to read. We had a bunch of books, some of them old seafaring stories. Might be some old ships' logs in the group, but I don't recall a Smith."

"Would you mind if I took a look?" It seemed like a long shot, but she didn't want to give up too soon. Not when the Emerson mill was at stake.

Strom led her to a back storeroom, which was filled with boxes, old bed frames, broken lamps, and assorted items that had seen far better days.

The thought of searching through all the junk was daunting.

Strom pointed to a pile of boxes. "If we have what you're looking for, it would be in one of these boxes."

"Then I guess I'd better get started looking."

"I'll give you a hand." He lifted a couple of boxes down to the floor. They each opened one and started to search through the contents.

Some of the books had been attacked by bookworms that had gnawed their way through the pages. Almost all were damaged beyond repair. Still, Mary pressed on, checking each book title. When she finished with one box, she dragged out another.

The third box didn't contain published books but rather bound journals. She picked one up and read the cover: Captain's Log, *Good Hope*.

"Here's one," she said out loud.

"Let me see." Strom took the log from her and flipped through a few pages. "Aye, this is the sort of thing you're looking for. But your man Irving Smith was not the captain."

Disappointment tightened in her chest even as she checked another log. "*Princess II*. Would that be Smith's boat?"

"I have no idea, but I do have a list of all the ships that sailed from this port. I'll be right back." He got to his feet with amazing agility for a man his age.

Strom returned quickly. "I found him. Irving Smith, captain of the *Jolly Mae*."

"The *Jolly Mae*. That must have been named for his wife." She eagerly sorted through the remaining contents of the box. Not finding the *Jolly Mae* log, she moved on to a fourth box.

Moments later, she announced, "I've found it!"

Excitement building, she sat back on her haunches, opened the log, and started to read.

It didn't take long for Mary to become engrossed in the log of the *Jolly Mae*. On each journey to sea, Captain Smith noted time of departure, destination, compass course, wind force, and the state of the sea. But most fascinating were the remarks. Sick crewmen. Tons of fish caught. Loss of nets. Even arguments among the crew.

She easily found the entries of early October 1841, which said they had set sail at 1900 hours, 7:00 PM, on the evening of October 3, 1841. But she couldn't stop reading. Although the entries were brief, she could clearly understand the hard life of those who went to sea to earn their living.

It occurred to her that even now, a century and more later, the life of a commercial fisherman was still both hard and dangerous. Suddenly, she felt a rush of sympathy for the long line of Hopkins family members who had gone to sea to fill their holds with fish for others to eat.

She also felt a bittersweet emotion, because she could now check a murder suspect off her list.

EIGHT

A fter closing the shop, Mary headed home to report her discovery to Betty. She found her sister kneeling on a rubber mat in front of a bed of colorful Johnny-jump-ups in the front yard. Betty appeared to be tidying up for the day. She paused to rub the small of her back.

"Hi, Betty," Mary greeted her, concerned about her sister's physical health. "Let me take over for you."

"Thanks," Betty said. "I'll let you this time. I've been feeling great, but I'm definitely ready to quit for the day."

"I know exactly what you mean." Searching for information on the Web and at the Seafarers' Hall might not be physically tiring, but it was wearing.

She picked up Betty's tools and placed them in her gardening basket.

"How about some leftovers and iced tea for dinner?" Betty said, heading into the house.

The idea sounded perfect to Mary. She put the basket of gardening supplies in the garage and followed her sister into the house.

After they prepared their food, they took their dinner out to the sunroom, and as they sat, they almost simultaneously sighed with the satisfaction of finishing a busy day. Mary was about to tell Betty about her trip to the Seafarers' Hall, when Betty spoke up.

"I've been thinking about the shop's backyard and what to plant," she said.

Mary took a sip of her iced tea. "How exciting. The plants you've already put in are doing well. Rebecca has been so reliable about keeping them watered. Or rather Ashley has," Mary said with a smile.

"She is a sweetie, isn't she? But it has occurred to me that you don't want the yard to be too high maintenance. I'd thought of making flower beds along the back wall, but I've changed my mind."

"Oh?" In contrast to Mary's black thumb, Betty could grow almost anything and had a wonderful ability to design a garden to be beautiful all year long.

"What would you think of putting in a patio back there, probably brick to match the building? You could have an umbrella table with chairs where people could read comfortably. And you could even have readers' groups meet outside when the weather was good."

Mary brightened. "I love that idea."

"I'm glad." Pleased, Betty placed her hand on her chest as though she'd been afraid Mary would object to the concept. "I'll call Kip right away. And I thought for color, we could get a couple of big tubs and plant annuals in them. The nursery could deliver the tubs already planted, and I just have to keep the flowers trimmed. That would cut down on the amount of maintenance that would be needed."

"Sounds ideal. But are you sure you're not taking on too much—the shop's backyard plus your own gardening here at home?"

"I may be." Betty laughed. "But I love the work. I'll take it slow."

Mary nodded and left it at that. She knew she could trust Betty to know her own limits. "Well," she said, changing subjects, "I think I can eliminate one of our suspects."

"Oh?" Betty shot her a surprised look. "I do hope it's William Emerson."

"I'm afraid not yet." Mary ran her fingertips up and down the cold sweat on her glass of iced tea. "It's the ship's captain, Irving Smith. The man who'd had a fight with Caleb earlier on the day he went missing."

"How can you suddenly know he didn't kill Caleb?"

"I visited Seafarers' Hall today. Strom Engle has boxes and boxes of old books the fishermen read. He also had some old captains' logs, including Irving Smith's log for the *Jolly Mae*. It made fascinating reading. I felt almost like I was on the ship with him."

"Getting seasick?"

"Practically." Mary chuckled. "According to his log, the *Jolly Mae* set sail at 1900 hours, that's seven o'clock, on the evening of October 3, 1841."

"So? What does that prove?"

"The newspaper account said Caleb was last seen around midnight of that same night. Irving Smith had already set sail by then. Therefore, he couldn't possibly have killed Caleb. He had an iron-clad alibi."

"Although"—Betty considered that for a moment—"he may have lied in his log to give himself that iron-clad alibi."

"I suppose that's possible. But the log entries were very detailed. They left the harbor heading north-northeast to fish the outer banks around Nova Scotia. The seas were heavy, waves washing over the gunnels. The barometer falling fast. Seems hard to believe a captain would make that up in his log. It would be too easy to check. In fact, the newspaper reported a terrible storm had passed through Ivy Bay on October 3."

"That still sounds odd to me. The fishing fleet usually leaves around one or two o'clock in the morning, don't they? Then why did this Smith fellow leave at seven?"

"Good point." If Irving Smith had fabricated his logbook, that meant he could be guilty of murder. Mary looked at her sister with a weary smile. "For now, I'm too tired to think straight."

Betty took her sister's hand and squeezed gently. "Have I mentioned lately how much I love you?"

Chuckling, Mary said, "Probably, but I don't think we have to say the words. Just being here together speaks volumes."

Yes, Mary's decision to move in with her sister after John died had been good for them both. Neither of them had to rattle around in a house much too large for one, and they provided companionship for each other.

Smiling, Mary thought of her favorite old adage: A sister is a forever friend.

———

The following morning, shortly after Mary opened the shop, Jill Sanderson walked in, a pleased smile on her face.

"Good morning, Jill!" Mary was genuinely pleased to see her.

Jill's smile grew wider and a little conspiratorial. "I found the picture you wanted."

A burst of adrenaline accelerated Mary's heart rate. "Caleb and his wife, Martha?" she almost whispered.

Jill nodded with a hint of accomplishment in her expression. Mary couldn't help but feel another tug of gratitude for the young woman. Of course she'd been hesitant to divulge any information about her family to Mary; familial politics were tricky, especially in this case. But Mary hoped Jill knew that she certainly understood Jill's lack of total allegiance to her grandfather-in-law, and would absolutely keep a tight lip about the help she had offered to Mary.

"I dug into that old box of photos in the attic, and I found a few things," Jill said. "I think it might be the same sea chest Daniel found the bill of sale in when he was storing his things in our attic. Fortunately, either my mother-in-law or someone else had labeled most of the pictures and even dated some." She placed a small miniature painting in a gold frame on the counter. "It was kind of fun looking at my husband's ancestors. There's even a resemblance between him and Caleb."

Gingerly, Mary picked up the portrait. Martha stood next to a seated Caleb Hopkins. As was the custom of traveling portrait painters, the heads of the two subjects were proportionally larger than their bodies, their expressions somber. Mary couldn't be sure the painter had captured a good likeness of the couple, but they both looked to be in their thirties. Mary supposed the painter had purposefully made them look younger than they really were, though.

"This is wonderful to see what Caleb must have looked like," Mary said. "His wife too."

"I thought my Harry's resemblance to Caleb was mostly in the eyes."

Mary studied Caleb, then his wife. "How big a man do you think Caleb is?"

Tilting her head, Jill took another look. "Hard to tell with that funny perspective."

"Martha's head is only barely above Caleb's, and she's standing," Mary said. "She looks quite petite. But I guess it's possible the painter made her look that way on purpose."

"Yeah, she looks really tiny there." Jill looked up at Mary. "But here, I found this as well. This may be more useful." She laid a small framed picture on the counter. It had a metal back and was covered with a thin sheet of glass. "I think it's a photograph of the family."

Mary leaned in to get a closer look and squinted against the glare in the glass. Caleb and Martha were standing, ramrod straight, staring at the camera. Two teenage boys and two young girls stood around them, with the same somber look on their faces.

"It's actually too early to be a photograph. It must be a daguerreotype," Mary said, touching the edge of the metal gently.

Jill looked at her blankly.

"It was an early kind of photography," Mary said. She'd recently read a historical mystery where a daguerreotype was a major clue, and the author had included lots of fascinating details about the process. "It was done by exposing a silver-surface copperplate to a lens and then exposing it to mercury."

Jill nodded, but she looked like she was trying to follow. "So it's old then?"

"Very. The process wasn't invented until the late 1830s. It would have been very new and not very common when Caleb died. It must have been done fairly soon before he disappeared."

Mary studied the photo. Caleb stood almost a full head taller than Martha, and he was thick. Martha was indeed much smaller than her husband, and Mary had the proof in the form of a photograph taken not long before he disappeared.

"So, does this help you?"

"Yes," Mary said. "Thank you so much." Considering Martha's small stature, Mary's question about her part in Caleb's death remained. If Martha had killed Caleb, how could she have disposed of his body? She didn't see how the tiny woman could have budged him—much less put him in a wagon to take the body somewhere else.

She thought about Jill's comment about Harry's bulk. "Jill, out of curiosity. If you had to pick up or drag Harry somewhere, could you manage?"

The young woman let out a guffaw. "Heavens, no. I'd need a block and tackle to even get him off the ground. He weighs a good two hundred pounds, and it's all muscle."

With the hard labor Caleb did as a fisherman, and the typical diet of the 1840s, Mary doubted he would have weighed quite that much. Still, given a muscular body, he'd be way too heavy for such a small woman as Martha to manhandle into a wagon alone, no matter how many laborious chores she was responsible for herself.

With a sigh that was close to regret, Mary tentatively eliminated Martha Hopkins from the suspect list. The woman's size wasn't absolutely proof she wasn't involved, but nonetheless, it was telling. "Thank you for bringing these to me."

"Oh, it's no problem. I'm just glad I found them. They're family heirlooms I'm definitely going to hold on to for my children and grandchildren to enjoy. You're welcome to hold on to them for a while, if that will help you." Then she sobered. "Just ... don't let Grandpa know I tried to help you. He'd be furious."

Mary touched Jill's shoulder and gave her a reassuring look. "My lips are sealed. I promise." At that, Jill left the shop and Mary returned to her post behind the counter.

Although Mary had now made some progress investigating the murder, she still couldn't see how the answers were getting her any closer to countering Daniel's lawsuit.

She hadn't been able to find any trace of a title change, despite Daniel's claim of a bill of sale. In fact, she'd found evidence that the Emersons had continually operated the gristmill from the earliest records until well past 1792.

She also hadn't found a signature or handwriting example of Isaac Emerson at the clerk's office or in the library archives. Neither had Rob's assistant.

For all intents and purposes, she'd hit a brick wall.

She laid the portrait and daguerreotype on the counter and tried to shake off her discouraged mood. Jill had found a valuable heirloom in that old chest. It would be a lovely way to pass family history to her children. And a daguerreotype that old was probably worth a fair amount, if she ever cared to sell it, though Mary was sure she wouldn't get rid of that piece of family history.

Mary was reminded of how she had traced her father's side of the family, the Nelsons, back as far as Plymouth,

England, in the 1600s, although the name itself was originally from the Anglo-Saxon tribes in England. The Fishers, John's family, were originally Normans who arrived in England after the 1066 Norman Conquest. They had a long, proud history to pass on to her children and grandchildren.

The adrenaline Mary had felt at seeing the miniature of Caleb and Martha slowly drained away. She had no idea how to prove or disprove that the barkeep at Horse Head Tavern was involved in killing Caleb. And now that she'd pretty much eliminated Martha and Irving Smith . . . .

Gus jumped up on the counter right in front of Mary and bumped his head against her chest.

"You sense I'm discouraged, don't you?" She scratched the top of his head and smoothed the soft fur over his back. "I hate to think William was guilty, almost as much as Betty does. But I'm running out of ideas."

He bumped her again, harder this time.

"Augustine Fisher, what is it you want?"

He canted his head, gazing at her with blue eyes that suggested she was the thickest human he'd ever met.

"I'm not a mind reader, you know."

Tensing, he poked the daguerreotype with his paw.

She was about to shoo him off when she realized, as silly as she knew it was, that he was trying to tell her something. "You want me to look at that again?"

Nonchalantly, he began to wash his face with his paw.

"So we're going to play twenty questions, huh?" Maybe Gus simply felt a need for a face wash and decided—

She gasped as realization struck. "It's true that Martha couldn't have moved Caleb's body on her own. But she could have moved it with some help."

Lifting Gus, she put him on the floor, sat down on the stool in front of the counter, and stared at the picture. Of course. Maybe Martha had a helper right in her own household, a son who had witnessed Caleb hurting his mother one too many times. The newspaper article had mentioned Martha and her *son* had both been questioned at length.

The door chimed. She looked up to see Bob Hiller had arrived with the mail.

"Morning, Bob. How are you today?"

"All is well here, Mrs. Fisher. My granddaughter Isabella's T-ball team won their game last night, so that's given me an extra hop in my step, you might say."

Smiling, Mary clapped her hands. Isabella was in Ashley's grade, and so Mary had spent some time with the girl. "Here's to the win!"

Bob gave a deep nod. "You look busy. So I'll leave you to it."

"Thanks, Bob. See you soon."

She looked back down at the picture. The older boy looked to be in his late teens, maybe even early twenties.

"What do you think of that, Gus?" She looked around, but her cat had returned to his favorite napping spot by the window. Apparently, he'd done enough work for the day.

Leaning back, she imagined Caleb's oldest boy had already been to sea with his father as a member of the crew. He'd be a strong young man. Maybe even the second boy had developed a few muscles by working on the boat. Sons could be very protective of their mothers. And the way Caleb's children had grown up, watching and hearing Caleb mistreat his wife, all four of them could have had anger and resentment boiling in their hearts. Perhaps the boys had eventually gotten big enough to do something about protecting their mother.

In her mind's eye, she pictured Caleb staggering into the house, wet from the storm, drunk, and still angry because of the argument he'd had with William. As he had many times, she wondered if he had vented his fury on his wife. This time, however, perhaps Martha fought back. As Mary had imagined it before, perhaps Martha did, in fact, take the knife to Caleb's chest.

But Mary took the scenario further this time. By the time Martha had theoretically killed Caleb, her sons had perhaps been awake. They came into the kitchen and understood that what had happened was done in self-defense. They resolved to help their mother appear innocent.

Even on a stormy night, Mary realized it would have been possible, with the help of a strapping teenager or two, to cover Martha's tracks. Neighbors would have been hunkered down in their homes during the storm, not peering outside. Certainly after midnight, the townspeople would all be in bed.

Satisfied with the possibility of that scenario, Mary nodded her head.

"Well, then, Martha and now her sons go right back on the suspect list. Thank you, Gus."

In response, Gus stood, turned around as though taking his well-deserved bow, and curled up in his spot again.

"Don't get too proud of yourself yet, Gus. We still have one more problem to solve. How do I prove that's what actually happened?"

The phone rang, interrupting her train of thought. She answered with a cheerful greeting. "Mary's Mystery Bookshop, Mary speaking."

"Hi, Mary. It's Chief McArthur. My clerk found the police report you wanted."

Her spirits perked up. "That's wonderful, Chief. Thank her for me."

"I will. She's left them at the front desk for you. You can drop by anytime you'd like."

Mary glanced around the bookshop. Rebecca would arrive soon. "I'll be there as soon as I can get away."

NINE

❖

The inside of the police station had sage-green walls and wide-plank floors. Sturdy wooden tables and chairs were arranged in the reception area.

The clerk handed Mary a brown folder that contained the old 1841 police file. Mary found a seat at a scarred table where she could study the contents. Instead of boxes in which to make entries, like the modern report Chief McArthur had filled out when her shop was broken into, this report simply had a blank area for the constable to fill in his report. The paper had yellowed with age, each sheet so fragile she feared it might crumble when she touched one.

Constable Greenstock's signature appeared on each report, as well as the date. His handwriting wasn't easy to read, but she managed to get the gist of what he'd done. The interview with Martha Hopkins and her son Peter. Another interview with Mountie Baker, the Horse Head Tavern barkeep, and witnesses to the argument between Caleb and William Emerson, with the notation that no blows had been struck during the dispute.

The interview with Emerson was apparently lengthy, worth several pages of handwritten notes, concluding there was no evidence that Emerson had killed Caleb, but that he was a primary suspect in the case.

Mary winced. Not a good sign for William. Or Betty.

As she read on, the report mentioned Irving Smith, the fisherman Mary had already cleared as a suspect with an iron-clad alibi.

Overall, the reports provided no new information beyond what she'd already discovered from the *Ivy Bay Observer*.

She returned the file to the clerk, thanking her and then walked back to the shop. The temperature had warmed again, and beads of perspiration formed on her forehead and under her arms. Hot summers might be fine for tourists, but she was already looking forward to fall.

———

Later that afternoon, Betty showed up at the shop with Kip Hastings in tow.

"Hi, Bets. Hi, Kip!" Mary glanced past her sister to the man wearing overalls who was with her. "It's so nice to see you. How's married life?" Kip Hastings and his sweetheart Heather had just recently wed in the area, although Mary hadn't attended. She knew they had planned a very small wedding because Heather had wanted something intimate, and they also were pretty short on cash.

The beginning of Mary's and Kip's friendship had had a rocky start—he had stolen a framed photograph from Mary's store before her grand opening, as a favor to his grandmother-in-law, knowing what she didn't: that there was money hidden inside it. But within a short amount of time, the whole thing had been resolved, and Kip had even donated the money that was stolen to a local charity. He and Mary had worked closely together with the renovating of her building, and he was a very talented handyman. Especially knowing that he was just starting off and trying to build a nest egg, she was always happy to hire him for projects.

"Nice to see you too, Mrs. Fisher." Kip, whose overalls were streaked white with mortar, touched the brim of his cap and gave a modest smile. "Married life is great. It's nice to finally live in one place and get to share meals together without having to separate at the end of the day."

"I remember that feeling," Mary said. "It's such a relief to finally become official."

"You can say that again," Kip said and smiled. "Now, let's take a look at the backyard." He spoke in the clipped tones of a New England native.

"Thank you, Kip. Betty's the one with the idea for a patio, but I fully approve."

The three of them went out the back door, leaving Rebecca to take care of the two customers browsing the bookshelves.

Betty described her concept for the patio. "We have the wild raspberry bush we're going to keep along this wall. And the chokeberry opposite that, plus the two rosebushes. The raspberry and chokeberry will attract birds. The roses will smell especially lovely in the spring."

Kip knelt and scooped up a handful of dirt. "First thing, you'll need good drainage so you don't have rainwater or snowmelt running in your back door." He glanced around the yard. "We'll have to grade the patio so the water runs off to the side there and out to the street in front of your shop."

That made sense to Mary, so she nodded in agreement.

"I want to put a couple of tubs of flowers on the patio," Betty said. "And we'll have an umbrella table with chairs."

"That's no problem." Kip stood and paced off the breadth and width of the yard. "I'll need to spread sand around so I can get the bricks to seat good. Do you want them mortared or flush up against one another?"

Mary glanced to Betty for advice.

"Mortar always crumbles after a while. Will they stay flush, or will weeds grow up between them?"

"If it was me, I'd do them flush back here. Give you a nice, smooth surface to walk on. When I do it, bricks stick right together like they were glued that way."

Smiling at his self-confidence, Mary glanced down and found Ashley standing next to her, waiting patiently to interrupt.

"What is it, honey?" Mary asked.

"Mother asked me to tell you that Henry's here. She thought you'd want to say hello."

"Thank you, honey. I'll be right in." She turned to her sister. "You work out the details, and we'll talk about the cost later when Kip brings us the estimate."

She thanked Kip for his time and slipped inside right behind Ashley to find out if Henry had enjoyed the latest book she'd sold him.

"Hi, Henry. How was that Scottish mystery?"

Wearing wash pants with frayed pockets and scuffed work boots, he grinned almost sheepishly. There were streaks of dirt on the shoulders of his cotton shirt. "I haven't quite finished it yet, but it's going well. All spooky fog and rattling noises down in the dungeon of the old castle. Although nothing's as scary as the crawl space I just saw this morning." He shook his head in dismay.

"Oh? Let me guess . . . . Dorothy's?"

"Yep, I'm afraid so." Henry looked at Mary hesitantly for a second, as if he didn't want to gossip. But then, clearly needing to vent, he continued. "The foundation seems to be settling. That's why her windows and doors aren't fitting well. I just feel so bad because it's not something I'm qualified to fix. I gave her the name of a contractor friend who I think she ought to call, but she seemed disappointed."

Mary knew there was more than one reason Dorothy would have been disappointed, but she simply said, "That sounds like a major project."

"It is. I've actually heard about several of the historic houses around the Cape that are having troubles like this. The foundations need shoring up, and the house needs to be releveled. Otherwise the house will fall down of its own weight."

"That would be terrible." She felt bad for Dorothy and also wondered if the gristmill had similar problems. No doubt that would have a major impact on the decision to restore or destroy the old place.

"Anyway, like I said, that's a job well beyond my pay grade. I wouldn't even know how to begin." While Henry was exceptionally good with his hands, he was a fisherman by trade and inclination.

As Mary contemplated Dorothy's problem, Henry gestured toward the back door. "What's Betty up to out there?"

"Oh, we're putting in a brick patio. We'll have tables and such for folks to sit and read or visit. I'm really excited."

"Sounds great to me. All those big bookstores in the city have coffee bars and lounge chairs for studying, so you'll be right up to date."

"I hadn't thought about it like that, but my goal has always been that this is a comfortable place where people can enjoy themselves."

Henry's eyes twinkled and he smiled. "With you around, it's sure to be."

Her cheeks warmed ever so slightly, and she laughed.

When Henry left, he got into his spiffy 1953 Chevy Bel Air, which was parked at the curb. Outside of his boat, Mary knew that the car was one of his favorite toys. He'd restored it to near-showroom condition and showed it at car clubs and other special events around the Cape.

By the time Mary closed the shop, clouds had crept in, bringing with them the first drops of rain that was predicted to last all night. She hoped the summer storm would cool the overheated air and reduce the humidity that had been plaguing the Cape for several days.

When she reached home, she parked and pulled her jacket up over her head to ward off the light shower and hustled inside with Gus in his carrier.

"Betty? You home?" she called.

"In my room."

Shrugging out of her jacket, Mary followed the sound of her sister's voice. Betty had converted her husband's former office on the first floor into a bedroom for herself so that she wouldn't have to climb stairs.

At the moment, Betty was sitting at her small desk, re-reading Daniel's lawsuit. She looked up. "Kip's going to bring us an estimate by tomorrow or the next day."

"Good. Thanks, Bets." She walked across the plush carpet to the desk. "I have something that might interest you."

"About the mill?"

"Not directly. It's about Caleb's murder. I had pretty much written off Martha Hopkins as the culprit, but she's back on the suspect list."

"So you think Martha did it?" Betty said, her expression a mix of regret and hope.

"I think she's still a viable suspect, but at this point, I can't prove it one way or another."

"At least William isn't the only one left on the list."

"That's true. In fact, I read the official police report this morning at Chief McArthur's office, but it didn't provide any new information."

"This whole suit business is so troubling."

Mary rested her hand on Betty's shoulder as a gesture of support. She knew how strongly Betty felt about her family. Even so, Mary hadn't been able to eliminate William yet, and he had been the prime suspect.

Soon, she should take another walk over to the gristmill. Maybe she'd missed something, another lead, although she couldn't imagine what it might be.

Betty sighed. "My goodness, Mar. I feel like our lives have been taken over by this thing. I'm sorry it's been so crazy. But I'm also really thankful for your help."

"Don't mention it, Bets. It has been pretty intense, but hopefully soon, this whole lawsuit business will be resolved and we can return to our normal . . . What am I saying? Our lives are never exactly *normal*. But that's one of the things I love about living here with you."

"I couldn't agree more. For now, I'll take solace in the gardening—it's been such a nice distraction."

"Speaking of distractions . . . How's that quilting mystery I lent you?"

"Oh! I just started last night. And I'm pretty sure it was Jacob who stole Evelyn's quilt. Her own son. I'll bet you that's who it was."

Mary laughed. "I'm not saying a word." Although she was impressed; Betty was right.

They talked a little longer about the book, then Mary went to her room to clean up and get ready to prepare dinner. The rain was falling steadily now, drumming on a metal shed in the backyard. She hoped that the storm and the skies would clear for the prayer group.

Lynn Teagarden had one of the nicest houses in Ivy Bay. Situated on a large lot surrounded by woods, the front had three dormer windows and a welcoming front porch.

Carrying a bowl of fresh fruit salad in a yogurt dressing, Mary walked up to the door and raised the brass knocker. Lynn quickly responded.

"Come in, come in, Mary." She gave Mary a polite kiss on the cheek. "I'm so glad to have a prayer meeting here."

Mary stepped into the foyer, which had a high ceiling and hardwood floor. "Oh, Lynn, what a beautiful home. You're so nice to invite us."

Lynn waved off the compliment as if her home was nothing special, then reached for the salad bowl. "Let me take that from you. Go on into the living room. Several ladies have already arrived."

As Mary headed toward the living room, she continued to take in the house. The light green carpet was so lush it was

like walking across a field of spring grass. Original oil paintings of the area hung on the walls, and a grand piano sat on a
raised portion of the living room. Tea and coffee had been set
out on a cherry-wood credenza beneath the paintings.

Mary greeted the ladies already present. "This is a tiny bit
fancier than the church chapel or the all-purpose room."

"It's a lot fancier than my *house*," another woman said
with mock envy.

They all echoed the same good-natured sentiment, including Tricia Miles, who lived in the parsonage provided by
the church.

More members of the group arrived in twos and threes, all
smiling and chatting, buoyed by the bright, sunny day. They
helped themselves to coffee or tea and found chairs.

Dorothy Johnson seemed unusually quiet as she arrived
and took a seat next to Mary.

"How are you, Dorothy?" Mary asked, genuinely concerned for Dorothy after hearing about the repairs her house
needed. Of course, Mary wasn't planning to mention that she
knew anything about it.

"Quite well, thank you." Her cryptic response suggested
she was in no mood for idle conversation, and Mary didn't
necessarily blame her. Still, this was their prayer group, a
place where they could share their struggles. Mary wanted
Dorothy to feel comfortable opening up. "How has Henry's
handiwork gone?" Mary asked, hoping her question would
encourage Dorothy to share.

Dorothy's face turned red and her lips narrowed. "I really
don't want to talk about it, but if you must know, my house is
a huge disaster. It's damaged to its very foundation." After she
blurted out the words, she covered her mouth with her hand

as if realizing that her comment may have been misinterpreted as a negative reflection on Henry. "Of course, Henry did a very fine job with what he could. It's just that my house is beyond the help of even someone as strong and skilled as him."

"I'm so sorry, Dorothy. If Henry can't fix the problem, it must be pretty major. Please let me know if there's anything I can do."

"Yes, it *is* major, and no, there's nothing you can do. I'm sorry. I'm simply not able to talk about it." Her spine ramrod straight, she lifted her chin and turned away from Mary.

All during the meeting, Dorothy never bent from her rigid posture. She neither spoke nor bowed her head in prayer. Her body language clearly said she was in pain of some sort.

As soon as the group adjourned for lunch, Dorothy left, not staying long enough to eat.

Lynn had noticed Dorothy's abrupt departure. "Is she okay?"

Mary didn't know how to respond. "I'm not sure," she finally said.

"Perhaps she wasn't feeling well," Lynn suggested, then went back to her hostess duties.

As the others went to help themselves to lunch, Mary turned to Tricia, the pastor's wife, and said quietly, "After lunch, could we chat?"

Her forehead furrowed in concern, Tricia nodded. "Of course."

Finally, after they had all enjoyed a delicious meal, and most of the others departed, Mary took a moment to talk with Tricia. "I know Dorothy is having some problems." Mary didn't want to gossip, but she decided this was a worthy conversation and that Tricia Miles was the right person to talk with. "From what I understand, her house is in pretty serious disrepair, including the foundation. I'm wondering if we can figure out a possible way to help her."

Tricia studied the last bite of strawberry pie on her plate. "I'm not sure Dorothy would want me to share this, but I do know that she's concerned about her finances. Apparently, her savings took a real tumble during the recession and haven't yet recovered."

"Oh my." Mary could understand why Dorothy has been so chilly lately.

"I suspect she's afraid she'll have to downsize and sell her house," Tricia went on.

"And with a foundation that's crumbling, she certainly won't get top dollar." Mary shook her head. "I just wish we could do something for her. It's a lovely, old historic house, and she's kept everything authentic over the years."

"I wish we could too, but I'm not sure what." Tricia's lop-sided smile was both sad and wistful. "I guess we'll both have to pray about it."

"Let me know if anything comes to you," Mary said. "And I'll do the same. For now, Dorothy is officially a regular on my prayer list." *She should have been there long before now*, Mary realized with regret. She should have recognized Dorothy's attitude wasn't just because she was jealous, but because she was afraid for her own future.

———

Still pondering how she could help Dorothy, Mary headed for the bookshop.

"Everything all right?" she asked Rebecca, who was be-hind the counter, helping Ashley stamp the insides of new books with Mary's signature logo.

"Lots of browsers, but not many buyers," Rebecca said.

"It happens that way some days." Mary hung up her jacket in the back room and returned to the front of the store. "Speaking of buyers, riddle me this: If you needed a lot of money in a hurry, what would you do?" She was really asking, of course, about Dorothy's situation.

"*Mmm*, rob a bank?" Rebecca said with a playful smile.

"Mommy!" Ashley gasped. "That's against the law."

Mary coughed. "That's not quite what I had in mind, and I think your mother was teasing."

Then, with a tilt of her head, Rebecca looked at her with a frown of concern. "If you're running short—"

"No, no, it's not about me, although I appreciate your concern. I have a friend who is facing a serious financial expense, and I'd like to help her, but I don't know quite how to do that without offending her."

Rebecca blew out a sigh. "Well, I'm at least glad you're doing all right, but I'm sorry for your friend. I suppose . . . there's always a yard sale to raise a few dollars, or, maybe sell some jewelry?"

Interesting ideas, Mary thought, recalling Dorothy's table of antiques at the summer festival at the park. She was sure Dorothy would need more money than selling a few antiques or having a yard sale would generate.

The bell over the door chimed, interrupting Mary's thoughts and giving her pause as a stranger stepped into the shop.

TEN

◆◆◆

The newcomer, an older man, his back hunched with osteoporosis, glanced around, surveying the shop. Despite the August weather, he wore a black raincoat that nearly touched the floor and a matching black rain hat. He lifted his hat, revealing a scant covering of silver hair. He peered through glasses so thick it was impossible to make out the actual shape of his eyes.

He acknowledged Mary and Rebecca with a nod.

"Ladies." Carrying an old-fashioned briefcase, he spoke in a voice far stronger than his physical appearance might suggest. "I'm looking for Mrs. Mary Fisher, the proprietor."

"You've found her. I'm Mary." More than a little curious, she stepped toward the gentleman.

"It's nice to meet you, Mrs. Fisher. I am Lincoln King."

"Oh, Mr. King. Good to see you. I wasn't quite sure what time you'd arrive." Smiling, she extended her hand. The document expert had finally arrived. His hand was smaller than hers and icy cold. No wonder he was all bundled up. He must not have any circulation at all. "I really appreciate you taking the time to come, Mr. King. This is Rebecca Mason."

"How do you do?" he said.

Rebecca nodded politely, then looked at Mary. "Unless you need me for anything else, I'll take off for the day."

"Go right ahead, Rebecca. See you tomorrow."

Rebecca smiled at the guest and went on her way.

"I'm so glad you could come, Mr. King."

"Just Lincoln. No mister required." His exceptionally narrow lips curled into what Mary took as a smile.

"Now then, I believe you have something you wanted me to examine, Mrs. Fisher."

"Mary, please. That's what everyone calls me." Their gazes met and they both smiled. Lincoln even chuckled a little.

She walked over to the counter to retrieve the ledger. "I found this at the Emerson gristmill, which is one of the oldest buildings in Ivy Bay, though it's in disrepair now. I believe it is a ledger of some sort. It was wrapped in oilskin when I discovered it."

"It would be my pleasure to tell you what I can about your ledger." He bowed slightly and his narrow lips lifted again.

Anticipation rippled through her chest. Maybe the ledger could tell her something about the mill's history and the reason for the feud between the Hopkinses and the Emersons.

Not to mention the alleged murder of Caleb Hopkins.

"Let's sit over there where we can be more comfortable." She pointed toward the pair of upholstered chairs at the back of the shop.

Following her, Lincoln said, "You have a lovely little bookstore, Mary. I do love a mystery, and a whole shop full of mysteries is an extra bonus."

"I imagine your work has always been about solving puzzles." She waited for him to be seated.

"Indeed, it has been about puzzles and mysteries of one kind or another." After getting comfortable in his chair, he took the ledger and turned it carefully in his hands. He sniffed the cover. "This is definitely later than the 1700s. Mid-1800s, I would think."

Mary was immediately impressed, as she'd hoped she would be when she'd found out about Lincoln in the first place. "You know all that simply by looking at the cover?"

"I would be happy to substantiate my reasoning, if you'd like. But I will warn you, I can be quite enthusiastic and long-winded about these things."

Mary beamed at the man. "That is exactly why I reached out to you."

He nodded resolutely, took a deep breath, then began to explain. "Well, first, the binding is, of course, the primary clue. And if you smell it"—he sniffed the ledger again—"it is definitely glue utilized in the 1800s. There are other clues, if you'd like me to elaborate further." Mary nodded, and he continued to talk about the thickness of the cover, its coloring, and the size of the book in general.

As Lincoln spoke, Gus leaped up onto the arm of the chair, which startled the man. Mary picked up her cat and held him. "Sorry about that," she said. "You're not to bother Lincoln when he's working," she admonished Gus in a loving tone, then set him down on the floor.

Recognizing the cat was under control, Lincoln opened the ledger to the first page with the elaborate handwriting. "Ah, I was not far off. Clearly the author has identified the year for us: 'In the year of our Lord eighteen hundred forty-three.'"

How had he read that so quickly? Mary had stared at those words many times and couldn't come up with anything but "Lord," and that was all thanks to Rebecca. Then something hit her: 1843. *Two years after Caleb's death.* Hope stirred in her chest. Not only could the ledger ultimately be helpful in understanding the mill ownership, but it could also contain clues about the alleged murder. And maybe even the feud.

Mary leaned toward Lincoln to get a better look. "The only word I was able to make out of those squiggles was *Lord.*"

"Understandably. The scribe who penned this bit got somewhat carried away with her Spencerian ladies' hand."

"Spencerian?" *Ladies'?*

"The style of handwriting. It became popular in the mid- to late 1800s. But to have a sample of this sort, written by a woman on a business ledger, makes it quite unusual. Although, education for women was increasing in that day and age, typically it was only those from the wealthy class. Many ordinary people, such as farmworkers, fishermen, and laborers signed their name with an *X.* Or at the very most had a rough education no greater than third grade. This woman, on the other hand, was quite well trained."

Mary pondered that revelation for a moment. It meant Betty's husband had a female ancestor who was highly educated. She wondered if the writer was the wife of William Emerson.

"What about the notations on the inside?" she asked. "I haven't been able to make heads or tails out of them."

He carefully turned one page and then another. Then he retrieved his large magnifying glass from his briefcase and reexamined the first few pages of the ledger.

He lifted his head. "These marks were not made by the same woman who wrote the words on the title page. In fact, I would guess this person, probably a man, could not write at all. I suspect it was his own code."

"Any clue as to what the markings mean?"

He returned his magnifying glass to his briefcase. "I confess I do not know, and probably only the worker who made the marks could read and understand them."

Mary's shoulders slumped, though she hoped Lincoln couldn't see her disappointment. She'd been so hopeful he would provide her with answers to the meaning of the ledger entries. Unfortunately, that was not to be.

She pulled back her shoulders and gave Lincoln a grateful smile. "Well, I appreciate you taking a look at the book." She slipped the ledger back into its oilskin covering. "At least I know the year it was written. That's a start." But less than she'd hoped for.

She handed him the selection of books she'd handpicked for him. "As promised," she said. "I think you'll enjoy these. One of them centers around ancient diaries, another is a biography of a 1920s New England professor, and another is a fun collegiate mystery."

"Thank you very much, Mary. It's been a pleasure. As far as the ledger, you might try to find an expert in codes and hieroglyphics, which are definitely not my forte. I focus on actual handwriting, as well as paper and ink."

That reminded her. "Come to think of it, I wonder if you might have time to check out some old records at the county clerk's office? My sister, who owns the gristmill I mentioned, is being sued. The man claims to have a bill of sale from 1792, although I couldn't find any record of the property transfer."

"Then perhaps his claim isn't valid," Lincoln said.

"That's what we're hoping, of course." She hesitated a moment, not wanting to take advantage of Lincoln's time but knowing his expertise could help Betty win the suit. "And when we get to actually see the presumed bill of sale, it would be enormously helpful if someone like you could evaluate the paper and even the ink to tell us whether it is a forgery or not. I figure, if you can evaluate paper from the same time and place as the plaintiff suggests the bill of sale was written, you could be an expert witness to deem whether the paper is authentic. And since you're in town. . . ."

"As a matter of fact, an attorney named Rob Dunlap has already contacted me. I believe it is regarding the same case you just described."

"Oh, that's perfect. Mr. Dunlap is my sister's attorney. Evidently he's one step ahead of me."

"It is reassuring to have an attorney who is working so diligently on your sister's behalf."

"I certainly agree." He stood and picked up the books and his briefcase. She walked him to the door. "Do drop by the shop again. I'm sure I can find other books you'd enjoy."

"It would be my pleasure, Mary."

They shook hands, and he slowly made his way to his car, a pewter-silver 1957 Cadillac with huge shark fins. It looked brand-new, as though he had just driven it off of the show-room floor.

She smiled as she locked up the shop and headed to her own car, thinking how Henry would have loved to have seen Lincoln's car.

———

When Mary arrived home after work, Betty was resting in the living room, reading the quilting mystery. Mary let Gus out of his carrying case, and he immediately jumped onto Betty's lap. "Hey, little guy," Betty said, setting her book down and petting the cat. It tickled Mary that Betty and Gus had developed so much affection for each other.

"How's the book?" Mary said.

"It's going well. The author is trying to throw me off, but I'm still convinced." She continued to pet Gus, who purred loudly. "Kip gave me the estimate today for how much the brick patio would cost. The estimate is on the kitchen table." She set the cat down. Mary followed her into the kitchen and pulled out a chair.

The price was about as high as Mary had expected, but since she had some extra funds left over from her original budget, she was happy to spend them on something as valuable as a functional backyard.

"This looks fine to me, Betty. I'm so excited about it. Will you let Kip know that he can move forward? And please buy whatever supplies you need for your gardening."

"It will cost a bit to buy the tubs for the annuals, but it will be worth it."

"No problem. I'm just grateful you're taking care of everything for me," Mary said. "And now, in other news, I *have* to tell you about the character I met today." She went on to tell Betty about Lincoln, the date of the ledger, and the strange markings inside that even Lincoln couldn't discern.

"As it turns out, Rob Dunlap has already hired Lincoln to examine Daniel's bill of sale to authenticate the paper and ink. That's assuming we ever get to see the record."

"That's wonderful, Bets. I'm sure Rob knows what he's doing."

Mary could only hope Lincoln would discover that Daniel's bill of sale was a fake.

"Meanwhile, I'm going to keep digging into the whole thing about mill ownership and the presumed murder of Caleb Hopkins." Tomorrow, she was going to visit the gristmill again. Now that she knew more about the Emersons and Hopkinses, maybe she'd notice things she wouldn't have before. She was also going to see if she could find someone to help her decode the markings in the ledger. And she would to think through the murder suspects.

But for tonight, she intended to relax. She and Betty would eat out on the deck, enjoy the summer evening, and listen to the birds calling to one another across the expanse of neighborhood yards. She couldn't imagine a more perfect night.

———

The following morning, Mary rose earlier than usual. The late summer sun was up, promising a midday temperature in the high eighties. She wanted to be on her way as soon as she finished breakfast.

Dressed in her robe and slippers, Betty came into the kitchen. Her hair was mussed and she hadn't put on her makeup yet.

"Morning, sleepyhead," Mary said with a grin as she poured herself a cup of coffee from the pot. "Want some coffee?"

"Sure, but what are you doing up so early? Come to think of it, what am *I* doing up so early? Oh, that's right, that *cat* of yours woke me," Betty said in mock irritation.

"Sorry about that." Mary laughed and handed her sister a cup of coffee, with lots of milk and lots of sugar, as Betty preferred. "I'm going to go back to the gristmill and take another look before I go into the shop. I've been wondering if there's more to discover there."

Betty sat down at the table with her coffee. "I can't think what. At this point, it's just a dirty, dusty old building."

"You never know. Maybe I'll see something I didn't see before." After finishing the last bite of her toast, Mary washed it down with a sip of coffee. "I'll wait if you'd like to go with me."

"Thanks, but I can't today. This is my morning at the church library. Pastor Miles, Dorothy Johnson, and I are reviewing some possible books we may want to acquire. There are a couple of recent releases about raising children in a Christian family and ways to use family vacation time as an opportunity to help others and bear witness to your faith."

"They sound like worthwhile books." Mary carried her dishes to the sink, rinsed them, and put them in that dishwasher. "I may not learn anything new at the mill, but maybe something will strike a chord. I'll see you this evening."

"Be careful," Betty warned. "Keep away from those rotting boards."

"Trust me, I plan to." Mary grabbed the heavy-duty flashlight they kept for emergencies, like power failures, and was about to go out the door when she saw Gus waiting for her next to his carrier.

"Sorry, Gus. You'll have to stay here for now. I'll come back after I explore the gristmill."

At the mill, she parked and walked across the logs to the other side of the creek. The recent rain had raised the water level in the creek. It poured down the run to the mill, churning white over rocks that protruded above the surface of the water. She imagined in a serious storm, one like the October gale of 1841, the creek would be brimming over the top of its banks. Whatever had bridged the run could well have been washed away by the hurricane forces that night.

Reaching the door, her breath caught and she halted abruptly. Someone had shoved open the heavy door.

Probably just kids, she thought.

She eased past the open door with care. Compared to the morning sunlight outside, the room was dim and filled with shadows. The place smelled dusty and dank with hints of rotting wood and tobacco smoke in the air.

She wrinkled her nose. Someone must have been smoking in there. She'd have to talk to Evan about securing the mill more carefully. Having anyone, let alone a child, injured here would be bad news on any number of levels.

A single column of sunlight spilled through the window on the east side of the building. Dust motes floated like tiny fireflies that had lost their sparkle.

She heard a noise in the corner of the room. A shuffle of feet. Dirt being ground into the old wood. Animal? Or human?

Air stuttered in her lungs, and youthful tales of the gristmill ghost raced through her mind. *A ghost and hidden treasure.*

She raised her flashlight to take a look. Before she could switch it on, a figure appeared from out of the shadows behind the buhr stone. Tall. Sinewy. A cold cigar tucked in the corner of his mouth.

Mary screamed. She took a step back and lifted the heavy flashlight in defense. Her heart thundered in her chest.

"Why, if it isn't Mrs. Fisher, sister to that Emerson woman, who's gonna prove we Hopkinses don't own what's ours by rights."

"Mr. Hopkins! What are you doing here?" She glanced toward the door. She could make a run for it but hated to give ground to the man. Yet she knew, despite his age, after years of fishing the seas, he still had more strength than she'd be able to muster to protect herself. She wavered on the brink of indecision.

"I'm just visitin' the *Hopkinses'* gristmill. Lookin' at the view. It's my right, ya know." His snide tone sent shivers down her spine.

"No, it isn't." Despite shaking knees, she used her sternest librarian's voice, one that unfailingly silenced rowdy patrons. She wondered how often Daniel had been coming to the gristmill. It seemed too great a coincidence for him to arrive on the one day she'd come back. "You're trespassing until a court says otherwise." She pulled her cell phone from her pocket and flipped it open. It glowed in the dim light. "I'm afraid you'll have to leave, Mr. Hopkins, or I'll call Chief McArthur."

"I've been coming here for years, woman. You're not going to keep me out of my own building." He sauntered toward her, his menacing gait rolling like he was on the deck of a ship.

Trembling on the inside, she stepped aside, leaving plenty of room for him to get out the door without coming any closer to her. She mustered her most confident voice. "Leave, Daniel. Now."

"I'm leaving. But there's no use in you snooping around in here. Soon enough, the mill and everything in it will be legally mine." He placed his hand on the giant stone buhr, patting it almost affectionately. "You mark my words, woman. This place belongs to me."

His warning, along with her rapid breathing, echoed in the empty mill as he stormed out the door.

Leaning back against the wall, Mary tried to calm herself. Daniel was nothing but a braggart and bully, she told herself. All bluster and no bite.

He'd come here often? To look at the view? How very strange he should say that. Not that the view overlooking the town and the marina wasn't lovely. It was. But it was a view that could be seen from any number of places in town. Why did he specifically come here to the mill?

Slowly, her heart rate returned to normal. She wondered what on earth Daniel had meant that the mill and *everything in it* would be his.

The huge buhrstone? That couldn't be worth much, assuming anyone could move it. And why would anyone want it, anyway?

She shined the light around. The beam touched the far corners of the room. She pointed the light upward, where there was a loft area, perhaps a place to stand in order to repair or oil the grinding gears or to pour the corn.

Slowly, she circled the room. Evan, or someone, had nailed a plywood sheet over the flooring she'd broken through and over another spot that must have been rotten. She flashed her light over the grinding stones' surface and stepped closer. It looked like generations of young people had scratched their initials on the stone, some couples circling their initials with a heart. A romantic notion in a decidedly unromantic place.

Mary preferred the red roses John had given her on every one of their wedding anniversaries.

She scanned the walls with the beam of her light. More initials and some graffiti, but nothing of interest that she could see.

Then her light caught an irregularity in a section of the wall down low next to the floor. She knelt and ran her fingertips over the mismatched wood. A small space, less than a quarter-inch wide, separated the two sections. The unmatched wood formed a two-foot square.

Like it was a hatchway to another room.

She glanced over her shoulder. After getting to her feet, she went to the mill doorway to see if Daniel was still around.

With no one in sight, she went back to examine the wall more carefully. Using the butt end of the flashlight, she tapped on what she thought might be a door and then on the undisturbed section.

The area behind the hatchway sounded hollow.

She ran her hand over the wood again. The edges seemed entirely flush with the rest of the wall. No knob or hinges were apparent.

Gnawing on her lip, she pushed on the top section. Nothing gave. She pressed on the bottom half. The wood gave a groan. She pushed harder.

Her hand shoved forward, which caused the top section to fall toward her.

"Oh my goodness!" She fell back. She hadn't really expected that.

Cautiously, she peered inside the empty space and discovered there was about an eighteen-inch gap between the interior wall and the exterior construction.

A false wall!

ELEVEN

◆◆◆

Mary gaped at the hatch and the wall behind it.

Had this been a place for early settlers to hide in case of an Indian attack? Or a place to hide their valuables from those who might steal them? She'd heard of such things but had never expected to find a secret hiding place in the old mill.

She peered in a little farther. To the left of the opening, she spotted what looked like an old cornmeal bag covered with dust.

Excited and anxious at the same time, she poked at the bag with her flashlight. The contents compressed slightly like a pillow does when punched.

She took a deep breath. "You can't just leave it there, Mary. You have to find out what's in the sack." To give herself courage, she whispered a favorite Bible verse. "Though an army besiege me, my heart will not fear; though war break out against me, even then I will be confident" (Psalm 27:3).

"No army here today. Just a dirty old bag," she told herself. She reached for the sack and dragged it out onto the mill floor. Years of dust and dirt blew up into her face, and she sneezed.

A narrow length of leather tied the sack closed. She worked the stiff knot with her fingers, finally loosening the leather, which she pulled away. The fabric of the bag was so old she was afraid it would rip apart. Painstakingly, she opened the sack's neck.

To her amazement, she found some sort of dark red fabric with what appeared to be an old pewter button with a stamped number, forty-three, attached.

She stared at the fabric and button without understanding for several seconds, her head trying to make sense of what she was seeing.

Could it be, however impossible it seemed, a British military uniform? That of a redcoat?

She tugged on the material gently to remove it from the sack. As she did, she heard the distinct sound of metal clinking against metal.

Was this what Daniel Hopkins had been talking about? Had he spent years searching for the treasure in the mill, or even stranger, had he known it was there?

Too aware that Daniel might still be nearby, she decided not to dump out the contents here at the mill. She stuffed the uniform back inside the sack and retied the leather fastener.

With her flashlight, she took one last look into the cubbyhole.

Her throat tightened. Another, similar sack lay almost out of reach behind the false door.

Lying flat on her stomach, she eased past the hatchway and closed her hand around a corner of the sack. Slowly, she edged backward, pulling the bag along until she could get to her knees again.

This sack wasn't as full as the first and wasn't tied closed. Perhaps the contents had been hastily hidden behind the false wall. Folding back the opening, she let the sack fall open around the contents.

A boot? Leather. Twisted out of its shape as though it had been in the water a long time.

Why in the world would anyone hide a boot? A single boot, not even a pair?

Gingerly, she picked it up to examine the wear on the sole. An object fell out of the boot and clattered onto the floor. For a moment, she stared at what appeared to be a salt-encrusted pocket watch with a cracked face and a few links of broken chain attached.

One more look behind the wall revealed nothing more hidden there. She'd lingered at the mill long enough, risking Daniel's return or the appearance of someone else tempted to sneak past the No Trespassing sign.

Perhaps she should leave the items at the mill, she reasoned. But then, sympathetic thoughts for Betty and Evan and the Emerson family history made her change her mind. Daniel Hopkins was not going to bully them. And she certainly wasn't going to let Hopkins steal Emerson property.

It was time to get these treasures safely back home.

Mary restored the hatch to its proper place. Nervous about being observed, she carried the two sacks to her car and drove home. In the back mudroom, she spread newspapers on the floor, then carefully removed the contents of the first sack. She wished Betty was here to go through the bags with her, but Mary didn't want to wait for Betty to be finished at the church library.

She started by examining the red jacket she'd seen earlier. The wool fabric felt coarse between her fingers. Definitely not the kind of jacket you could buy at Cape Cod
Togs in town. It was more like one you'd see in a museum of
American history about the Revolutionary War.

Or one worn by reenactors. But in that case, there would
be no reason to hide the uniform behind a false wall in a
decidedly old cornmeal sack.

Gus strolled into the mudroom to see what she was up to.
He sniffed at the jacket and pants.

"What do you think, Gus? Do you think this uniform dates back to the Revolutionary War?" Of course, the
Revolutionary War was well before the date when Caleb
went missing. But could Daniel have believed that these treasures were somewhere in the mill? It could certainly explain
why he'd been so eager to claim ownership. Mary doubted
he had enough money to restore the place, but perhaps he
had planned to tear the building to shreds until he found the
valuable treasures.

Gus began sniffing the second cornmeal sack.

"I'll get there, I'll get there," she said with a pat on Gus's
head.

She spread out a white vest next to the jacket and matching white pants on the newspapers. Had the British really
gone to war in white? She definitely wouldn't have let her
son Jack out to play in the woods wearing white. She'd had
enough trouble getting dirt stains out of his white Little
League pants.

Finally, she pulled out a squashed tricornered hat with a
feather on top.

She stared at the collection of clothing, wondering why someone would want to hide it. It was hard for her to believe there were many upstanding reasons for such a carefully masked hiding place. She supposed it could have been a deserter wanting to hide his identity. Or a British soldier who stayed in America after the war and wanted to keep his military days a secret. Or a worse scenario, a patriot who had killed a British soldier and didn't want anyone to know what he had done.

She shuddered at the thought.

The sound of her cell phone startled her, and she flinched. Taking a breath to settle her nerves, she pulled the cell from her pocket and said hello.

"Mary, are you okay?" Rebecca asked. "It's almost eleven."

"Oh, Rebecca, I'm so sorry." She glanced at her watch to verify the hour. "I, um, got so involved in something, I wasn't watching the time. I'll be there as soon as I can."

"No hurry, really. I was just worried about you."

"Thanks, Rebecca. I'll be in soon." Not for a minute could she have guessed what an engrossing treasure she would find at the mill.

After she got off the phone, Mary started to stuff the uniform back into the sack only to realize there was still something inside. Something relatively heavy compared to the uniform.

She held up the sack to let the contents slide out. A bag clunked to the floor.

Gingerly, she picked it up. A small leather pouch. The contents heavy in her hand. Untying the cord that closed the pouch, she poured the contents onto the newspaper.

Coins. More than a dozen of them spilled out, and the bag was still full. Not from the US mint.

She picked up a coin and turned it over. Given the uniform she'd found, she wasn't entirely surprised. Even so, she gawked at the profile of King George III and the date 1775 in amazement.

She began to think through what scenario would have brought this particular uniform to a random gristmill in a small town in Cape Cod. The image of British redcoats marching through the countryside. She pictured a soldier, a young man, who perhaps slipped away from his troop, hoping to escape the terrors of war, and found the gristmill as a temporary shelter.

An instant later, Mary frowned and the picture she'd created shattered into tiny pieces. As far as she could remember from her history books, there hadn't been any Revolutionary War battles on Cape Cod. Concord, Lexington, and Bunker Hill were a long march from the Cape.

Unless British troops passed through the area from Canada en route south to reinforce troops engaged elsewhere. Or perhaps simply a British patrol out scavenging for food. Still, they would have had to come a long way.

She shook her head. She didn't have time to worry about the source of the uniform now. She was ready to get to the bookshop and spend the day there.

Taking one coin, which she put in her pocket, she tied up the purse and put it, along with the uniform, back in the cornmeal sack.

Discovering the history of these items and determining if they had any connection to the ownership of the gristmill and how it related to the Emersons and Hopkinses in general would be quite a research project.

Particularly curious about the old watch, she dumped that out of the boot and looked at it again before putting it in her pocket along with the coin. She put the boot back in its sack.

She carried the sacks out to her car and put them in the trunk for safekeeping. If Daniel Hopkins really was after the coins, she didn't want to leave the telltale sacks laying around for him to find—or steal.

The sidewalks of Ivy Bay were busy with tourists wearing shorts, tank tops, and flip-flops, some women wearing floppy hats, when Mary arrived at the bookshop. A few of the tourists had wandered into the store to browse.

"Sorry I'm so late coming in," she said to Rebecca. Mary knelt to release Gus from her bag.

"It's fine. I was able to answer most of the questions, and with Ashley's help, we sold a bunch of children's books to one grandmother. I hope her grandchildren appreciate how much time she took to select the right one for each child."

Sitting behind the cash register, Ashley grinned. "She told me how old her grandchildren are and what they liked. Finding the right books was easy."

"Good for you, sweetie." She cupped the girl's cheek. "I'm going to have to put you on my payroll, after all."

Ashley seemed to like that idea, but her mother's quick shake of her head quashed the possibility. She glanced at Mary's slacks and lowered her voice. "*Umm*, Mary? The knees of your pants. . . ."

"Oh dear." Mary tried brushing away the dirt she'd picked up at the gristmill, but remnants remained. She'd washed her hands before she left for the shop but hadn't even thought of what a mess her pants had become. "I should've changed before I came in."

"It's all right. Nobody will notice if you stay behind the counter."

"I'm afraid that would limit the amount of help I could give customers."

Rebecca flushed. "I guess you're right."

Not wanting to run home to change, Mary said, "I'll try a damp cloth—see if I can make myself presentable."

As she went into the back room, she glanced out at the yard. Betty's plants were doing nicely, and she was anxious for Kip to get started on the patio.

Having done the best she could cleaning her slacks, she went back into the shop. Several people were browsing the shelves of mysteries. She put on her friendliest smile.

"Let me know if I can help you find something. We have both new releases and the old classics. Several local authors as well."

For the next few hours, she stayed busy helping customers and giving Rebecca a chance to take a lunch break.

By late afternoon, business had slowed and there were fewer people on the streets.

"Rebecca, I'm going to hop over to Gems and Antiques across the street. I have something I want Rich Tucker to take a look at."

"Sure. Go ahead. Almost time to close up anyway."

Mary knew that Rich was an ardent coin collector, and she wondered if he would have anything to say about these coins. She'd had other plans for the day, including trying to get in touch with someone who could potentially read the notations in the ledger, but she couldn't resist looking into the new treasure she'd found at the mill first.

At Gems and Antiques, she edged past an old footlocker decorated with ornate paintings of whales and ships at sea, and what looked to be a Tiffany table lamp.

Jayne was behind the counter. "Hey, Mary. Did you find out any more about that ledger?"

"I did, thank you for the recommendation."

"No problem. How can I help you today?"

"Actually, I dropped by to see your husband. I have a coin I'd like to show him."

"Oh, sure, he's in the back trying to restore the workings of an old clock. Just a sec."

Jayne let Rich know Mary was there, and he came out from the back room.

"What've you got, Mary?"

She placed the British coin on the counter. "I found this today," she said, careful not to mention where. "Any idea if it's authentic?"

His brows lifted. "Something you found around here?"

She nodded. "Nearby," she said, and she left it at that.

As Rich plucked a jeweler's eyepiece out of his pocket, Jayne joined him at the counter. He examined both sides of the coin.

"Interesting." He lifted his head. "A 1775 British farthing with dear ol' King George III on the front."

"Is it worth anything?"

"Indeed, yes. Although I don't recall any British coins from this era found locally." He took a book down from a shelf behind the counter and flipped it open. "During the Revolutionary War, it was pretty quiet in our neck of the woods."

That's what Mary had suspected. "But you do think it's real?"

"*Hmm*, I do." He skimmed down a page with photos of various coins. "Not terribly rare, of course, but still valuable. I'd have to get the latest quotes, but from what I can tell, this coin would be worth at least twenty pounds sterling. That's something a bit over thirty US dollars."

Mary's mouth flew open in surprise. Thirty dollars for *one* of those coins. Who knew how many of them were in that pouch. All together, they could be worth a fortune. "Wow! That's good to know."

"That's quite a bit for a coin originally worth less than a penny," Rich commented.

Jayne, who'd been listening with interest asked, "Did you find more than just the one coin?"

"I did," Mary admitted. "There seemed to be several different size coins, but I just picked up the one so I could bring it to you to check."

Jayne hopped up onto the stool behind the counter. "Sounds like you may have found your pot of gold."

And a likely motive for Daniel to be prowling around the gristmill. But if he'd visited the mill often, as he had said, why hadn't he located the false wall? If Mary found it, surely he could have. Couldn't he?

Or what about the children who had played in the mill through many generations?

Perhaps only now, with aging, the foundation of the mill shifting and changes in the weather, had the seam of the hatch she'd spotted become apparent.

"The higher the initial value and the better the condition, the more a coin will be worth. Are you interested in selling the coins?" Rich asked.

"Not right now. But I may want you to assess them for Betty." From Mary's point of view, they rightfully belonged to Betty and the Emerson family.

Rich closed the book. "I'd be happy to, anytime you're ready."

"Thanks, Rich. But there's more." She retrieved the watch from her pocket. "What can you tell me about this?"

"That it's not worth much in that condition," Rich said without hesitation.

"I'm sure that's true. But can you tell me anything else, like how old it is?"

"Maybe. Let me see." He rubbed the back of the watch with a cloth, dislodging some of the crusty covering. "It wasn't a particularly expensive watch originally. Gold-plated, most of which has worn off. From the workings, I'd say it was made sometime in the mid-1800s, but I can't be sure without doing some research."

Mid-eighteen hundreds. Awfully close to the time of Caleb's death, Mary thought.

"There are some initials here." He got out his eyepiece again. "Looks like CAH. Does that help?"

Mary's stomach rose up into her throat. *CAH? Caleb Hopkins?*

"It may help, thank you." Not wanting to divulge how important these items might be to the lawsuit, she kept her tone calm. Rich handed her the watch and coin, and she returned them to her pocket. Even though she hadn't told him much, she still needed to rely on his discretion. "For now, I'd appreciate it if you didn't mention the coins to anyone else. There may be someone else who's searching for the same pot of gold."

"Our lips are sealed."

Mary started to leave, then turned back. "Are you able to authenticate things like old buttons?"

Rich's blue eyes twinkled. "I say, you must have come upon a real cache of something. I'd love to take a look at whatever you have."

Mary left the shop with a simple thank-you.

———

Because of the warm day, Betty had set the table for dinner on the deck in the backyard. Trellises with climbing vines provided a privacy screen on one side of the deck, and a large umbrella could be adjusted to offer shade over the glass-top table.

Betty carried a bowl of chicken-apple-raisin salad out the door. Mary followed with a tray of lemonade, tumblers, and fruit salad.

"This heat wave is supposed to last for several days." Betty sat down at the table. "Personally, I'd rather have it cooler even if the tourists want it blazing hot."

"I hear you." Mary was anxious to tell Betty of her morning discovery at the mill. She said a brief prayer before the meal, then served her sister and herself a heaping spoonful of chicken salad, then took a bite.

"*Mmm*. This is delicious," she said, savoring the taste. "So, you'll never guess what I found this morning at the mill."

"*Ooh*," said Betty. "Do tell."

Mary told her of Daniel's presence at the mill, the false wall, the disguised hatch, and what she discovered behind it. "I even took a coin and the watch to Rich Tucker today to see if he could determine any value for them. Turns out, the one coin I took him—which was worth about a penny back then—is worth something like thirty dollars now."

"Oh my goodness." Betty looked as surprised as Mary had been. "Where did you store everything? I have to see them."

"Everything's in the trunk of my car. I debated whether to leave them inside or in the car. I chose the car, because I figured that way if anyone—and mostly I just mean Daniel—had seen me with the bags, that he wouldn't try to break into our house." Mary twisted her lips in thought. "But I'm second-guessing it now. Even if I parked in the garage instead of the driveway like usual, I almost think it would be better to rely on our alarm system, should Daniel dare try to intrude."

Mary wondered if she was being paranoid with all this worrying about a break-in. On the other hand, if Daniel had gone to such lengths as to file a lawsuit and use apparent scare tactics of loitering around places Mary and Betty had visited, she certainly couldn't put it past him to try such measures as breaking and entering.

Betty looked thoughtful. "I think you're right. You should bring the bags inside." She smoothed the pleats in her khakis, then she looked up again. "You have to wonder if all the fuss Daniel is making about owning the mill is really about those coins."

"I've thought the same thing. Even with those stories we all heard when we were children, why would he be so determined to believe them *now*? That there was something valuable *inside* the mill, more valuable than the mill itself and the land?"

"I don't know, except that it has turned out there is, or was, a treasure of sorts." Pensive, Mary ate a few more bites of salad. "Oh, and the old watch has the initials CAH."

Betty slanted her a curious look. "Caleb Hopkins?"

"Right."

"Okay, but why would Caleb hide his things in there? And where'd he get a Revolutionary War uniform?" Betty covered her mouth with her fingertips. "You're thinking the mill could be where Caleb was killed. And that Caleb's things were hidden because they were evidence."

Mary nodded. She noticed how Betty hadn't mentioned William as the guilty party, but it's what they both were thinking. The very thing they were afraid might be true.

Mary touched her sister's arm. "After we finish dinner, I'll bring the sacks with the uniform and coins and boot into the house. I'm going to see if Rich can tell us how much all the coins are worth. Perhaps he can even keep them in his safe."

"That's a good idea," Betty said. "I know Jayne puts her gemstones away every night. Their shop has great security."

"We'll both feel better knowing they are in a safe place."

Later that night, after Mary and Betty had pored over the treasures and continued to discuss the case, Mary went to bed with the coins and British uniform stashed in her closet.

Sometime during the night, after she'd long been asleep, a car alarm woke her. Occasionally that happened in the neighborhood. Someone would push the wrong button to lock their car. Knowing it would stop soon, she rolled over and went back to sleep.

———

While Betty and Mary were eating breakfast the next morning, there was a knock on the door.

Mary's eyebrows rose. "Early for visitors." She pushed back from the table and went to the front door. Their neighbor Sherry was there, a single mother who worked at the high school as a secretary.

"I'm sorry to bother you so early," Sherry said. She was usually trim and well dressed, but this morning she looked and sounded rattled.

"What is it, Sherry? Come inside."

"No, no. I'm waiting for the police. Someone broke into my car last night."

"That's terrible. Did they take anything?" Suddenly Mary recalled the alarm she'd heard.

"It looks like they tried to take the car radio but ran off when I turned on my porch light."

Still in her blue terry-cloth robe, Betty joined them at the door. "Who could have done such an awful thing? Our neighborhood is usually—"

"While I was outside, I noticed your car, Mary. It looks like the same person tried to get into your trunk."

Mary's mouth dropped open. "The trunk of my car?"

"I'm afraid so. It's all scratched up." She glanced toward her house. "There's Chief McArthur's car now. I called 911 right away."

Sherry headed his way, quickly followed by Mary. She'd parked in the driveway last night. Thank goodness she'd brought the treasure inside.

Mary gaped at the rear of her Impala. It looked as though someone had taken a crowbar to one corner of her trunk lid, bending it up. Having failed to open the trunk, they dragged the sharp end of the crowbar across the lid, gouging into the paint.

She felt sick to her stomach.

"Looks like they got your car too." Chief McArthur strolled toward her. He thumbed his uniform cap up farther on his forehead and studied her car. "We had some vandals breaking into cars earlier this week in the parking lot at the Chadwick Inn. Probably bored kids out to do some mischief. They didn't take anything except some change in the glove boxes."

A large part of her strangely hoped that this was done by kids, but it seemed far too coincidental to Mary. "Chief McArthur, the person who did this might . . . not be a kid."

He turned, frowning. "Oh? What makes you think that?"

"Well, it's about the gristmill suit I mentioned. I have reason to suspect that Daniel Hopkins could have tried to break into my car."

The chief frowned in disbelief. "You think old man Hopkins did this?"

"I think it's a strong possibility." Mary pursed her lips. "I was at the Emerson gristmill yesterday trying to help Betty by seeing if there were any clues that would point to ownership. Daniel was there when I arrived, and"—she shook her head at the memory of Daniel's rudeness—"after I told him he was trespassing and he had to leave, I found some items hidden behind a false wall. I thought he was gone by the time I carried what I'd found out to my car and put them in the trunk. He might have still been around and saw me."

Chief McArthur pulled out a notepad and took a few notes, though his expression was still dubious. "What did you find?"

She told him about the contents of the two cornmeal sacks and how she'd taken them inside last night.

"Interesting." He grew pensive for a moment and rubbed his chin with his fingertips. "You should come into the station and fill out a formal report. But first, I'll have to pay a visit to Daniel Hopkins and ask him a few questions."

TWELVE

————◆◆◆————

Mary was already at the shop when Rebecca and Ashley arrived that morning.

"What in the world happened to your car?" A worried expression on her face, Rebecca shed her sweater. "I saw it parked outside. Did you have an accident? Are you hurt?"

Looking equally concerned, Ashley came over to be close to Mary.

Mary put a reassuring hand on the child's shoulder, then smoothed a loose curl of her hair back from her face. "No, I didn't have an accident. And I'm fine." Irritated. Even angry. But physically fine. "Just a little vandalism," she said, trying not to worry Rebecca any further.

"I'm sorry, Mary. Makes you wonder what this world is coming to when people don't respect the property of others."

That was all too true. Yet the possibility that Daniel Hopkins, as angry and grouchy as he was, would have the nerve to break into her car still boggled the mind.

Just then, Bob Hiller came in and placed the mail on the counter. He eyed the doll Mary still had beside the computer. "What are you doing with an old tap? I haven't seen one of those in a long time."

Mary spun around. Her gaze locked on the porcelain doll she'd found at the gristmill. "A tap?"

"Yeah, you know, like on a cask of beer. You can tell by its shape. They're collector items now. I saw one like it on that antiques TV show." Bob gave an easy shrug. "Too bad she's chipped, though."

"Yes, it is," Mary said, still floored by the news. She looked up at Bob. "Thanks so much."

"My pleasure." He tipped his hat and went out the door.

Mary slipped around the counter to get on the computer. Nothing of interest had turned up when she'd checked the slogan "Only the Very Best." Now she needed to expand her search parameters and include words like *collection, antique, beer* and *eighteen hundreds*.

She clicked through one Web site after another. Finally, she found a site dedicated to the history of beer and ale in the United States. She read the part of the history that interested her: "For a brief period during the early to mid-1800s, Queen's Castle porcelain factory in England produced genteel dolls that fit over the spigots of kegs of ale, particularly specialty ales brewed in the United States. These dolls, which were stamped 'Only the Very Best,' became popular collector items and an early form of advertising."

"Yes!" Mary pumped her fist in the air.

"What is it?" Rebecca asked.

"I've found out what that little doll is all about." She explained briefly how the doll was used but didn't mention the Horse Head Tavern, which had to be the source of the doll she'd found.

Her forehead furrowed. But how would the doll have gotten to the mill, and why had it been hidden under the floorboards? Had William tossed it aside as trash? Or had the doll fallen out of Caleb's pocket during a fight with William?

Mary's stomach knotted on the fear the latter was the case. William could have been hiding the evidence that Caleb had been at the mill that night. He'd known there had been witnesses to the argument he'd had with Caleb.

Please, Lord, I don't want to have to tell Betty that her husband's ancestor could be guilty of a serious crime.

Later that afternoon, after she'd filed her report with Chief McArthur at the sheriff's office, Mary went home to retrieve the coins and British uniform, leaving the boot and watch tucked away in her closet.

She wanted the uniform and coins in Jayne Tucker's safe as soon as possible. And she would ask Rich to give her an estimate of their value. Then she would return to the bookshop until closing time.

Daniel Hopkins could trash her car all he liked and threaten her, but he wasn't going to steal what was rightfully Betty's treasure.

Before she left the shop that evening, she sat down with a pad of paper and pencil to list all the information she still needed about the gristmill and Caleb Hopkins' death.

- Find someone to interpret the markings in the ledger.
- Brainstorm alternative causes for Caleb's death or prove that William was not guilty.

In her sister's mind, the latter would be the most important point. And the hardest to produce.

In serious need of prayer and meditation in the presence of the Lord, Mary was eager to attend church Sunday morning. She drove Betty the short distance into town, only to find the parking lot nearly filled with summer visitors in addition to local churchgoers.

Inside, the walnut pews, worn smooth over the years, were equally full. Betty and Mary squeezed into a row near the front. A whole phalanx of yellow and gold chrysanthemums stood in front of the pulpit and the choir. The faint floral scent drifted over the congregation.

As they sat down, Mary noticed Dorothy Johnson sitting at the opposite end of the pew, her head bent in prayer.

Guilt pierced Mary's conscience. She hadn't given any more thought to how she could help Dorothy with her financial problems. Not that it was her responsibility, but Mary felt for the woman. Dorothy simply looked troubled.

With the organ playing, Mary lowered her head. *Please, Lord, help me to find a way to lighten Dorothy's burdens. Use my hands and my heart to do Your work.*

As Pastor Miles began the service, Mary opened her heart and mind to the will of God. If only she listened carefully enough, He would guide her.

Mary's mind began to drift during the sermon, when ideas began to stream in. Could she put donation jars in the shops in town, with the contributions going to restoring historic homes, houses like Dorothy's? She wondered if Dorothy would accept the charity. Clearly the woman was proud, and Mary didn't entirely blame her. It was hard for many people to admit when they're in trouble.

Mary thought again about the many historic buildings and houses in Ivy Bay, each of them a challenge to maintain, and each with its own story to tell. Even Grace Church had a history that went back to the 1800s. And there was her bookshop with its history as a depository of Ivy Bay archives and onetime auction house. The small houses that were once fishermen's homes and the lives they led were fascinating and the historic Emerson gristmill had a story to tell. Mary knew there were lots of historic places in Ivy Bay she hadn't even seen yet, stories she'd yet to hear. Then it hit her . . . .

"That's it!" she said out loud.

Betty looked at her, and so did the woman sitting in the pew in front of her.

Giving them each a weak smile, Mary's cheeks warmed in a blush and she slipped lower in the pew.

Despite her momentary embarrassment, she knew God had given her the answer. With the cooperation of downtown businesses and owners of historic homes, she was going to organize a walking tour of Ivy Bay. People would buy tickets, and there'd be volunteers at each location, usually the owner, who could tell visitors the narrative of their building or home.

And, if people would agree to it, the proceeds from the walking tour could go to Dorothy Johnson to defray the expense of restoring her home.

Smiling to herself, Mary relaxed.

Betty leaned toward her and whispered, "Are you all right?"

"I'm great, Bets. Thanks to the Lord's help."

After the service concluded and they were driving home, Mary was eager to share her revelation. When they got home, they prepared lunch together. Despite the late August heat, the table on the deck was shaded and a light breeze cooled the air, keeping the temperature comfortable.

Once they were seated and enjoying their meal, Mary told Betty her plan.

"I think it's a wonderful idea," Betty said when Mary finished. "I've known a couple of the members of the board of selectmen for a very long time. I can talk to them and hopefully get them to help support the effort."

"That'd be great, Betty. I should have thought to include them in the planning and organizing."

"How about including Dorothy in the organizing as well? She's done a terrific job putting together the Summer in the Park Festival. This is right up her alley."

Mary popped a seedless grape into her mouth and pondered the idea. "You know, I think if she was part of the program, she'd feel like whatever money we're able to pass on to her is less charity and instead something she helped to earn."

"I agree. But I do worry that you have enough to do. Are you sure you want to put this together while helping me deal with Daniel Hopkins' suit *and* running the bookshop? Of course, you know I'm happy to help in any way I can, but it's still a lot to take on."

Her sister had a great point. But Mary knew Dorothy needed financial help soon or she might be forced to sell her house at a big loss.

"I'll figure it out," Mary said. "And speaking of the lawsuit, has Evan given you word yet on when the court date will be set?"

She shook her head. "I actually just spoke with him this morning. No date has been set yet, but preliminary meetings are being scheduled right now. Rob Dunlap told Evan we'd finally get to see the bill of sale at that meeting."

If only Mary could gather some solid evidence of who owned the gristmill before that meeting occurred. But she was far shorter of adequate answers than she had hoped.

Mary almost laughed. Betty was right—she was in over her head. Somewhere in the middle of all of this, she was running a business. And this was the busiest season of the year.

Lord, I'd appreciate Your help to get me through the next few weeks. I'm really going to need it.

On Monday, Mary arranged to take her car to the body shop and rented a compact car. Her insurance company assured her that the repairs and car rental would be covered except for her deductible.

During the next several days, Mary spent much of her time organizing a committee for the historic tour of Ivy Bay. Among the businesses she visited, she went to Gems and Antiques to talk with Rich and Jayne.

Rich bounded out from the back room, a big grin on his face. "Mary, I was hoping you'd drop by. I've got great news."

"The coins?" She held her breath.

"The coins *and* the uniform. I'm used to dealing with valuable coins, but I had no idea there was such a market for authentic Revolutionary War uniforms. I checked online and then called a couple of guys I know who are in the business. It looks to me like that uniform could be museum quality."

Mary's mouth hung open for a moment before she could snap it closed. "What does that mean, exactly?"

"It means if you took it to the right auction house, you could make a bundle." He named an amount that made Mary's jaw drop again.

"Then when you add in the value of the coins"—he gave her a rough value—"you're going to come out with a tidy sum. Mind you, the coins aren't uncirculated, which would jack up their price considerably. But they're in better than average, even good condition for circulated coins from that time period. You found quite a treasure, Mary."

Her mouth went dry, and she swallowed hard. "I had no idea." It wasn't that Betty needed extra money. Edward had left her quite well-off. But to have that much "found" money to spend or save or give in any way Betty wanted would open up all sorts of possibilities.

Rich grinned even more broadly. "Looks like the cat's really got your tongue this time."

"I'm absolutely stunned." She frowned in thought. "How do you suppose that uniform and the coins made it to Cape Cod? There weren't any battles around here that I know about."

He eased himself onto the stool behind the counter. "I've been thinking about that too. The uniform belonged to an enlisted man, which means he probably came from the lower classes in Britain. If he didn't have much to go home to, maybe he deserted his company. Or when the British were retreating, he marched the other way planning to make a life for himself in this new country."

Mary had envisioned something like that herself. She wondered if the Emersons had helped the man get away.

She smiled a little. Maybe the British soldier was hiding out at the mill and that's what started the story about the building being haunted. "Well, thank you, Rich. For the work you've done and for keeping the items in your safe."

"It's my pleasure, although I'll be anxious to know more about where you found the treasure and who it belongs to, once you're ready to tell me."

I'm anxious to know who they belong to as well, she thought. But she simply said, "Sounds good, Rich. Your discretion means a lot to me."

"It's my middle name," he said with a chuckle.

She turned and walked through the narrow aisle, past a child's rocking chair and chest of drawers made in the Federalist style, to the door, where she stopped.

She whirled around. "For pity's sake, I'd forgotten why I came to see you."

"Not about the coins?"

"No, not really," she said walking back to the counter. "I'm glad to know their value, of course, but I wanted to ask if you'd serve on the committee to organize an historic walking tour of Ivy Bay?"

He blinked and his tall forehead pleated. "You're going to have to tell me more, Mary. I've never heard of a walking tour around here."

Yet another reason why it's such a good—or rather, a God—idea, she thought.

The street was nearly deserted as she walked back to the shop and something caught her eye. Two teenage boys skulking around the parked cars. They'd duck down, then pop up again.

Suddenly, one of them stood. He slammed what looked like a big wrench against the passenger window of an almost new Lexus. The car alarm screamed. The boy with the wrench reached inside and pulled out what looked to be a laptop.

"Stop!" Mary cried. She hurried after them, but the boys were too fast on their feet for her to catch them.

After halting beside the damaged car, she pulled out her cell and called the police station. "Chief McArthur, please," she said when the operator answered.

A few moments later, the chief said hello.

"Chief McArthur, this is Mary Fisher. I just witnessed two teenage boys breaking into a car on Meeting House Road. They stole what looked like a laptop."

By now, people had gathered on the sidewalk, and the owner of the Lexus had silenced the car alarm.

"We already got a 911 call on that," the chief said. "Sounds like the teenagers we've been having trouble with. Probably the same kids who tried to get into your car trunk."

The act of vandalism that she'd blamed Daniel Hopkins for.

Unwarranted disappointment crept into Mary's heart and shame heated her cheeks. She'd jumped to a conclusion and accused Daniel without any evidence.

"So it wasn't Daniel who tried to get into my car," she said in a faint whisper.

"Doesn't seem like it." He paused for a moment. "Can you stick around there? The responding officer should be there by now. He'll take your statement."

"Of course." She ended the call. How had she let herself forget her Christian duty and judge a man so unjustly? *Forgive me, Father.*

When Mary arrived home that evening, Betty's air-conditioned house felt heavenly. She set her handbag on the floor and released Gus from his carrier. Sitting erect on the plush carpet, he looked at her as though insulted he had been trapped in the bag for even a few minutes.

"I'm just keeping you safe, Gus. Wild animals do sometimes come into our area. Don't look at me as though I were some ogre who cages you."

"Bets," she called, chuckling at her prideful cat. "Are you home?"

"In the bedroom."

Mary found her sister at her desk paying bills. "I've got good news for you."

Betty looked up. "Daniel has dropped his suit?"

"No, not that good, unfortunately. But you've come into some valuable property." She sat on the edge of the bed and related what Rich had told her.

Betty's eyes rounded and her mouth opened much like Mary's had when Rich had told her the value of the coins and uniform.

"My gracious." Betty put her pen down and shook her head in amazement. "I had no idea."

"I thought the coins would have some value, but I wouldn't have guessed so much for the uniform. Rich says he'll arrange things if you want to sell it at auction."

"How nice of him. I'll have to think what to do and talk to Evan."

Mary couldn't think of any reason to hold on to the uniform, but there was no rush to sell it either.

Overall, the day had turned out better than she'd expected, considering it had started with a vandalized car.

THIRTEEN

Thanks to Eleanor Emerson Blakely, who was head of the chamber of commerce, the committee met in the chamber's renovated nineteenth-century carriage-house stable. The conference room had once been where the owner kept his tack.

Mary and Betty arrived early and set out a meeting agenda at each place, along with the names and contact information for the eleven members of the committee.

Several local businesses were represented, all of them housed in historic buildings. Dorothy Johnson had already lined up several owners of historic homes willing to open their houses to visitors and recruited two of them to serve on the committee. And, of course, Eleanor had agreed to serve on the committee as well.

Chief McArthur served as an ad hoc member of the committee to help with planning for traffic control and pedestrian safety, and his sister Cynthia, who had a strong interest in the history of Ivy Bay, was here as well.

By 8:10 AM, all the committee members had arrived. Mary asked them to introduce themselves, then briefed them on the concept of the walking tour. The members had agreed that the proceeds would go to Dorothy, but she'd only been told that the profits would be dedicated to the "preservation of historical homes and buildings." Mary was both excited and nervous to ultimately surprise her with the news that the money was for her.

Throughout the meeting, Mary's goal was to delegate some of the responsibilities: publicity, building and home selection, development of a brief description of the properties and a route map, and ticket sales.

Randy Overholt, an Ivy Bay selectman, would arrange for official sanction from the town leadership; Chief McArthur would work with the routing map subcommittee.

In just over an hour, Mary adjourned the meeting, pleased with everyone's enthusiasm.

As she was gathering her notes, the police chief lingered until everyone else had left.

"Mary, if you've got a couple of minutes, I'd like to talk to you about the teenagers you spotted. We caught them."

"I'm glad. I don't know what gets into youngsters like that. I hope they've learned their lesson."

He shoved his hands in his pockets. "I kind of doubt it. The parents didn't think it was a big deal. I wrote them up but had to let them go under their parents' supervision." He snorted. "Not that the parents have done such a great job of supervising them so far. They did say their insurance would cover the damages." He handed her a note with the parents' names and insurance carrier, which she could pass on to her insurance representative.

She gave him a reassuring pat on his shoulder. "You did what you could. Someday, their behavior will catch up with them. I just hope they don't hurt someone else in the process."

They walked out of the building together and then went their separate ways. After work, Mary drove to the garage to pick up her Impala and then went home ready for a restful weekend.

By the time Mary got to work on Monday, Kip was already in the backyard. He and a helper named Ian were grading the patio and laying a wooden border.

She unlocked the back door and stepped outside. "Good morning, Kip."

He tipped his hat and grinned. "Hope you don't mind we got started early. On these hot days, I like to get as much done as I can before it warms up."

"I can certainly understand that. I'll leave the door unlocked." She checked the progress they'd already made, pleased with the flowing shape of the patio as it was emerging. "You're welcome to come inside to get a drink of water or to cool off whenever you'd like."

"Thanks, Mrs. Fisher. We might just do that a time or two." Leaning on his shovel, he surveyed the patio area. "Do you want me to lay the bricks in any special way? Maybe a herringbone pattern?"

"That would look nice, I think."

"Good. Then that's what we'll do. The bricks are gonna be delivered tomorrow, early."

Definitely no moss growing under Kip's feet. "Sounds great. Just let me know if you need anything."

She stepped back inside and found Rebecca and Ashley had arrived. Ashley was already settled in the children's reading area, and Rebecca was in the process of checking the cash register.

"Patio going in?" she asked.

"Yes, indeed. I think Kip may have it all done by the end of the week."

"That's exciting. Maybe for the walking tour, we could serve punch and cookies on the patio. That would bring folks into the shop. If their interest was piqued by the tour, they might buy a book or two about Ivy Bay."

"What a good idea! I can order the cookies from Sweet Susan's." Although, Mary didn't want to treat herself to Susan's bakery goods *too* often or she'd have to buy all new clothes in a larger size.

"I know you're likely to be busy that night with all the organization of the walk, so I'll take care of the punch," Rebecca said. "I've got a couple of nice recipes with sherbet and sparkling soda."

"That'd be wonderful. You get whatever you need, and I'll reimburse you." Mary went behind the counter and sat at the computer. "But what about Ashley? I thought you were going to take her around on the tour."

"I talked to her about that. Turns out she'd rather come here to the bookshop and stamp the tickets of the visitors who drop by."

Mary chuckled and shook her head. "You can never tell what's going to appeal to children, can you? Or how often they'll change their minds."

The punch and cookies at the bookshop sounded like a good plan. In fact, at next Friday's committee meeting, Mary would make the suggestion that the businesses on the tour route might want to do something similar.

Rebecca and her daughter set about rearranging books to even out the shelf space, while Mary caught up with paperwork on the computer.

Idly, she picked up the ledger she'd found at the mill. Staring at the cover, she tried to picture what had happened on October 2 and 3, 1841. The storm must have been horrendous, blowing business signs down and toppling trees. Rain would have been coming down in cascades, to the accompaniment of thunder and lightning.

She wondered how Caleb Hopkins and William Emerson could even hear each other in the cacophony of noise. Surely they'd both wanted to get out of the rain and wind; William to the mill, and Caleb home or back to the tavern.

So how did the boot and watch end up hidden in the mill?

The chime over the door sounded. Mary stopped her musings as Bob Hiller strolled into the shop. "Looks like you're doing some work around the old place." He put the mail, including a couple of catalogs, on the counter and picked up the outgoing mail.

Mary began sorting through the envelopes—mostly bills and advertisements. "We're putting in a brick patio. It'll be a quiet place to read or visit with friends."

"Sounds good. When you get it done, I'll slip out there one day and take myself a break." He shifted his weight from one foot to another. "These feet of mine are getting older by the day."

"I can imagine." There were days when Mary's feet hurt too, from standing most of the day. She glanced at the ledger again and thought about that long-ago fateful night. "As a child, I mostly visited Ivy Bay in the summer. But you've lived in Ivy Bay a long time. What's it like when a hurricane comes through here?"

His eyes widened. "Is there one coming our way? I hadn't heard anything—"

"No, Bob, it's okay. Don't panic," she said with a laugh. "I'm just doing some research. I'm wondering what the town would be like if several inches of rain fell in only a few hours."

"Well, now ..." He removed his cap and ran his palm across the top of his receding hair. "When it gets real bad, the streets overflow their curbs. In fact, the streets that run down toward the marina turn into rivers, and some of the shop owners have to sandbag their doors so they don't get water inside."

"What about the pond and the race at the old gristmill? Does that usually overflow too?"

He paused again to contemplate her question. "I don't generally work the route out that direction. In fact, if there's a hurricane coming through, we don't deliver."

"None of this 'through rain and sleet' business for Ivy Bay mail carriers, huh?"

His cheeks darkened with a blush. "That old saying has sort of been replaced with safety first."

"Smart plan." She smiled to let him know she'd only been teasing. "Do you think the pond overflows in a heavy rainstorm?" she repeated.

"Oh yes, indeed. The pond breaks over its bank, and the race past the mill becomes a regular Mississippi River, covering a whole lot of land. When I was growing up, us kids would go over to take a look after the rain stopped. You didn't dare get too close to that river of water or you'd be washed right out to sea."

"Really?" During her summer visits, she recalled only a few times when it rained. She had never seen anything like what Bob had described.

"Absolutely. That rushing water would pick up anything in its way—garbage cans, bicycles. I saw a picnic table float away once. I heard it turned up a couple of days later on the beach at Provincetown. The owner went over to bring it back, but it was pretty well broken up."

If a storm could sweep a picnic table out to sea, would the power of a hurricane be enough to wash a full-grown man away? A man who was drunk?

"I'd best be on my way." With a grin, he touched his fingers to his cap and walked out the door.

Mary picked up the mail and started opening envelopes. An invoice from the wholesale book distributor. An electric bill, higher than usual because they'd been running the air conditioner a lot. A notice from her dentist that it was time for a checkup.

As if she had a lot of spare time for that, she thought with a sigh.

Frowning, she considered what Bob had told her. What if . . . A scenario began to form in her mind. What if Caleb had followed William Emerson back to the gristmill after their argument? It was raining hard. Caleb confronted William again, and they continued their argument. One of them threw a punch. Caleb fell or was pushed into the roaring water and was washed out to sea. His body, too, might have washed up on a nearby shore.

Later, after the storm had passed, William could have discovered Caleb's boot and his watch, which had been lost as Caleb battled in the rushing water to reach safety.

Of course, Caleb could have fallen into the race all on his own. William later found the evidence of Caleb's presence. Knowing he would be a suspect, he hid the boot and watch behind the false wall at the mill in order to protect himself and his family. That would explain why she'd found the porcelain doll too, because that also tied Caleb to being at the mill.

But why was the ledger hidden in the same place as the spigot for a keg of ale?

As Mary paused to consider those two possibilities, she realized there was yet another possibility. Not far from the gristmill, there were marshes; marshes that were quite close to where Caleb Hopkins lived.

With such a heavy rain, the marsh could have overflowed just like the race at the gristmill.

What if Martha had stabbed Caleb with the bloodied butcher knife? She and her son could have dragged or carried Caleb to the marsh under the cover of darkness and the roaring noise of the storm. If they'd dumped him in the marsh, his body could have sunk to the bottom and still be there buried beneath the silt, mud, and goo. Or maybe his body had washed out to sea like the picnic table.

Washed all the way to Provincetown?

Gus leaped onto Mary's lap, startling her. "What is it, Gus? Do you think I'm on the right track now?"

He nudged his head under her chin.

"You're right. It's a lead I should at least follow."

But how? She couldn't go digging up the marsh looking for old bones in the mud. Nor did she want to.

Apparently, no one in Provincetown had reported finding Caleb's body. So maybe that wasn't what had happened.

Or perhaps it was, but the body had never been identified. Communication between the Cape and the mainland in the twenty-first century was far better than it had been in the 1800s.

A steady stream of customers began to drop into the shop, requiring Mary's attention. Kip and his helper came inside to cool off and eat their lunches. Rebecca and Ashley took a quick break as well.

Finally, when it was well after two o'clock, Mary decided to dash over to the library.

She made her way to Victoria, who was at her desk. "I seem to have become a bad penny that simply keeps on showing up."

Her friend laughed and her blue eyes sparkled behind her cat's-eye glasses. "I love pennies like you, Mary. Always so full of questions, you keep me on my toes."

"This one may be harder than most. Do you have old papers from Provincetown?"

She stood. "Are we going back to the 1840s again?"

"I'm afraid so," Mary admitted.

"I don't think I have a complete set, but let's see what I've got on microfilm."

Mary followed her into the room that held the micro-film records she'd read of back issues of the *Ivy Bay Observer*. Victoria went directly to a different cabinet.

"The Provincetown *Inquirer and Mirror* has been in publication since 1820, which is quite an accomplishment for a newspaper. Papers don't make a very large profit." She skimmed down the labels on the shallow drawers. "The records from that long ago are spotty. Lots of missing issues. But, let's see . . . . Here we go." She pulled out a drawer. "What date are you looking for?"

"Early October 1841."

"Oh yes, around the October gale disaster."

"That's right. I heard today, that in a big storm, the mill race can overflow. Whatever the water catches can wash out to sea."

"A big nor'easter storm can make a pretty big mess here on the Cape."

"I'm wondering if Caleb Hopkins might have fallen in and been washed out to sea."

"I suppose anything is possible." Victoria carefully searched through the microfilm rolls, checking dates. "I've got September 30, October 1 and 2. Then it jumps to October 4."

Mary leaned over Victoria's shoulder. "The storm came in on the third. They might not have been able to publish that day. Certainly distribution would have been nearly impossible."

"Okay, then." Victoria straightened and handed Mary the roll of film. "I leave you to it. Hope you find what you're looking for."

Mary hoped so too. She sat down and threaded the film through the machine. She found the October 4 edition and skimmed down the front page. It was filled with stories about the storm, the lost fishing boats, and the serious damage done to homes and businesses in Provincetown.

Carefully scanning the headlines, she read through several editions looking for a story about a body being washed up on the shore. Someone resembling Caleb. Although she didn't find anything right off, she still didn't give up and kept on reading.

Finally, a full week after the storm, a two-inch story reported an unidentified adult male had been discovered washed up in a rocky area north of town. The Provincetown constable suggested the man was likely a fisherman who had been lost at sea during the hurricane.

Her heart skipped a beat. She was guessing the deceased was a fisherman, all right, but he hadn't been out to sea. Either someone had killed him, or, drunk as he'd been, he'd fallen into fast-moving water and was dragged out to the ocean.

All she had to do now was determine if the man could actually have been Caleb. If so, she needed to know the cause of death—a stab wound, injuries that suggested a beating, or drowning—and she'd be one step closer to resolving that mystery.

But no closer to proving who owned the gristmill, she thought with a groan.

She made some quick notes about the report, returned the roll to its proper place, and thanked Victoria for her help. Then she hurried over to the police station. She wanted to catch Chief McArthur before he went home for the day.

Minutes later, Mary stood in front of the police chief, who was seated behind his steel desk, shaking his head.

"Now let me get this straight. You want me to call the police chief in Provincetown and ask him to find the medical examiner's records of an unidentified man who died in 1841."

"Exactly. I'd call myself, but I'm afraid he'd think I was a nut case." She ignored Chief McArthur's nod of agreement. "I assume you know the Provincetown police chief and have had dealings with him previously."

"I do. Chief Duncan and I meet a couple of times a year about the mutual-aid agreements between all the departments on the Cape and disaster planning for the area."

"Perfect." Mary slipped into the chair in front of his desk.

He leaned forward and gave her a hard stare. "You're not going to go away until I make that call, are you?"

She grinned sheepishly. "Tenacity has always been one of my finer qualities."

He shook his head again and picked up the phone. "Tell me what you want to know."

She told him to ask if the man had sustained injuries from a knife or due to a fight, or if he had simply drowned. "One other thing. Ask if the man was missing one boot."

"Missing a boot?" Chief McArthur visibly did a double take before punching in the phone number. Mary sat back to listen to his side of the conversation. There were several pauses. Benjamin, the dear man, finally convinced an apparently reluctant fellow police chief to do this favor for him and said he'd reciprocate in kind in the future.

He disconnected the call and looked at Mary with weary eyes. "Duncan says he'll check but makes no promises. He'll get back to me when he can."

Mary wanted to do a little jig but restrained herself. With a bit of luck, she'd make real progress toward discovering what happened to Caleb.

"Thank you, Chief. I can't tell you how much I appreciate your help."

Standing, he grabbed his cap. "I'm on the way home. Can I give you a lift to your shop?"

She thanked him but declined his offer. She suspected Police Chief McArthur had seen enough of her for one day.

FOURTEEN

———◆◈◆———

"Look what Eleanor brought over." Betty thrust a bulky book into Mary's hand.

Mary had just come in the door after seeing Benjamin, and her head was still considering the possible cause of Caleb's death and what she might learn from the Provincetown police. She set Gus's carrier on the floor, released him, and stared dumbly at the book in her hand.

"What is it?"

"It's a Bible." Eleanor, who was seated on the living room couch, spoke up. "I finally had time to look through some of those boxes in the attic I mentioned. I had no idea I'd find a family Bible."

"How interesting." Mary flipped the book cover open and turned to the first page. There, in a Spencerian hand, someone had written the words: "For my dearest friend, Martha Hopkins, with eternal love, Elizabeth Emerson." It was dated January 1843. The writing was lovely and seemed similar to the one on the ledger, even if it was less elaborately flourished.

Stunned, Mary sat down heavily in a nearby chair. "That's two years after Daniel claims William Emerson killed Caleb Hopkins."

Gus climbed up in Mary's lap to sniff the Bible.

"Yes, I know. That's why I brought the Bible over immediately." Sitting primly with her hands folded in her lap, Eleanor said, "Look at the signature. Those two women were obviously close friends. One probably the wife of William, and the other Caleb's widow, don't you think?"

Tilting her head, Mary continued to study the handwriting. "They could be. The census from that period doesn't list any names except the heads of households, virtually all of them males. I haven't come up with any genealogical records. The woman who wrote this must have been unusually well educated for the time. She writes a beautiful hand."

When Lincoln had examined the inscription on the ledger cover that Mary had found, he concluded the handwriting was that of a woman. Elizabeth Emerson? The miller's wife? Entirely possible. How many women in Ivy Bay in 1843 wrote such a fine hand?

Mary doubted there were many.

"If her husband's ancestor had sold the gristmill, it was likely his only means of supporting his family," Betty said. "I can't imagine Elizabeth Emerson would feel all that cordial toward the family who had bought the mill, which might well have made her and her family paupers."

"I quite agree," Eleanor said.

"Nor would Caleb's widow feel kindly toward the wife of the man who supposedly killed him," Mary added. She paused in thought, then continued. "The relationship between the two women does seem odd if either of those scenarios is true."

"Most certainly odd," Betty continued in a firm voice. "Which is one more reason we know Daniel is lying."

Eleanor nodded in agreement. "Lying because he is greedy and opportunistic."

Mary pursed her lips. "It's circumstantial evidence, I agree." But not proof. It would take much more than a signed Bible for a judge to agree that the two families were such close friends that one wouldn't buy property from the other. Business deals happen between friends all the time.

And more often than they should, turn out badly.

She handed the Bible back to Betty. "You hold on to this. You'll want to give it to Rob Dunlap."

Betty gave a quick nod. "I know you're not totally convinced about any of this, but I am, Mary. And so is Eleanor. Think about it. We haven't found a single piece of evidence that Hopkins bought the mill or that William Emerson killed anyone, and we're not going to." She put her hand over her heart. "I believe that with every bit of faith I have in my husband's family."

Eleanor stood. "No Emerson would have ever murdered another soul. We are and always have been a good Christian family."

Mary sincerely hoped she was right.

———

Mary arrived at work the next morning to find a large truck in front of the shop, blocking several parking spaces. Kip and Ian were unloading bricks, using wheelbarrows to carry them to the backyard.

After unlocking the front door of the shop, Mary went inside and walked to the back door to observe the activity.

Ian was stacking the bricks alongside the chokeberry bush. A big pile of sand had been dumped in the center of what would soon be the brick patio.

"Good morning, Mrs. Fisher." Sweat already glistened on Kip's darkly tanned face, despite the comfortable temperature. "After getting the sand spread around, we can start laying the bricks. Then you'll be able to see how nice it'll look."

"I'm sure it will be a great improvement over what I have now." She stepped back into the shop to find that Rebecca and her daughter had arrived. "Good morning to you both."

Ashley skipped over to her. "My grandmother sent me a present!"

Mary knelt down to Ashley's level. As she did, she released Gus from his carrier. "What a nice grandmother. What did she send you?"

"A bookmark!" She thrust the bookmark at Mary. "She and Grandpa went to Yellowstone. That's a long way away, and they saw Old Faithful."

"They did?" Mary looked at the bookmark, which was a holographic-style picture of Old Faithful. As she turned the bookmark one way or the other, the geyser erupted and then retreated. "What a wonderful bookmark. You're a lucky girl."

After more conversation about the bookmark, all three of them went to work. Mary busied herself straightening books that patrons had left unshelved.

The chime over the door sounded. Mary smiled as Dorothy Johnson walked in the door, her stride determined, her head held high. Mary could hardly remember the last time the woman had visited her shop.

"Good morning, Dorothy. You're out early this morning."

"I simply couldn't wait until the Friday meeting. I've already lined up fifteen lovely, lovely homes for the walking tour."

"So quickly? You've definitely been working hard." Betty had told her that Dorothy was a good organizer, and Mary had known that was true.

"It's been fun." She placed a list of homes that she'd recruited on the counter. "And I've given some thought about showcasing my own house." She lifted her chin in a slightly defensive way. "I do have some nice things, one-of-a-kind handcrafted statuettes, fine china decorative pieces, not to mention some original paintings. Some of the smaller pieces I plan to put away. I also thought I'd put up some velvet ropes across doorways so the visitors can look but not go into certain rooms."

Mary was so glad Dorothy was on board. "That's an excellent idea."

"Yes, I thought so. It's what they do in museums, you know." She eyed Mary. "I've suggested to the homeowners they consider something similar. I'd hate for anyone to have some priceless object stolen during the historic tour."

"Sounds perfect."

"I agree. That's why I've asked Henry to be at my house during the tour to help me keep an eye on things. He's such a close, good friend." A smile that looked more like a smirk tilted Dorothy's lips.

Mary forced herself to keep a straight face. "I'm sure Henry will be of great help to you, and you'll be able to rest easy while he's there."

"Yes, I am relieved he'll be there." She glanced toward the back door. "My goodness, what's going on back there?"

"I'm putting in a brick patio. Betty's already done some landscaping, and I plan to buy an umbrella table and some chairs so people can read or chat comfortably outdoors when the weather's good." Which reminded Mary she should start looking through catalogs and checking for sales for a suitable table. With the end of summer nearing, she might be able to pick up something for a good price. "For the walking tour, I plan to serve punch and cookies on the patio to anyone who drops by the shop."

Dorothy's shoulders straightened. "I hadn't heard anyone was planning to serve refreshments," she said.

"I'm going to mention the idea at our next committee meeting. It might help draw people to the businesses that are participating. The homes too. Purely optional, of course."

Dorothy huffed out a breath. "I'll be sure to inform the homeowners of that option, even though I hadn't previously been told about it."

A customer came in the door, and Mary felt as though she'd been rescued. "You're doing a wonderful job, Dorothy. I really appreciate all your efforts for the walking tour." She pointedly glanced toward the customer who was examining books in the cozy-mystery section. "I'll see you at the Friday meeting."

As Mary turned to greet her customer, she heard Dorothy promise to be at the meeting.

Please, Lord, help me to remember to be kind to Dorothy. As vexing as she can be at times, I know she mostly means well.

Later in the day, Mary picked up the ledger and turned to the pages of symbols. When Lincoln had visited, he suggested an expert in code breaking or hieroglyphics could possibly help her. At this point, Mary wasn't sure deciphering the hieroglyphics in the ledger would make a difference. Still, if there was a chance to ensure the suit would come out in Betty's favor, she'd have to make the effort.

But the ledger, like a good many of the clues she'd found, could easily point the other direction.

Ashley came around to Mary's side of the counter. "You're frowning, Mrs. Fisher. Is something wrong?"

"Not exactly wrong." Mary smoothed Ashley's flyaway blonde hair. "More like a puzzle or a code I can't seem to figure out."

"I read a book about a code breaker the other day. It's a kids' story, but they said the author was a real code breaker in World War II."

"Really?" Mary's interest perked up. "Can you bring me the book? I'd like to take a look." She'd also love to find a code breaker to resolve her questions about the ledger.

Ashley dashed off to the children's section and returned quickly. "Here it is."

"Thank you, sweetie." Noticing the author's name, Arnold Binghamton, on the cover, she flipped to the back of the slender book to read about him. There was a photo of a very distinguished gentleman and notes about the work he'd done during the war. But the last part of his biography was what most interested her. "Major Binghamton currently resides on Cape Cod."

Knowing many World War II veterans had passed away, she quickly checked the date the book had been published. Only two years ago. So he was alive two years ago, at least. Maybe he still was.

"This is perfect, Ashley. Thank you."

It couldn't be that difficult to find one person on Cape Cod, could it? Mary sat down at her computer, her fingers resting on the keyboard, trying to think of where to start. A quick search turned up listings for his book, but no contact information. She pulled up the publisher's Web site. She found information about the book there, but nothing more about the author himself. She did find a link to a page where she could contact the publisher's authors, and she typed out a quick message and sent it in, but she had little faith that it would actually reach him.

If he was still on the Cape, where would he be likely to live? There were retired folks all over. But Mr. Binghamton would be quite elderly at this point, probably in his eighties. There was a good chance he'd be in a retirement community or nursing home now.

Mary typed in the phrase "nursing homes Cape Cod" and quickly pulled up a list of more than a dozen facilities.

There was no way to tell from his author biography which town on the Cape he lived in, so Mary decided to start at the top. She dialed the number listed for Abingdon House assisted care facility in Hyannis. The woman who answered the phone was brisk and professional, and told Mary that she couldn't reveal whether someone by the name of Arnold Binghamton lived there or not. Mary had expected as much.

Next on the list was Bay View retirement complex. Mary had been to Bay View. It was a nice facility right here in Ivy Bay. She dialed the number, and since the receptionist recognized her name, she told Mary that no one named Mr. Binghamton lived there.

Halfway down her list was the Roxbury retirement center in Chatham. After a few rings, someone picked up. Mary explained why she was calling, and she was put through to Mr. Binghamton, who sounded both pleasant and alert. He invited Mary to visit him on Sunday afternoon.

With any luck, Mr. Binghamton would provide the answers to this part of the gristmill mystery.

The Friday morning meeting of the walking tour committee went quite well. Even though the members were pressed for time, wanting to get to their businesses, Mary made sure Dorothy had ample opportunity to share her success with the historic homes portion of the tour.

The business side of the planning was going a little more slowly, but Rich Tucker from Gems and Antiques thought more businesses would sign on in the next day or two.

Cynthia McArthur had put together some information on the history of Ivy Bay's downtown shopping district for business owners to hand out during the tour, and she gave copies to everyone to look over.

Art Shirk presented a sample of the tickets for the event, which was approved by the committee. They'd be available for sale at the participating businesses in town.

As Mary picked up her notes and extra copies of the agenda, Chief McArthur hooked a hip over the meeting table next to her.

"Chief Duncan in Provincetown couldn't find what you were looking for. But he said the Forman Mortuary has been in business since the early 1800s, a family-run business. They've always had the contract for burying paupers and indigents." Benjamin handed her a slip of paper. "That's their phone number. He suggested they might have records back that far."

Disappointed the Provincetown police chief hadn't come up with what she needed, she looked at the phone number for the Forman Mortuary. "I'll give them a call and hope for the best."

"Good luck." Placing his cap on his head, Benjamin headed out the door.

Mary sat back down at the table. She needed to know if the unidentified body was Caleb before she'd be satisfied she could unravel the mystery of Caleb's death.

After picking up her cell phone, she punched in the number Benjamin had given her. "Forman Mortuary, Mildred Forman speaking," a professional-sounding female voice answered.

Mary introduced herself. "I'm looking into the death of a man who was washed ashore in 1841. I understand your mortuary handled burials for indigents at that time."

"Yes, we did. We have since the company was founded by my great-great-great-grandfather." Pride in her family's history was clear in her voice. "Are you working on your family's genealogy?"

"More like my sister's family, but it is important."

"Of course. Tell me exactly what you need to know. We have a strict policy of retaining our records. The oldest records like you're looking for have all been scanned and saved on CDs."

"That's wonderful." Mary explained what she needed and about the body that had washed ashore.

"May I e-mail you the records when I find them?"

"Yes, please do." Mary gave the woman her e-mail address. "I really appreciate your help."

"We're always glad to help those who come to us, whatever the reason."

Mary terminated the call, optimistic that she'd be receiving the information soon.

After picking up her committee materials, Mary walked back to the bookshop. Several customers were browsing the shelves, and Rebecca was at the cash register ringing up a sale.

Mary stepped into the back room to leave her committee materials. She glanced out the back door. The patio was taking shape nicely, and she thought Kip would finish soon.

When she returned to the front, Rebecca asked, "How's the tour committee doing?"

"Things are nicely falling into place. I think it's going to be a wonderful event for the town." And prayed it would raise enough money to give Dorothy a good start to cover the cost of repairs to her house.

Mary spent the next hour flipping through publishers' catalogs and making a list of books she'd include next time she placed an order. Then she turned back to her computer.

Although Mary couldn't imagine the woman at the mortuary could have responded this quickly to her request for information, she booted up the computer.

To her delight, she had an e-mail from the Forman Mortuary. She read the pleasant note from Mildred, then downloaded the attachment.

Mary stared in amazement at the scanned sheet of paper, a handwritten mortician's report. "Unidentified male, approx fifty years old, height five ten, weight 180 pounds. Except for minor contusions, no trauma visible. Cause of death—drowning. Personal possessions included no identification; missing one boot. Deceased buried in pauper's grave #231."

Her heart jumped at the reference to the boot. And no visible trauma had to mean no stab marks on the body or signs of a fight.

Mary continued to puzzle over the report. If Caleb hadn't been stabbed, that meant the butcher knife with blood on it the constable found at the Hopkinses' house was not the murder weapon. Mary felt confident she could eliminate Caleb's wife Martha and her son as suspects.

She had been unable to prove the tavern keeper had any hand in Caleb's death. Nor did the police report or newspaper account indicate the tavern keeper was in any way a suspect. So only two other possibilities remained.

Either it was an accidental death, a result of the storm that caused him to fall into the fast-running race by the mill. Or William Emerson was a murderer who had thrown Caleb into the race and then hidden the evidence so his guilt wouldn't be discovered.

⁓

When Mary arrived home after work, Betty met her at the door and told her Evan had called.

"The lawyers have worked out a time for depositions," she said. "A week from next Wednesday at ten o'clock in the Ivy Bay county building."

"Finally." Mary released Gus from his travel carrier. "At least we won't have to drive to Boston." It was a congested drive on the best of days.

"Evan says Daniel's attorney will bring what Daniel purports is a bill of sale. In which case, your Mr. Lincoln will be able to show it's fake and a fraud."

Mary picked up the mail from the candlestick end table by the entry. She immediately spotted a note from her granddaughter Daisy, her son's sixteen-year-old, who had been at summer camp all month. The quick note indicated she'd been riding a horse named Peaches all week and loved him. A friend of hers named Johnny hit his head diving into the pool. He was taken to the hospital. And finally, please send her some cookies. The food was terrible!

Chuckling, she brought her thoughts back to the upcoming depositions. "I wish I had more to say that would counter the bill of sale if Lincoln decides it could be legitimate."

"You can certainly say there's no evidence of the sale being recorded."

"Yes, I can do that." But would that be enough?

FIFTEEN

◆━◆━◆

After church on Sunday, Mary hurried home to have a quick lunch before driving to Chatham.

"Are you sure you don't want to come with me?" she asked Betty as she put together two sliced turkey and cheese sandwiches on rye for their lunch.

"No, I promised I'd go with Sherry next door to a miniature show up in Plymouth. She says there's a seller who has some wonderfully detailed Victorian homes in one-inch-scale kits, including all the traditional furniture. They even have miniature wallpaper appropriate for the era, and handwoven rugs."

"Sounds like you're about to apply your decorative skills to a dollhouse."

"Well, Christmas isn't all that far away, and I do have two lovely little granddaughters who are old enough to appreciate the finer things now."

Mary nodded in understanding. She always looked for something special to give to her grandchildren. That reminded her she'd have to bake some cookies tonight to send off to her granddaughter first thing tomorrow. "That would be a wonderful project for you."

206 C SECRETS of MARY'S BOOKSHOP

"I'll have to decide *if* my poor old arthritic fingers wouldn't tire out too fast using those small tools." She flexed her hands for emphasis.

"Even if you decide not to buy, I'm sure it will be a fun outing for you and Sherry. Since she has two boys, she'd probably love to make something frilly and feminine for herself."

Betty chuckled. "As dear as her boys are, I do get the feeling she sometimes tires of robots, monster trucks, and alien war machines."

As soon as Mary finished her lunch, she changed into slacks and a loose cotton blouse for the drive to visit Arnold Binghamton. She tried not to be too optimistic. It seemed a long reach from German code breaking to deciphering an 1843 gristmill ledger.

Sunday traffic was heavy, and it took her almost an hour to reach her destination.

The main building of the Roxbury retirement complex was a one-story structure painted in blue and gray, echoing the colors of the independent-living duplexes scattered across a well-kept landscape. Attractive flower beds lined winding walkways that led to and from the central buildings.

Somewhere on the property, Mary was pretty confident there was an assisted-living facility and a central dining area.

With the ledger tucked under her arm, she walked toward the main building.

Inside, Mary found a comfortable lobby with conversational groupings of chairs and tables and potted plants strategically placed. The ambience of the lobby was what she would expect in a high-priced hotel. A grand piano sat quietly in

one corner of the spacious room; two gentlemen were playing chess beside a window that looked out onto an outdoor
patio.

Graceful living as we age, she thought, suspecting the cost
was equally high-end.

A slender, gray-haired gentleman, who had been seated near
the entrance, stood with the help of a walker. "Ms. Fisher?"

"Mr. Binghamton." She walked toward him with her hand
extended. "Thank you for meeting with me." His handshake
was firm. His light-blue eyes, although a little watery with
age, sparkled with intelligence.

"I've been told by my loving children that my driving is
hazardous to the lives of others, so I fear others must come
to me."

"I was happy to come."

He gestured toward the chair next to his, and she sat
down.

"Now tell me again how I can help you."

Briefly, she told him of the dispute over the gristmill and
how she'd discovered the ledger. "This may or may not have
anything to do with the ownership of the mill, but until I
know what the symbols mean, it's a loose thread I'd like to
tie up."

"I understand completely, my dear." He pulled a pair
of glasses from his shirt pocket and slipped them on before taking the ledger from Mary. "I confess it's been a
long time since I've attempted to decipher any notations
as old as 1843, but I'm certainly willing to try. Good way
to keep the synapses in the old brain working, don't you
know."

Mary was immediately enamored with Arnold Binghamton. He might be well past ninety years, but he seemed as alert as a much younger man and had a good sense of humor as well.

"I assume these notations have something to do with selling cornmeal," he said.

"I'm assuming so. I don't know why else the ledger would have been in the mill."

"*Hmm.*" He ran his finger across the rows. "When decoding a message, you first look for repeated words or symbols. And then patterns begin to reveal themselves." He looked up from his study of the ledger and peered at her over the top of his glasses. "Most older codes, when you get down to it, are deceptively simple."

She nodded to show her interest, and he returned to his study of the ledger, turning to the next page and then the next.

Mary waited quietly, noting the people that passed through the lobby. Mostly well-dressed senior citizens, including a few who had apparently just returned from a round of golf. From a room behind the lobby, she heard laughter, and she had the feeling it must be happy hour at Roxbury.

Arnold removed his glasses. "I think I may be of some help. If you'll take a look."

Mary leaned toward him.

"The first pattern I see is these little squares that appear regularly. Sometimes there is one square inside the column, other times two or three. I take that to refer to the number of bags of cornmeal the author of the ledger sold to the individual involved."

Squinting, Mary followed his finger down the columns. "Oh yes, wow. I see what you mean. That's very logical." Even though his comments made sense, she was sure she would have never been able to come up with his conclusion on her own.

"These things usually are quite logical," as if disagreeing with her thought. "Now then, notice there's a column of these squares followed, most often, by a column of hatch marks that are related in number to the squares."

Mary nodded. She'd never realized the pattern, but she could see it now.

"I can't be completely sure, of course, but my best guess at this point would be that the tally marks represent how much an individual paid for the cornmeal he purchased."

"Okay, I see. That makes sense." She was fascinated.

His smile broadened. "You're a perceptive student, my dear. You may also note that some tally marks are not preceded by what I believe represents bags of cornmeal. In that case, I suspect the individual in question bought cornmeal from the miller but had not raised the corn himself."

"Interesting. No wonder you were a code breaker."

"Simply a question of making assumptions and then testing them." He drew his finger from left to right across the page. "You'll notice there are gaps between the symbols over what has to be time. Two bags purchased and paid for here . . . . Another two bags possibly some days or weeks later here."

"Yes, I can see that now."

"Now, there are several things I can't yet discern. I can assume that the bags were of all equal weight. However, I don't know how much money each tally mark represents. There does appear to be some discrepancy in some instances."

"Why would that be?"

He shook his head. "I would need much more information about the particular situation to reach a conclusion about that. It seems in a case or two"—he pointed halfway down the page—"payment was not made for a sack of cornmeal. There are no tally marks. But we have an even more difficult problem."

Fearful that she'd come to another dead end, Mary pursed her lips and tugged at her earlobe. "I'm afraid to ask what the problem is."

"It may not be that dire, depending upon why you need this information." Reassuring her, he patted her hand. "The person who kept this ledger—I assume it was the miller—was apparently illiterate but quite intelligent. In this first column, he has identified his customers."

"Really?" She certainly hadn't gotten that out of looking at the ledger.

"Indeed. You see here what is clearly a cane." He pointed to the symbol halfway down the page. "It would be a reasonable guess that this customer used a cane."

Mary strained to see the figure he was referring to, which looked more like a candy cane to her rather than a walking cane.

"And here we see what amounts to a stick figure of a woman with, if I may be so unkind, wildly curly hair."

She laughed out loud, then quickly covered her mouth with her hand. She could only wonder what symbols William Emerson might have used to describe her and her sister.

"I do see what you mean there. Makes you want to let the woman borrow a comb from you."

"There are several reasonably clear signs or drawings, some less easily distinguished, but the difficulty is knowing who these people might be. Had we lived in the village in 1843, it would have made the task much easier. We'd know our neighbors and recognize their characteristics."

Leaning back, Mary contemplated how she could determine which Ivy Bay family had bought cornmeal at the mill and how that knowledge might help her regarding the mill's ownership.

"I am sorry I haven't been able to tell you more about your ledger," he said.

"No need to apologize. You've been very helpful." She took the ledger from him and stood. "You've certainly figured out more than I ever could have, and I appreciate your help."

With the help of his walker, he stood. "It's been my pleasure, my dear. I've enjoyed your company as well as the mental workout."

They parted on that note, and Mary walked to her car still wondering how she could use the information she'd been given. After driving back to Ivy Bay, she still hadn't come up with a plan.

Betty wasn't home from Plymouth when Mary returned, so she took the opportunity to whip up a double batch of chocolate-chip cookies, which she'd pack up and send to Daisy at camp tomorrow. She put the first cookie sheet into the oven.

Her grandmotherly duty under way, Mary poured herself some iced tea and refilled Gus's water dish, which he'd apparently tipped over. The house phone rang, and she picked up the extension in the kitchen.

"Hi, Aunt Mary. How are you?"

She smiled at the sound of her nephew's voice. "I'm fine, Evan. How are you and your family?"

"The girls are good. I think Mindy is eager for school to start again."

Mary laughed. Summers could get long for a mother of two energetic girls. "If you're looking for your mother, she took a run up to Plymouth to look at miniature dollhouses." She took a sip of her tea, and Gus decided to brush up against her leg, asking for attention.

"Actually, I think you're the one I need to talk to. It's about the lawsuit."

"Oh dear. Has something happened?" She knelt to pet Gus.

"The arbitrator we're using has asked that we move up the deposition date to a week from Monday."

A ripple of panic raised her pulse rate. "Evan, I'm concerned about the hearing. I can testify there is no evidence in county records that the mill was ever sold, but if Daniel really does have a bill of sale, my statement won't be enough to invalidate his claim."

"You haven't been able to find a sample of Isaac's handwriting or signature?"

"No, there's simply no place else to look. I've searched all the property records that might apply. I was hoping Rob's assistant would turn up something."

"I'm afraid not," Evan said.

Thinking about the ledger, she frowned. "There is something that may help. I found a mill ledger dated 1843. The miller, who I'm quite sure was William

Emerson, wasn't literate, although his wife was. Possibly the daughter of a minister or schoolteacher who insisted she learn to read and write. And I'd guess William's wife was busy raising their children and didn't take an active role in the workings of the mill. I think it's safe to say that Isaac was illiterate too. Which means that he probably wouldn't have signed his name anyway. He likely would have simply used an *X*."

The timer on the oven dinged. Still holding the phone, Mary pulled the cookie sheet out of the oven. The delicious smell of the cookies made her mouth water. She'd have to save a few cookies for her and Betty to enjoy.

"Sounds like if the bill of sale is signed with an *X*, we may be in trouble." Evan sounded discouraged.

"Exactly."

"Have you found anything else that could help our case?"

"Well, US census records show the Emersons consistently lived on the mill property as far back as 1790. If possession is nine-tenths of the law, we'd have that in our favor."

"I certainly hope so. Can you bring a copy of the census to the hearing?"

"Of course. I'll print out the records of the subsequent six or seven census periods. They all show an Emerson operating the gristmill."

"That's great, Aunt Mary. I know Rob's been working the case hard, but I'm really impressed by what you've been able to find."

She sipped her tea again to moisten her dry throat. "There is something else you should know."

"That sounds ominous."

"Not exactly ominous, however, Daniel has loudly claimed William Emerson killed Caleb Hopkins, his great-grandfather several times over."

"Yeah, Mom told me about that. Aunt Eleanor too. None of us believe it, though. We think Daniel's blowing smoke."

"Well, Daniel claims the reason why Caleb was murdered was about the mill ownership. I've been investigating, trying to disprove Daniel's statement. I've pretty well eliminated all the suspects I can, except William. That incident could have been what started the feud between the two families and what makes Daniel so determined to claim the gristmill." Although the two wives involved didn't seem to be feuding, she noted. In which case, the coins and uniform she'd found might well be an added incentive if Daniel believed in the old tales of hidden treasure at the mill. But if that were true, why hadn't he ransacked the mill years ago?

"You can't believe that guy's crazy story, can you?"

"I have no actual proof that there was a murder. It could have been an accident, for all I know. And I certainly hope that was the case. The report I received from the funeral home indicated an unidentified man, who I believe is Caleb, had drowned. But there is quite a bit of circumstantial evidence pointing to William. It's still possible William could have pushed Caleb into the flooded race."

Evan muttered something under his breath. "I don't think we ought to bring up this fake story of Daniel's. It has nothing to do with who owns the mill."

"Of course. I completely understand." Except she believed getting to the bottom of Caleb's death could shed a good deal of light on the situation. The wrong kind of light, if she proved William was indeed the murderer.

Evan thanked her for her help and asked her to pass on the change of date for the hearing to his mother. Mary said she would.

Troubled by the phone call and her inability to be of more help to save the mill for the Emerson family, she finished baking the rest of the cookies. She'd box them up for mailing after they cooled.

She took her tea and a sample cookie and went out to the deck. There was a light breeze blowing off the bay, keeping the summer temperature comfortable.

After pulling out a chair at the umbrella table, she sat down and opened the ledger. Because Arnold had shown her the patterns, they were now easier for her to identify. But that first column, the description of William's customers, was far harder to interpret.

Yes, there was a cane and a curly-haired woman. The outline of a fish in one square could easily mean the person in question was a fisherman. But Ivy Bay must have had dozens of fishermen that called the town their home in 1843. Besides, the squiggly line could instead be a bow tie. Whatever that might mean, Mary had no idea.

A small cross could be the local preacher; he was one who paid for cornmeal but hadn't brought William any corn to mill.

By the time Betty returned home, Mary's glass of iced tea was empty and she had stared at the ledger pages so long she felt like her eyes were permanently crossed.

"Yum," Betty said. "These cookies are delicious." She popped the last bite of one into her mouth.

"I'll mail them to Daisy in the morning. She says camp food is terrible." Smiling at her granddaughter's complaint, so common among kids off at a summer camp, Mary removed her glasses and rubbed her eyes.

"Assuming I can resist eating them all myself," Betty said with a teasing glint in her eye.

"Did you bring home a dollhouse?"

"I'm afraid not. They were quite lovely, but I think too delicate for the girls to play with, after all." Betty sat down next to her and stretched out her feet. "The unfinished kits take a great deal of work. In all honesty, I'm not sure either my patience or my hands would last long enough to get the job done." Betty glanced at the ledger in front of Mary. "Did your code-breaking gentleman come up with any helpful revelations?"

"Enough that I understand the notations better. But I'm still trying to figure out who the marks in this first column represent." She showed her sister the symbols Arnold had identified. "I think I could get further if I knew what the residents here in 1843 looked like or their occupations. And the 1840 census didn't ask for that information."

Frowning, Betty skimmed down the page and pointed at one figure. "Is that a cow?"

Mary looked more closely. "It could be. You think he was a dairy farmer?"

"It'd be my guess, or maybe that's a pig instead of a cow, but who knows?"

A name instantly popped into Mary's head. "You know, I bet Bea could help me out. She certainly has a wealth of records. Property records might give me a hint about a person's occupation." Bea always welcomed her so warmly that Mary didn't think she'd mind yet another visit to the basement records.

"Excellent idea." Grimacing as if in pain, Betty stood up slowly. "I'm afraid I overdid at the miniature show. I got so engrossed I didn't want to miss anything."

"You go rest a bit. I'll fix us a light supper, and then we can both relax for the evening." Although Mary feared she'd be seeing strange symbols in her dreams tonight, which wouldn't make for a restful sleep. "Oh, I almost forgot. Evan called. The deposition meeting has been changed to a week from tomorrow."

"That soon? Are we ready to prove Daniel doesn't know what he's talking about?"

"Not entirely," Mary hedged. She was anxious to get a look at the bill of sale, but she only had a week to come up with more substantive evidence.

Suddenly, a week didn't seem like nearly enough time.

The week started with several local business owners dropping into the bookshop to see how plans were going for the historic walking tour. It seemed the idea was catching on and enthusiasm building. Even a couple of business owners who didn't operate out of a historic building wanted to know how they could help.

She referred those owners to Rich at Gems and Antiques.

Meanwhile, Kip had almost finished laying the bricks for the patio.

Mary realized she'd have to order a table for the patio soon. If she had to have it shipped, that might take a week or more. She didn't want to risk not having it here by the day of the walking tour.

When the flow of customers began to slow, she sat down at the computer. The first thing she needed to do was print out the census data she'd promised to Evan.

When she completed that task, she searched the Internet for the kind of table she wanted. She found the perfect one on sale at a big-box store that had an outlet in North Dartmouth. She could order it to be delivered to the store, but first she'd have to check with her sister. She didn't want to make a big design decision like this without Betty's approval.

She sent the link in an e-mail to Betty, then called her sister asking her to log on and have a look. She hung up the phone and began scanning a few invoices. A few minutes later, she got Betty's reply: "I love it. Your design eye is getting sharper, Mar, and believe me, I take all the credit." Then Betty had typed a smile emoticon. Mary smiled back at the e-mail, then she returned to the Internet browser and placed the order.

With that done, she glanced at her watch. Plenty of time left in the day to visit Bea at the clerk's office. Hopefully her records would provide some insight into who the townspeople were in 1843.

SIXTEEN

❖◆◆❖

After so many visits to the basement of the county clerk's office, Mary was beginning to feel strangely at home. Which, in a way, was truly frightening. She didn't want to adjust to life in a dim, almost dank room with only stacks of files for company.

She found the box of property records that included 1843 easily enough. Hauling it over to the table, she settled down to see what information she could uncover.

She'd brought the ledger, her notepad, and the plot map from the shop so she could identify the location of property listings. Removing a handful of records, she studied them. Individual records identified the land use of the property— residential, business, or agricultural. Not as many specific land-use subdivisions as she would like, but it would have to do.

What a world of difference computers would have made in 1843.

Since cornmeal was such a staple in the diets of early Americans, for the moment she would assume all the residents of Ivy Bay at least bought cornmeal from William Emerson, even if they didn't raise any corn to be ground.

The first record read "Abmie, Frank," followed by a plot number with the notation "Residential."

She glanced at the ledger and the column of doodles she was supposed to decipher. How in the world could she pick out the symbol related to Mr. Abmie? He could be anything—the handlebar mustache William had drawn, the top hat, or any number of other symbols she couldn't interpret.

Setting that record aside, she found the next. "Adair, Mitchell," a plot number on the edge of town and described as a blacksmith. Slowly, she scanned the ledger symbols again.

A hammer. A neatly drawn sailing ship.

Her eye fell on a horseshoe. That had to be the blacksmith Mitchell Adair and his family.

Eagerly, she scanned across the horseshoe row. From what she could tell, the individual had purchased cornmeal at fairly regular intervals but had never sold corn to William Emerson.

Tentatively, she jotted down the row number and Mr. Adair's name. At this pace, it would take her days, if not weeks, to match names to the symbols for the gristmill's customers. And how did she think that information would get her closer to the cause of the Hopkins-Emerson feud or the ownership of the mill?

She removed her glasses and rubbed her eyes, which tired quickly in the dim light.

Deciding to take a different approach, she searched for the record of "Emerson, William," who was clearly noted as the owner of a plot identified as a business. And it looked as though he was all paid up on his taxes.

She found the Hopkinses' record next. This listed "Hopkins, Martha" as the owner of residential property.

Caleb had been gone for two years; now a widow, the property belonged to her.

What would William have used for a symbol for a widow whose husband he may or may not have murdered?

She shuddered. "Don't even think about murder. Not in this dreary basement."

If she'd known how to translate the ledger when she'd been looking at the property records weeks ago, she could have checked for this detail as well.

She drew her finger down the column of symbols again. The woman with curly hair was drawn in simple lines. But several spaces below that was a woman drawn more carefully. She clearly wore a black skirt and a black bonnet.

A widow!

Forcing herself to take a breath, Mary checked the rest of the symbols all the way to the end. There was no other female figure dressed in black.

She turned back to the row of what she was almost sure was the record of Martha Hopkins' cornmeal purchases. What she found stunned her.

Periodically, William had drawn tiny *o*'s, or possibly zeros, where Mary would expect to see a tally mark indicating Martha had purchased a bag of cornmeal. But not a single tally mark appeared over a span of time that must be at least a year.

Did that mean William was giving Martha bags of cornmeal at no charge? If so, why? Out of charity, was he helping a widow faced with hard times?

Or was his generosity based on guilt for having killed her husband?

Walking back to the bookshop, the significance of all the evidence she had uncovered weighed heavily on her conscience.

All she could say for sure about the mill ownership was that she hadn't found any record of a sale to James Hopkins or anyone else.

But the cause of Caleb's death was still unclear. Yes, he could have accidentally drowned on the stormy night of October 3. Heavy drinking was likely a contributing factor to his end, no matter how it came about.

The argument he'd had with William could have equally as well become a fight. Without meaning to, William might have pushed Caleb into the overflowing race beside the mill. That, too, could have been an accident. Or in the worst case, manslaughter. Not first-degree murder.

If Martha Hopkins had believed her husband, abusive or not, had been killed by William, how could she have stayed such close friends with Elizabeth Emerson, as evidenced by the Bible that Eleanor had discovered? Was it because William had been so generous, giving her cornmeal to feed her family?

Evan wanted Mary to keep quiet about Caleb's death during the deposition meeting. She understood why. It would muddy the waters and divert attention from the issue of ownership.

But could she, in good conscience, keep silent if the issue of the feud came up? Or the cause of Caleb's death?

The Bible says: "So I strive always to keep my conscience clear before God and man" (Acts 24:16).

Whatever happened, Mary vowed to keep the word of God as she understood it.

She reached the bookshop and stepped inside. Ashley was playing a game of hopscotch in the aisle between the cozies and thrillers. She stopped. Standing on one foot, she grinned. Mary returned her smile. There were no customers around, so no harm done. The sweet girl was so good all day long, reading and actually helping customers, she needed a chance to use up some of her pent-up energy.

Rebecca was behind the counter, tidying up for the night.

"I wasn't sure you'd get back by closing time," Rebecca said.

"My errand didn't take quite as long as I had feared." But it had left Mary confused about her role in the lawsuit and how much she should reveal about her discoveries.

Returning the plot map to the map display, Mary said, "Why don't you go on home? I'll finish closing up."

"You're sure?"

"Yes." She waved Rebecca and Ashley to be on their way. "Go home and be with your family."

After they left, Mary lingered, deep in thought about the future and what would happen at the deposition.

Before she shut down her computer for the night, she checked her e-mail. The umbrella table she'd ordered that morning had already shipped and would be at the shop in a few days.

Over dinner on the back deck, Mary told Betty that the table would arrive shortly. Betty was glad it would be set up in time for the walking tour, and said she'd been back to Tanaka Florist and Garden Center and asked to have tubs of flowers delivered later in the week.

"And I had an idea about the tour," Betty said. "The gristmill isn't too far to walk from town for most people. Since it's one of the oldest structures in Ivy Bay, and one of the most important in its day, I've been thinking that it ought to be on the tour."

"No one would be able to go inside. It's too dangerous."

"I know. But I was talking to Evan about my idea. He thinks we can blow up old photos of the mill I found up in the attic and mount them so visitors could see what it looked like before it got so run-down."

Mary nodded. "That sounds like it would work. Someone would have to be there to explain the mill's history."

She set her napkin aside. "If you have no objection, I'd like to do that. I can dress up in period costume. Even if Daniel wins his lawsuit"—her words drifted off—"it might be the last time I'll ever have a chance to tell the history of the Emerson gristmill," she finished weakly.

A lump filled Mary's throat, and she agonized for her sister and the vow she'd made to herself to restore the mill to honor Edward.

"I think that's a wonderful idea. Maybe we can even write up a brief history of the mill that could be handed to visitors who drop by."

"Good idea. I'll get started on that tomorrow."

Sleep did not come easily to Mary that night. She churned in bed trying to come up with what she had missed. What new avenue of research she could follow that would prove conclusively that the Emersons had always owned the gristmill.

She'd searched all the public records she could think of, and nowhere had she found any indication that an Emerson had ever sold the mill.

The connection between the Emersons and Ivy Bay, where their roots ran deep, was so strong it was impossible to believe any Emerson had even considered selling the mill.

Meanwhile, generations of Hopkinses had gone to sea, first in sailboats, then in trawlers where they were long-liners fishing from dories. More recently they went farther to sea in larger trawlers and brought home ever-larger catches of cod, redfish, flounder, and haddock. Then overexploitation caused the catches to shrink and the fishing fleets to slowly fade away.

Caleb Hopkins and his descendants continued to cling to their fishing tradition.

Why would Daniel Hopkins want to own a gristmill, particularly now in the twenty-first century?

Mary's eyes popped open, and she stared into the darkness. What would the gristmill land be worth if it was sold to a developer? Was simple greed really the crux of the lawsuit? And was Daniel not after the coins at all but rather something even more valuable?

What did they always say in murder mysteries? *Follow the money!*

Mary got up and dressed far earlier than usual and was downstairs drinking her morning cup of coffee when Betty strolled into the kitchen in her robe and slippers.

"My, you're up early. Is anything wrong?" Betty asked.

Without responding to her sister's question, Mary asked, "Have you had any offers to buy the mill property?"

Betty retrieved a mug from the cupboard and poured herself some coffee. "Not recently. Not since Edward passed away, that I can remember. He used to get queries from time to time, but he was never interested in selling. Why do you ask?"

"Last night I got to thinking this whole lawsuit thing might not have anything to do with Isaac selling the mill to James Hopkins. Or the accusation that William murdered Caleb Hopkins."

"Which he didn't do," Betty interjected as she sat down at the table.

"But the point is," Mary continued, "this could be a land grab, pure and simple. Daniel has almost admitted as much."

Betty peered at her over the top of her mug. "What do you mean?"

"Say, if Daniel had gotten wind of some developer wanting to build condos or something on the mill property, he would use any ploy he could think of to get his hands on that land and make a killing selling it to a third party. Jill told me her children are all excited about the possibility of the family becoming really wealthy."

Wrapping both hands around her coffee mug as though she'd felt a sudden chill, Betty said, "Do you think that's really what is behind this lawsuit?"

"I don't know." Mary drank the last of her now-cold coffee and wrinkled her nose at the bitter taste, the same bitter taste Betty would experience if she lost the gristmill. "But I'm going to find time today to see Lori Stone."

"The Realtor?"

"Right. Lori always has her ear to the ground. She can tell me if there's been recent interest in the property and where that interest is coming from." Mary had been very impressed with Lori when she handled the purchase of the bookshop property for her. She was one sharp woman. Mary was sure she would have answers.

———

Mary had already opened the bookshop that morning when Rebecca arrived breathless, her hair mussed as though from sleep.

"Sorry I'm late." She stowed her lunch in the small refrigerator in the back room and waved hello to Kip, who was already working in the backyard. "Ashley and I finally got around to putting the snapshots of our trip to Boston into an album, and I lost track of the time. Anyway, I had a terrible time waking her up to get to work this morning. I finally decided to leave her with her dad. Russell didn't have to go to work today."

"No matter. Recalling good memories of family times is always important." Mary gave her employee an encouraging smile.

"Except when you're seven years old and are grumpy because you didn't get enough sleep."

"Oh dear. I remember days like that. When my son Jack was a teenager, it would take two alarm clocks and the threat of a bucket of ice water to get him up in the morning." Mary chuckled. "I have to talk to Kip to see how he's doing. I'll be out back."

She went out the back door and stood for a moment, amazed at how far the backyard had come. Once taken over by weeds, it was now an elegant space. The red-brick herringbone pattern of her new patio was gorgeous, and she loved how the surface was as smooth as a concrete floor but far more attractive. The contrasting green foliage of the chokeberry, raspberry and rosebushes seemed to make the bricks look even brighter and more cheerful.

"Hey, Mrs. Fisher." Kip, who was wearing stonewashed jeans and a light gray T-shirt, gave a wave around the garden. "What do you think?"

"Oh, Kip, I think it's perfect. What a lovely spot this will be to sit and read or talk with friends."

"That's what I've been thinking too. Heather will love this place."

"I'd love for her to visit," she said. "So when do you think it will be finished?"

"Should have it all cleaned up by tonight. I'm going to leave you a few extra bricks alongside the building in case some of these crack or get broken. That way, when we have to replace the old ones, the new ones will match just right."

"Sounds like a good idea." Although she hoped no one would drop anything on the patio heavy enough to break a brick. "Whenever you're all squared away, give me your invoice and I'll write you a check."

"Happy to, Mrs. Fisher." Mary and Kip shared a knowing smile. It wasn't too long ago that she had asked for an invoice for his work, only to have the request ignored. Of course, soon enough she'd learned that he hadn't charged her for the work he'd done because he'd broken into her store. She was so glad all of that was now water under the bridge.

Mary stepped back into the shop and noticed that there was little pedestrian traffic on the sidewalk out front and no customers had come into the bookshop yet. Midweek was usually quieter than the weekends when out-of-towners filled up the local bed-and-breakfasts and hotels.

"Rebecca, I need to run out to Stone Realty for a few minutes. It doesn't look like we'll be busy this morning."

Rebecca hitched herself up onto the stool behind the counter. "Sounds good, Mary. See you soon."

"I shouldn't be gone long."

Because Stone Realty was located on Route 6A just as the road entered Ivy Bay, Mary drove the few miles to see the Realtor.

A small Victorian home had been converted into a real estate office. It was painted dove-gray with white trim, and attractive landscaping and ample parking on a gravel lot welcomed visitors. Except for Lori's midsize SUV, there were no other cars in the lot. Mary pulled in beside it.

A buzzer sounded somewhere in the building when Mary opened the front door. In the entry, a large bouquet of fresh flowers rested on an early-American pine sideboard and flyers featuring homes and property for sale were displayed.

The click of high heels on the hardwood floor preceded Lori's appearance. She was carrying Bitsy, her adorable schnauzer in her arms.

"May I help . . . Mary! How nice to see you." Tall and quite slender, Lori wore her pecan-brown hair in a loose knot at the back of head. The warmth of her smile and the sparkle in her ginger-colored eyes embraced Mary with pleasure. "What can I do for you?"

"I need some real estate advice, so I thought I'd impose on your time and expertise."

"For you, it's no imposition at all. Come into my office."

Lori sat down in a swivel chair at her desk, which was cluttered with assorted escrow and appraisal forms and more flyers describing property for sale. Various awards and photos of the Little League team that Stone Realty supported decorated the walls.

Mary sat in the guest chair next to the desk.

Lori put Bitsy into her doggy bed, then turned back to Mary. "Now, tell me what kind of advice you need."

"I assume you're familiar with the Emerson gristmill and the property it's on."

"Of course. I've always hoped the Emersons would restore the mill. It would be a great tourist attraction. Some of the restored mills in New England have been turned into living-history exhibits, gift shops, and even restaurants."

"I think Betty's hoping that will become a reality one day."

"That would be so special, both for the Emerson family and the town."

"I was wondering if you have heard of anyone who wants to buy the land for development purposes?"

Her brows lowered as she considered Mary's question. "I haven't heard any rumors about a prospective buyer lately. But the fact is, I don't know what kind of development they'd be thinking of. Several years ago, the board of selectmen approved a long-range planning document. The mill and the land around it, including the mill pond, is zoned for open space and recreation."

Surprised, Mary sat back in her chair. "You mean no one could build condos or a big hotel on the property?"

"Only if they got the zoning changed or a waiver from the selectmen. As longtime owners, the Emerson family might

be allowed to do something with the property, if it was con-
sistent with the overall long-range plan. Like restoring it in a
way visitors could learn about the mill's role in Ivy Bay history. But some big condo development or something like it?"
She shook her head. "Getting approval for that would be a
long shot."

Mary leaned her elbow on the arm of the chair and
rubbed her temple with her fingertips. It sounded like she'd
been way off track. She had started to believe that Daniel
Hopkins was after the land because he's greedy, not because
he really wanted to own an old, run-down gristmill.

"Well, I appreciate the information, Lori. If Betty does go
ahead with plans to restore the mill, I do hope the selectmen
will approve the proposal."

"I'm sure they will."

The two women stood and shook hands. "Let me know if
there's anything else I can do for you," Lori said.

"I will." Mary walked back to her car. If Daniel couldn't
develop the property, what made him so determined to own
it? Was it possible Daniel believed the stories about buried
treasure at the mill, after all? Treasure that Mary had actually
found and stashed safely away?

SEVENTEEN

❖━━◆━◆━◆━━❖

Friday morning, Mary called the meeting of the walking tour committee to order. Eleanor had seated herself at the head of the table, with Mary on her right-hand side.

"Good morning, everyone. Let's get started." Mary turned to Dorothy first.

"I have more than a dozen beautiful homes that will be on the tour." Dorothy passed copies of the list of homes and their addresses around the table. "I've suggested that owners be cautious about their possessions. All the tours will be on the main floors. For security reasons, no one will have access to the second or third floor of any house."

The members of the committee, including Eleanor, gave Dorothy a nod of approval.

"That's wonderful, Dorothy. Thanks," Mary concurred.

Mary turned to Rich Tucker. "How is the business community responding?"

"They've been terrific. We've got a dozen participating businesses, including your bookshop." He grinned in Mary's direction.

Betty raised her hand. "In addition to the homes and businesses, the Emerson gristmill will be on the tour. My son Evan and I will act as docents to explain the mill."

"As the principal member of the Emerson family," Eleanor said, "I will also share the docent honors."

"Yes, of course." Betty's face flushed. "Evan and I had planned to wear period costumes."

"An excellent idea," Eleanor agreed.

"What?" Dorothy's voice squeaked. "No one said anything about costumes."

"It's purely optional," Mary said hastily. "Betty simply thought it would add a little ambience to the mill site."

"Well, I never . . ." Bending over the table, Dorothy began scribbling on a notepad. "I'll have to get back to all my people again."

Not wanting to get bogged down about costumes, Mary turned to Jerry Avakian, who owned Meeting House Print and Copy and had volunteered to act as treasurer for the event. "What about publicity and tickets?"

"We've got the tickets printed." He passed samples to the other members of the committee. "And we're also planning to post flyers in the windows of every store in town plus make them available at hotels and bed-and-breakfasts." He placed several attractive 8½" × 11" flyers on the table for everyone to pick up. "Jimmy volunteered to distribute the flyers and tickets to sell to local businesses and the visitor center next week." He gestured at Jimmy Shepard, owner of Jimmy's Hardware, who nodded.

"Jerry, sounds perfect. Thank you so much," Mary said. "And thanks to you too, Jimmy."

Despite Jerry's olive complexion, his face turned a deep shade of red. "It's for a good cause."

Pride in the committee's efforts, and building anticipation, pushed a broad smile to Mary's face. She rested her forearms on the table, her palms up as though encompassing everyone there. "It looks to me like we're going to have a wonderful event. All we need now are paying customers, and we'll have a nice chunk of money to help with"—she almost said Dorothy's house and stopped herself just in time—"restoration."

"Just over one week to go," Rich reminded them.

Just one week. Between now and the walking tour, she and Betty still had to face Daniel Hopkins and the lawsuit deposition.

⸻

When the meeting finished, Mary hurried to the bookshop. The table had been delivered, and Tanaka Florist and Garden Center had promised they'd have the tubs of flowers delivered before eleven.

A young mother with two youngsters was looking over books in the children's nook. Ashley was talking with the customer's three-year-old daughter, introducing her to some of her favorite picture books. The three-year-old's older brother had far more interest in the pedestal bathtub. He'd climbed in and was making sounds like he was on a rocket ship.

Mary smiled. She knew just the right book that would catch the boy's interest.

The time passed quickly, and before she knew it, a big stake-bed truck pulled up in front, blocking two parked cars. The logo on the side read Tanaka Florist and Garden Center.

Mary went outside to greet the two husky young men who had exited the truck. At the same time, Betty showed up on the sidewalk.

"I didn't want to miss the big unveiling."

Only moments behind her, Henry appeared. "Looks like there's some excitement going on."

Mary greeted them both with a smile. "You're both just in time."

To the men, Betty said, "Everything goes around back. You can use the walkway along the side."

"No problem." The older of the two powered down the tailgate and hopped up into the truck. He wrestled the first tub of flowers—a rustic half-wooden barrel—onto a hand truck and wheeled it onto the tailgate, riding it down to the ground. There the younger of the two men took charge.

Mary went inside to meet the young man at the patio, Betty following closely behind her.

As the young man settled the first tub in place, Betty clapped her hands. "Look at that. Zinnias, dahlias, pansies. Marnie outdid herself this time. Just lovely." Marnie Reid was the head florist of the Tanaka center, and Mary knew she'd done an especially good job for Betty, but Mary also knew that Marnie had been given great direction.

Mary slipped her arm around Betty's waist. "You're the one who had the vision to make this yard a special place, Bets."

In no time, the two men had the tubs arranged on opposite sides of the patio and the table set up with the umbrella unfolded.

Rebecca had been watching the operation from the open back door. "That looks so great. In good weather, I'm going to eat my lunch out here."

Picturing herself taking a break to enjoy the fresh air and peaceful ambience, Mary agreed. *The patio would be a wonderful place to pray and give thanks,* she thought as she counted all the blessings the Lord had given her.

By Sunday, a heat wave had settled over the entire East Coast. Although the interior of Grace Church was a few degrees cooler than outside, many parishioners were using the morning programs to fan themselves.

During Pastor Miles's sermon, Betty stopped waving her program and leaned toward Mary. "I think we should pray for rain."

"A cold front would be just fine with me." Mary had noticed Betty fidgeting all during the service and thought her sister hadn't slept well last night. Worrying over the hearing tomorrow, she imagined.

Mary was doing her own worrying. Knowing there was not an official record of a sale might not be enough to save the gristmill. And she had no idea what to say about the ledger showing William Emerson not charging Martha Hopkins for cornmeal. What would that have to do with the purported sale of the mill in 1792? Testifying about the ledger wouldn't do a bit of good.

Nor would mentioning her discovery of the British coins and military uniform. As for what could be Caleb Hopkins' boot and watch, she was almost sorry she'd found them.

Pastor Miles finished his sermon, and Mary realized with a spurt of guilt that she hadn't been paying any more attention to the minister than Betty had.

When they got home, they found Gus splayed out on the cool kitchen floor.

"Poor kitty." Mary bent down to give him a tummy rub. "This isn't a good day for a fur coat, is it?"

He squinted his eyes closed and stretched out his body even farther.

"A salad and then ice cream for dessert strikes me as a perfect lunch for a hot day."

"I think we still have some of your special peach and pralines ice cream."

Mary laughed. "I was hoping there was still a scoop or two left over."

Together, they made the salad, poured some iced tea, and took their lunch out onto the deck. Only the faintest breeze crept past to cool them. When they'd finished their salads, Mary took their plates inside and served up two dishes of ice cream.

Betty sat staring off into the distance, toward a pair of seagulls swooping through the air.

"Are you as worried about tomorrow as I am?" she asked.

"Pretty much," Mary admitted. "We just have to have faith that the Lord knows what He's doing."

Betty took a bite of ice cream and let it melt in her mouth. "It's not always easy to let go, let God, is it?"

From the troubled look in Betty's eyes, Mary knew she was missing Edward and wishing he was here to deal with the problem. Mary could have used John's help about now too. He'd been a wonderful man to bounce ideas off of and help her resolve problems.

During the afternoon, Betty lay down for a rest before she had to dress to attend a lecture by an eminent historian at the Old State House in Boston. Eleanor, a longtime

supporter of the historic organization, was on the foundation's board of directors. After the historian finished his
presentation, Eleanor, Betty, and other members of the
board would take him out to dinner. They'd very likely be
late returning home. Because of that, Mary had begged off
attending the lecture. She suspected Betty would just as
soon stay home as well, but typically, when Eleanor invited
her, Betty could not refuse.

Mary settled in the sunroom with a book written by a
new mystery author. She was almost halfway through the de-
lightful mystery featuring a handwriting expert as the amateur sleuth when the doorbell chimed.

"Can you let Eleanor in?" Betty called from her bedroom.
"I'll be right there."

Marking her place, Mary went to the door.

Eleanor was dressed in an elegant, pale gray summer suit,
accessorized with an exquisite gold necklace and earrings. She
stepped inside as soon as Mary opened the door.

"Good. I'm glad you're here." Eleanor thrust a small,
leather-covered book toward Mary. "I recalled my mother
passed along a steamer trunk of family memorabilia years ago.
I hadn't stored that in the attic. Instead, dear Richard stuffed
it in the overhead storage area in the garage. I asked a neighbor to help me get it down. I knew you'd want to see this."

Betty walked into the entry. "I'm ready to go if you are,
Eleanor."

Mary looked at the book in her hand. "What is it?"

"I believe it's a diary of a young girl, but I really haven't
had time to read it," Eleanor said.

Betty peered over Mary's shoulder. "Who was she?"

"An Emerson, of course." Eleanor reached back to open the door. "We really must leave now. You know how terrible Sunday traffic is going into Boston this time of day. We don't want to arrive late for our speaker."

Looking a little flustered, Betty told Mary good-bye and hurried out the door behind Eleanor.

Curious to know the contents of the book, Mary turned back the cover. On the first page, she read *Diary of Alice Emerson, In the Year of our Lord, 1843.*

She drew in a quick breath. The diary held firmly in her hands, she sat down in the nearest chair and continued to read.

My mama gave this diary to me for Christmas. She says I am to write down my thoughts and what happens each day and then I shall have a record of my life. I do not believe it will be a very interesting record. Today, it has rained all day, and I had to stay inside. Moses and Eldon teased me about the biscuits I burned for breakfast.

My mama's best friend is Martha Hopkins. Mother worries about her because she is a widow. Sometimes she takes an extra meat pie to Martha. I like to go with her because sometimes Peter is there, and he winks at me.

Mama told me often how she and Martha read the Bible together on rainy days in the mill loft . . . .

EIGHTEEN

The following morning, after Mary finished combing her hair and putting on a touch of makeup, she grabbed her purse and then hurried downstairs for breakfast.

"Good morning to you both." She greeted Betty and Evan; Evan had come by to drive them to the hearing. She slipped a piece of toast into the toaster. Betty had already cooked soft-boiled eggs for them and looked no worse for the wear after her night out in Boston.

"You look very professional in your suit, Aunt Mary. You must be planning to wow the opposition forces," Evan said.

With a troubled heart, she turned to look at her sister and nephew. She hadn't told Betty last night about the diary; it had been too late when Betty had arrived home. The truth was she hadn't known just what to say or how to reveal what she'd discovered. In fact, she'd been awake most of the night rereading sections of Alice's diary and praying about what she should do.

So I strive always to keep my conscience clear before God and man (Acts 24:16).

Those words had come to her a dozen times during the night. Before she gave her testimony today, she would swear to tell the truth, so help her God.

In so doing, she would deeply hurt her sister and the legacy of the Emerson name.

But how could she not tell the truth?

The toast popped up. Putting the toast on a plate, she spread it with butter. Her stomach roiled at the thought of eating anything. But going into the deposition on an empty stomach seemed like an invitation for disaster.

She poured herself a mug of coffee and carried that and the plate to the table.

"Don't you want an egg, Mary?" Betty had dressed in a lovely robin-egg silk suit that made her look very sophisticated.

"I'm too nervous to eat."

"No need to be nervous, Aunt Mary. Rob Dunlap is still hoping the so-called bill of sale will turn out to be a forgery."

Although the toast tasted like sand, Mary forced herself to eat and washed it down with coffee, grateful that she didn't gag.

A local Ivy Bay attorney had allowed them to use his conference room for the meeting. The large walnut table in the room was polished to such a high sheen that the overhead lights were reflected like it was a mirror.

In contrast to Rob Dunlap, the opposing attorney Marc Dougher was much younger. Blond and blue-eyed, with a quick smile, he looked more like a fraternity boy than an experienced attorney.

The Hopkinses were represented at the table by their attorney; Daniel, who wore a suit and a perpetual sneer; Jill Sanderson, who had found the old pictures of Martha Hopkins; and Jill's husband, Harry, a very sturdy-looking fisherman with massive hands roughened by years of hard work.

In addition to Rob, Mary, Evan, and Betty, Eleanor was seated on their side of the table.

Lincoln King arrived a little breathless, wearing his trademark black overcoat, completing the Emerson team.

Martin Goodhue, the arbitrator, sat at the head of the table, and a court reporter was seated to his right with her own chair and a stand for her stenotype.

"Good morning, ladies and gentlemen." Goodhue spoke with a tone of authority, yet his voice was calm, in control. "I'd like to start with a few ground rules. First, all of you will be sworn in and your depositions recorded by Ms. Stanley." He nodded toward the stenographer.

"When a person is testifying, no interruptions from the opposition will be permitted," he continued. "Attorneys may pose questions to their own clients but will restrain themselves from giving testimony. After an individual has completed his testimony, the opposing attorney may cross-examine."

Mary twisted her hands in her lap, fussing with the pearl ring John had given her as an anniversary present. Alice Emerson's diary was in her purse, the words the twelve-year-old had written in conflict with what Betty had believed about the gristmill.

Help me, Lord. What should I do?

"When this hearing is finished," Goodhue said, "I will make a ruling within thirty days. If either party objects to the ruling, you have the right to proceed to trial. If the parties can reach an amicable agreement prior to my ruling, the case will be concluded."

His ground rules completed, and everyone sworn in, Goodhue turned his attention to Hopkins' attorney. "Mr. Dougher, your client has made a claim of ownership of the Emerson gristmill. You may proceed."

"Thank you, sir." Mr. Dougher began by asking Daniel some basic questions about himself, how long he'd lived in Ivy Bay, and his former occupation. "Now, Mr. Hopkins, I believe in the course of your usual activities, you discovered a bill of sale dated 1792 indicating one Isaac Emerson had sold the gristmill to your great-great-grandfather James Hopkins for the price of five British pounds. Is that correct?"

"It is," Daniel responded. Although his face was etched with the evidence of long years of heavy drinking, he sounded perfectly sober.

"Tell us how you came to be in the possession of this bill of sale."

"I was getting ready to move to my grandson's house." He nodded toward Harry. "I was cleaning out a closet filled with old junk. I came across a big sea chest someone had stuffed in there I don't know how many years ago. Stuck way down at the bottom, I found this here bill of sale. Clear as anything it proves that me and my kin have owned that mill since James bought it from Isaac."

Betty hissed under her breath.

"Would you please show us the bill of sale, Mr. Hopkins?" Mr. Dougher asked.

"Yes, sir, I have it right here." Hopkins slapped a clear plastic file folder with a letter inside on the table. "This ain't no forgery, neither." He glared across the table at Betty and Evan.

"Mr. Goodhue," Dunlap said. "Since we have not had an opportunity to examine the purported bill of sale, we'd like that opportunity now."

"Request granted." Goodhue indicated Hopkins should pass the folder to the Emerson side of the table.

Each of the members of the Emerson team took a look, then passed the folder along. When it was Mary's turn, she had to swallow a dispirited groan. Where Isaac Emerson's signature should be, there was a primitive drawing of a water-wheel much like the drawings in William Emerson's ledger that identified those who bought cornmeal from him. A technique no doubt passed down from father to son. A notary had carefully written Isaac's name beneath the symbol.

She thought for sure that this was indeed an authentic bill of sale for the gristmill.

Lincoln removed the bill of sale from the folder. He sniffed at it first, then studied every inch of the paper with his large magnifying glass.

Daniel began tapping his fingers on the table.

The knot in Mary's stomach tightened.

Betty's hand covered her mouth while she waited for Lincoln's conclusion.

Next to the arbitrator, Ms. Stanley waited patiently for Lincoln to speak.

He finally slipped the paper back into the folder and looked up. "The paper and ink used for this document appear appropriate for the period, most likely imported from Great Britain. However, I am not able to authenticate the signatures as I have no exemplars with which to compare them."

Betty exhaled and her shoulders relaxed. She gave Mary a tentative smile, but Mary was unable to return her expression. She was too sick at heart because she knew the truth.

Rob Dunlap spoke up. "My office has made an extensive search of records in an effort to discover any record of transfer of title to the property or the deed. We have found no such record. Mrs. Mary Fisher, the defendant's sister, has made an independent search for those records. Mary, were you able to find such a record?"

"No, sir." In response to Dunlap's further questions, she related what she had done to establish the ownership history of the mill. "From what I researched, I concur with the findings of your office. It's clear the Emerson family has operated and been in sole possession of the gristmill since the earliest records were established."

"That's a lie!" Daniel pounded his fist on the table.

"Quiet, please," the arbitrator admonished him.

"You seen the bill of sale? That place is ours."

Daniel's grandson tried to calm him down, but Daniel fumed and shouted, his face turning redder by the minute.

"Please." Mary interrupted his diatribe, her voice a little shaky. "I believe, despite there being no record of a title change, that Mr. Hopkins' bill of sale is a legal contract."

Everyone in the room gaped at her.

Betty whirled toward Mary. "What on earth are you talking about? You just said you hadn't found any record of a title change."

"If you'll let me explain . . ." She pulled the diary from her tote and waited for a nod from the arbitrator.

"Eleanor Emerson Blakely, Betty Emerson's sister-in-law, discovered this diary yesterday among some family memorabilia," Mary began.

"I did not expect that diary to be used against us, Mary. If I had, I certainly would not have passed it on to you."

"I understand, Eleanor. And I'm truly sorry." Mary briefly described the author of the diary and the young woman's relationship to William Emerson.

"He's the one what killed Caleb!" Daniel burst out, and his grandson grabbed his arm to hush him up.

"Actually, that's not true." Mary stared Daniel down for a moment until he stopped trying to yank away from Harry. "If I may, I'd like to read a few passages from Alice's diary."

She had marked the telling pages and opened the book. She read, "August 24, 1843: At dinner tonight, Mama asked Daddy why he wasn't charging Mrs. Hopkins for cornmeal. Mama usually has sympathy for the widow Hopkins, and they're really good friends, but she has been cranky all day. He told her that he was returning a favor owed to the Hopkinses, who once saved our family's skin. I didn't know what he was talking about and neither did Mama. Daddy explained a long time ago, when times were really hard, somebody named James Hopkins helped Isaac Emerson—that's Daddy's great-great-granddaddy—by giving him some money to feed his children. He had a lot of them."

Mary looked up from the diary. Everyone was listening intently, gazing at her like children used to when she'd been doing story time at the library. Unlike the children, however, they were not smiling or squirming in their seats.

"I can confirm from the census record that Isaac had twelve children, which you'll agree is a lot of mouths to feed," she continued. "I believe the money referred to is the five British pounds, which the lawsuit contends James Hopkins gave Isaac Emerson to help him take care of his family. It appears Isaac very likely signed over the bill of sale as collateral."

With a shocked expression, Betty leaned away, putting some distance between herself and Mary. "What are you doing? The mill is ours. It's the Emerson mill and always has been." The deep hurt of betrayal rang through the conference room.

"I'm sorry." Tears of regret burned the backs of Mary's eyes as she retrieved the mill's ledger from her tote.

"Like I said, the mill ain't yours!" Daniel muttered.

The arbitrator held up his hand for silence. "Please continue, Mrs. Fisher."

Pressing her lips together, Mary took a moment to control her emotions. She cleared her throat. "From reading this diary, I've concluded the two families were such good friends and neighbors that James Hopkins refused to record the sale of the mill. He was, after all, a fisherman by trade. What would he have done with the mill? Chances were good he knew nothing about grinding corn."

Mary swallowed and continued. "That would explain why I was unable to find any record of a title or deed transfer. I do have a ledger written by William Emerson that confirms what Alice wrote in her diary. Her father was not charging

Martha Hopkins for cornmeal. I believe that William Emerson made the effort to pay back that debt many times over by providing cornmeal to Martha Hopkins at no charge over the years."

Mary placed the ledger on the table and showed how she had reached that conclusion by identifying the sketch of the woman in black. "The lack of tally marks indicates that the widow made no payment for the cornmeal."

"Then if William paid off the debt," Eleanor said, "the Hopkinses have no claim on the mill or the land."

"This William fellow didn't pay back Isaac," Daniel insisted. "So it doesn't matter one whit what William did."

"Mr. Goodhue," Rob interrupted. "I think it is obvious from both the facts and the statement in the diary that Mr. Hopkins' intent was not to own the gristmill. County records clearly indicate the Emersons have paid property taxes each and every year since the earliest records, which is reason enough to establish their ownership. And, as we all know, possession is nine-tenths of the—"

"I disagree," Daniel's young attorney interrupted. "Mr. Hopkins has presented a valid bill of sale. That the transfer of title was not recorded does not change the facts. Isaac Emerson, in good faith and in exchange for value, sold the mill to James Hopkins. The mill should therefore rightfully belong to the descendants of James Hopkins."

Everyone on both sides of the table started talking at once, shouting to be heard over one another.

Feeling like a traitor, Mary returned the diary and ledger to her tote. She prayed Betty would forgive her, although she knew it might take time.

Meanwhile, Daniel was looking ever so proud of himself. Although the arbitrator hadn't ruled yet, Daniel looked confident he'd won.

But why does he want that run-down mill? she wondered yet again.

She leaned forward. "Daniel, what do you plan to do with the mill?"

He cut her a look. "What's it matter to you?"

"I'm curious. And I think the Emersons deserve an answer."

He wiped the back of his hand across his mouth. "I know a guy who wants that land. He's gonna build some fancy condos. He'll turn a pretty penny on the deal, but he's gonna pay me a bundle first."

Betty gasped, and Evan put his arm around his mother's shoulders.

Mary tilted her head in thought. "Have you spoken to the city planning department about the condo idea?"

"Nope. No need to. My buddy will take care of that."

"Maybe not, Daniel." She told him and the others about the zoning restrictions. "Your friend won't be able to build anything on that land, so he isn't going to buy the land. Instead, you'll probably have to pay to tear down the mill because it's a public hazard. That will cost you a lot of money."

"Thousands of dollars, according to the estimate I got," Evan added.

Daniel snarled at her. "That's another one of your lies."

"No, it isn't." Mary checked up and down the table. Harry Hopkins seemed like a reasonable man. Certainly his wife was.

She turned to the arbitrator. "If I may, I have a suggestion that may satisfy both parties in this matter without costing either of them a great deal of money."

"I'm all ears, Mrs. Fisher."

She acknowledged his permission with a slight dip of her head. "Assuming Mr. Goodhue will be ruling in Mr. Hopkins' favor, Daniel will find himself liable for the destruction of an unsafe building. Meanwhile, the Emersons will lose a beloved part of their heritage. I'm sure you've all heard the story of Solomon in the Bible when he was confronted by two women who both claimed to be the mother of a certain baby."

Everyone nodded, except Daniel, who continued to look at her with suspicion and distrust.

"Solomon, in his wisdom, decided that since the women could not reach an agreement, he would cut the baby in half. The baby's real mother immediately stepped forward and pleaded with Solomon to give the baby to the other woman so her child could live, even though she'd lose him to another. While our current situation isn't quite the same as the one Solomon faced, I think we can apply his wisdom to resolve this."

The Hopkinses glanced at one another. Goodhue seemed willing to listen.

"I have not revealed to Mr. Hopkins that I found something in the mill in addition to the ledger. Hidden behind a false wall, I discovered some valuable coins and a British uniform."

"If they were in the mill, they're mine," Daniel blustered, his determination twisting his features into an ugly mask. "You can turn them over to me right now."

"I think not, Daniel. The coins are dated 1775, well before Isaac needed money to feed his family and sold the mill to your ancestor. Therefore, the coins and British uniform from the Revolutionary War belong to my sister. Their combined value is such that it would provide a very good start for restoring the mill."

Evan confirmed that would be true.

"What if I just want to tear it down?" Daniel asked.

"Then you would be liable for the cost, wouldn't you?" Mary replied blandly. "But if you and the Emerson family could share in the ownership and operation of the mill, then the Emersons can restore it, and the mill might become known as the Emerson-Hopkins gristmill in Ivy Bay and would probably be listed as a registered historic landmark."

Shaking his head, Daniel muttered under his breath again.

Betty said, "Oh, I don't think that would work at all."

Mary looked to Goodhue for help.

"Ladies and gentlemen, Mrs. Fisher has proposed a very interesting compromise, which I feel has a great deal of merit. I think each side should take a minute to consider her suggestion."

Daniel, his grandson, and their attorney huddled on the opposite side of the table.

Betty, Evan, Eleanor, and Rob Dunlap did the same on the Emerson side. Mary sat staring off into the distance, worried about what she had done and the effect it would have on her sister and their relationship.

Lincoln touched her arm. "Well done, Mary. A smart solution, in my mind. A fine old building restored, and no harm done to either side. Your efforts would set an example for others in the antiquities business."

She thanked Lincoln, but her heart still ached.

The discussion between Daniel and his grandson grew heated. After a bit, Daniel stood and slammed his chair back against the wall. "Do any fool thing you want. I wash my hands of the whole thing. It's your worry now." He snatched the bill of sale, slapped it down in front of Harry, and stormed out the door.

After a quiet moment, Harry said, "I apologize for my grandfather. He shouldn't have made such a scene. He's been pretty emotional about the mill."

"No need to apologize," Goodhue said. "But since your grandfather has left matters in your hands, we'd be interested to know what your decision is."

Harry took his wife's hand. "Jill and I don't have any interest in tearing down the old mill. But it sounds like we have some responsibility toward the place since somehow we seem to own it now." He looked directly at Betty. "Seems to me our two families were close at one time, then things sort of got out of hand and a feud started up. I think if we could work together, our kids would be right proud to have the Hopkins name on the mill beside the Emersons."

"I agree with my husband," Jill said, directing her words to Mary. "I think the Lord had a hand in you finding a solution we can all live with."

Jill's support meant a lot to Mary, and she smiled in gratitude. "I have some information about that feud, if you'd like to hear it," Mary said.

Harry glanced at Jill, who nodded.

"From what I understand, Caleb Hopkins went missing the night of the October gale in 1841. Over time, some members of the community, probably someone in the Hopkins family, began to blame William Emerson for Caleb's death. As I can best reconstruct what happened, Caleb—who had been drinking at the Horse Head Tavern, which was close to the mill—argued with William and probably followed him home.

"The rain was coming down very hard; visibility must have been poor. Caleb made a misstep and fell in the race by the mill. Few fishermen at that time could swim, so he was dragged out to sea. His official cause of death, according to the funeral home in Provincetown where his body washed up sometime later, was accidental drowning." She passed a copy of the report across the table. "For the sake of family harmony, it's worth considering."

"And that's what my grandfather's been raging on about all these years?" Harry asked.

"I'm afraid so."

The young man blew out a sigh and looked at Betty. "So what do you think, Mrs. Emerson? Can we work together on this?"

Her features were strained and her eyes puffy. "I think it's high time that the Emerson and Hopkins families put the past behind them, Harry." She produced a wavering smile for him and Jill. "And I think Elizabeth Emerson and Martha Hopkins would be the first to tell us so."

NINETEEN

———◆◆◆———

The mid-September weather cooperated to provide a perfect day for the Ivy Bay Historic Walking Tour.

Tourists began to wander into the bookshop starting about two o'clock. Ashley faithfully stamped the walking tour tickets as the guests entered. Rebecca had made her daughter a colonial costume with a puffy white hat.

Mary, whose costuming effort was limited to a long cotton skirt and blouse, provided commentary for those who were interested in the building's history.

"This building was constructed over two hundred years ago using handmade bricks. For those of you who know something about bricks, these are slightly smaller than the current standard size."

At this point in her talk, one man actually got out a measuring tape and started measuring the bricks. Mary couldn't help but smile.

"Until recently, the building housed the town's archives, all the property records, titles and transfers, and tax records. That information is now stored in the county clerk's office down the street."

Mary intentionally skipped the history of her own uncle George having an auction house in this building. The details of that were too complicated to relate in a few short minutes. "Before that, this was an apothecary. We have several books on the history of Ivy Bay and Cape Cod."

Mary had made sure she had a full display on hand. "Plus we have replicas of early plot maps of the town and surrounding area."

As she finished her general talk, she chatted informally with visitors and invited them to help themselves to punch and cookies on the back patio.

By late afternoon, her voice was giving out and she was curious to see how the tour was going elsewhere. She left Rebecca to handle the tour-guide role and stepped outside.

The sidewalks were even more crowded with pedestrians than on a typical summer weekend, many of them checking the maps Jerry Avakian had printed for the tour.

She walked across the street to Gems and Antiques, only to find the store so crowded she couldn't get in the door.

After checking a few more shops, the owners happy with the number of visitors they'd had and accompanying sales they'd made, Mary decided to check on Dorothy Johnson.

Because of the line waiting to enter Dorothy's house, Mary slipped around to the rear of the house and entered via the back door. She followed the sound of Dorothy's voice to the great room. Dorothy was dressed in fine Victorian style; her gown had a voluminous skirt, snug bodice trimmed in lace and ribbon, and wide pagoda sleeves. Even her shoes were period style, white kid with side-laced boots. She was talking to a group of tourists.

"When guests arrive, they are greeted in the foyer and then escorted into what is called a great room, which you might call a living room." She gestured with a gloved hand at the paintings on the wall. "All these paintings are original oils, many by local artists. There are several fine galleries in Ivy Bay and elsewhere on the Cape that you might wish to visit."

Mary spotted Henry and eased across the room to stand next to him. "How is it going?"

He grinned and winked. "I've rarely seen Dorothy this happy. She's eating up all the attention."

Mary smiled back at him. "I'm glad. Looks like her house is a popular stop on the tour." She listened as Dorothy talked so proudly about her 1892 home for a few more minutes. Among the crowd, she spotted Lincoln in his dark raincoat. She smiled, and he nodded in return.

"Be sure Dorothy makes it to the special committee meeting tonight," she whispered to Henry. "Jerry Avakian will have a check for her."

"So soon?"

"He's already tallied the expenses, so once the ticket sales are added, we'll know what the profit will be."

Henry glanced toward Dorothy. "I'll be sure she gets there. She's going to be very surprised. Earlier today, she told me she was thinking about selling her house and moving into a condo."

"Now she won't have to." Mary let herself out the back, the same way she had come in. She wanted to visit the mill to see how Betty, Evan, and the Hopkinses were getting along. Betty had been cool toward her since the hearing. That worried Mary. Would their relationship ever return to the warmth they'd had before the deposition?

Evan had created a very nice display of the old gristmill photos, plus he'd mounted an artist's rendering of what the Emerson-Hopkins gristmill would look like after restoration.

Apparently, there hadn't been any need to worry about the two families getting along. Betty and Jill Sanderson were passing out pieces of cornmeal-mush bread made from an original colonial recipe. Meanwhile, Daniel, dressed in his fisherman's overalls, was strutting around explaining how people lived in the 1600s as if he'd been there himself.

Mary plucked a piece of bread from Betty's tray. "Are you doing all right here?"

"We are." She glanced around at a crowd of maybe twenty people who were examining the photos. "Do you know the best part of this?"

"The money we're raising for Dorothy?"

"That, too, but I was thinking about the feud between the Emersons and Hopkinses." She gestured toward Evan, who was talking to Harry Hopkins like they were old buddies. "Whatever misunderstandings and hurt feelings there were between the two families is now in the past. The feud is over."

That news warmed Mary's heart, but she still wondered how Betty felt about her and the revelation about mill ownership at the deposition. They hadn't really talked about the meeting yet or its outcome.

"You're the one who ended the feud, Mary." Betty set her tray down on a table. "I owe you an apology for being so upset during the deposition. You found out the truth and you had to tell us. It was the right thing to do. The Christian thing to do."

Tears filled Mary's eyes. "I was so worried you'd resent me, Bets. I didn't know what to do."

The sisters fell into each other's arms, hugging and crying, without saying a word. Their family ties were too strong for a dispute over an ancient mill to break them apart.

———

The special meeting of the walking tour committee was called for eight o'clock at the bookshop. As the members squeezed inside, they were all jabbering about the success of the event and talking about repeating it next year.

Dorothy arrived, still in her costume, which now looked a little rumpled, as did her blonde hair. She and Betty took seats in the comfortable chairs at the back of the shop.

"All right, everyone." Mary waved her hand for attention. "I know you're excited about our success, but it's getting late. We have one big chore left to do. We have to vote on who should receive the proceeds from the tour in order to restore a historic building in Ivy Bay. Do I have a nomination?"

Betty's hand shot up as she and her sister had planned. "I nominate Dorothy Johnson and her exquisite 1892 Victorian."

Dorothy's eyes registered surprise, and she opened her mouth to say something, but she was cut off by Benjamin. "I second that."

"All in favor?"

A chorus of ayes carried the unanimous vote.

"But—" Dorothy protested, her cheeks flushing.

"Jerry, would you please present Dorothy with her check?"

"Happy to." He held up the check and announced the amount. Everyone except Dorothy, whose jaw seemed to have come loose, cheered. "Because of your outstanding contribution to the success of the walking tour, I'm proud to hand you the check for the proceeds, with the committee's deepest thanks."

With a trembling hand, Dorothy took the check with just two fingers as though it might burn her. "I didn't ... I had no idea."

"You weren't supposed to know," Jerry said.

Blinking back tears, Dorothy looked up at Mary. "You did this, didn't you?"

"We all did it together, Dorothy. You're an important part of this community, and your home is part of Ivy Bay's history."

Tears began to spill down Dorothy's cheeks, and Mary realized that by sharing the Lord's grace with Dorothy, she had received the greater gift of His love.

———

By the time Betty and Mary got home, it was ten o'clock. Both of them slipped off their shoes the moment they stepped inside the house.

"I don't know about you," Mary said, "but I'm exhausted. I could sleep for a week."

"You'd deserve it. You pulled the tour together in record time."

"I had a lot of people helping, including you." She picked up her shoes. "Well, I'm off to bed."

"Me too." Betty turned toward her room and immediately halted. "Oh, I forgot to tell you the most interesting thing I learned about the mill tonight." Her eyes glittered with the hint of a secret to be shared.

"What's that?"

"Daniel and I were talking earlier this afternoon. He told me he'd wanted the mill land to sell to that developer, but he never intended to get rid of the buhrstone."

"Why on earth not? What was he planning to do with it?"

"If you can imagine, Daniel wanted to keep the buhr-stone for sentimental reasons. He'd proposed to his wife one Sunday afternoon when they'd walked up to the mill. He'd been courting her for some time. After she said yes, he carved their initials in the stone."

Ironically, it was the same place where Edward had proposed to Betty. Although when Mary mentally tried to picture Daniel doing something so romantic, the image failed to appear. "Their initials?"

"He showed me. He'd carved 'DH + JC' inside a heart. Isn't that sweet?"

Mary's brain struggled to process what Betty had said. "Maybe that explains why he always seemed to be at the mill when I showed up. He was visiting the spot where he'd proposed to his wife. He wasn't looking for the treasure at all." She gasped when another thought occurred to her. "One time when he was leaving, he patted that old stone with his hand. A loving caress where he had carved their initials, perhaps."

"Entirely possible."

"Goodness! Who knew that cranky old man was a secret romantic?" She shook her head and laughed. "I misjudged him terribly, didn't I?"

"I'm afraid we all did." She hugged Mary. "But now we know he was doing all he could to cover up the fact that he's lonely. I think maybe I'll invite him to go to church with us one of these days. Maybe we can coax Henry into getting Daniel active in the men's group."

Mary chuckled. "Betty Emerson, you are one of a kind and so dear to me; I don't know what I'd do without you."

"You know," Betty said quietly, "I think Edward would be pleased how this has all worked out, both for the families and the mill."

"I do too, Bets."

They hugged again. Then it was time for them both to get a good night's sleep. Mary suspected it wouldn't be long before another mystery popped up.

ABOUT THE AUTHOR

An author of more than fifty romance, cozy mystery, and inspirational titles, Charlotte Carter lives in Southern California with her husband of fifty years and their cat, Mittens—an equal-opportunity lap cat. They have two married daughters and five grandchildren. When she's not writing, Charlotte does a little stand-up comedy—G-rated humor for grown-ups—and teaches workshops on the craft of writing.

Visit her Web site at www.CharlotteCarter.com.

A CONVERSATION WITH CHARLOTTE CARTER

———◆◆◆———

Q: *What draws you to Mary's Bookshop as a writer?*

A: I live in Southern California, and I've never visited Cape Cod. It was wonderful to learn more about the beauty of that area. I see a trip to the "real" Ivy Bay in my future.

Q: *Which character in the series do you most relate to?*

A: I loved writing about Mary, a mature woman who is an amateur sleuth and good at it too. She'd make a good role model for our younger friends.

Q: *If you could open a bookshop anywhere, where would it be? And what kind of bookshop would it be?*

A: I'd open a bookshop on the beach in Redondo Beach, California. The only problem I'd have would be responsibly staying in the shop instead of taking a book out on the beach to read while watching the waves lapping against the shore. The book might be romance, adventure, suspense, or even a good biography.

On second thought, maybe I'd have my bookstore in the mountains. The scent of pine trees and the wind whispering through the treetops . . . .

Q: *What is your favorite mystery book/author? Why?*
A: I read most of James Patterson's books and particularly enjoy the Women's Murder Club series.

Q: *Have you ever had to solve a mystery? Tell us about it.*
A: The biggest mysteries my husband and I ever solve are finding an important paper that we've put down somewhere, where we've left our dark glasses, and discovering what happened this time to the little pocketknife he carries in his pants pocket. Guess we live a pretty quiet life!

Q: *Mary loves to make new ice-cream flavors and enjoys reading mystery novels. What are some of your hobbies?*
A: I've never been good at crafts; my feet perspire when I knit. So I write and read, a lot, and sometimes I perform stand-up comedy. Having an audience laugh at my jokes is a wonderful experience.

Q: *Mary's two favorite confidants are her sister Betty and her old friend Henry. Who are your greatest confidants?*
A: I've fairly recently reconnected with a few of my high school friends, which has been great fun. I have another group of friends who I worked with in the late 1950s. We get together three or four times a year for lunch. And, not surprisingly, I have made exceptionally good friends through my writing group.

Q: *Please tell us about your family!*

A: I'm particularly proud of my grandchildren. (No surprise there, huh?) Our oldest granddaughter is in college on a full-ride volleyball scholarship. Our oldest grandson, still in high school, performs in a group that provides youth programs at church camps all across California. The three youngest boys all have special talents that they're developing to match their older siblings.

CRANBERRY-BANANA JAM

Since there are cranberry bogs in Ivy Bay, I so wanted Mary to make some cranberry-banana jam, a recipe I picked up when my husband and I were living in Anchorage, Alaska. But the season was wrong in *Reading the Clues*. But I'll share the recipe with you anyway. The bananas take the tang out of the cranberries, making for a delicious addition to your toast or bagel.

> *3 cups cranberries*
> *1 cup mashed banana*
> *7 cups sugar*
> *1 package of Certo or other fruit pectin*

Clean and sterilize your canning equipment. In a large saucepan, combine the cranberries, banana, and sugar. Bring to a rolling boil on high heat, stirring constantly. Stir in the pectin. Remove from heat and run a metal spoon over the top to skim off any foam. Ladle the mixture into prepared jars, leaving ⅛ of an inch of room. Wipe jars and cover with lids; screw on tightly. Lower jars into your canner. Add boiling water—make sure water covers the jars by two inches. Cover and bring water to a gentle boil. Leave for ten minutes. Remove and cool jars.

FROM THE GUIDEPOSTS ARCHIVES

⎯⎯⎯•◆◆•⎯⎯⎯

Seek ye out of the book of the Lord, and read . . . . —Isaiah 34:16 (KJV)

I love books. Books stack up at my bedside, in my study, in my closet, in the cellar. Not to mention the books in the trunk of my car.

"Oscar," I told myself one day, "you need to find something to do with all these books."

That's when I discovered the book stall that sits in front of our supermarket. One day I gathered up two boxes of books and put them there. *It'll be weeks before anybody ever takes them*, I thought.

I picked up the things I needed at the supermarket and carrying my groceries to the car, I passed the book stall. To my amazement, half of the books I'd just donated were gone. In fact, the fellow who bagged groceries had dashed out of the store on a break and put some of my offerings in a bag for himself.

There are countless books out there and, to my delight, there are just as many readers. Giving them away, I've found, is almost as much fun as reading them.

Thank You for the pleasures, Lord, I get from reading.

—Oscar Greene

A NOTE FROM THE EDITORS

We hope you enjoy Secrets of Mary's Bookshop, created by the Books and Inspirational Media Division of Guideposts. In all of our books, magazines and outreach efforts, we aim to deliver inspiration and encouragement, help you grow in your faith, and celebrate God's love in every aspect of your daily life.

Thank you for making a difference with your purchase of this book, which helps fund our many outreach programs to the military, prisons, hospitals, nursing homes and schools. To learn more, visit GuidepostsFoundation.org.

We also maintain many useful and uplifting online resources. Visit Guideposts.org to read true stories of hope and inspiration, access OurPrayer network, sign up for free newsletters, join our Facebook community, and follow our stimulating blogs.

To order your favorite Guideposts publications, go to ShopGuideposts.org, call (800) 932-2145 or write to Guideposts, PO Box 5815, Harlan, Iowa 51593.